George P. Pelecanos is the author of *A Firing Offense*, *Nick's Trip*, and *Down By the River Where the Dead Men Go*, a trilogy featuring PI Nick Stefanos, as well as *King Suckerman*, shortlisted for the 1998 Crime Writers' Association Golden Dagger Award, *The Sweet Forever* and *The Big Blowdown*, all published by Serpent's Tail. Pelecanos has been hailed as "the coolest writer in America" (*GQ*) and "a literary Tarantino with added heart" (*Mail on Sunday*) who "makes Jim Thompson look like Barbara Cartland" (*Mirabella*).

Pelecanos lives in Washington, where he "has carved out a territory — the seedier suburbs of Washington, D.C. — and a language of danger and sadness all his own" (*Chicago Tribune*).

**Also by George P. Pelecanos
and published by Serpent's Tail**

The Nick Stefanos trilogy

A Firing Offense
Nick's Trip
Down By the River Where the Dead Men Go

The DC Quartet includes

The Big Blowdown
King Suckerman
The Sweet Forever

KING SUCKERMAN

GEORGE P. PELECANOS

A complete catalogue record for this book can be
obtained from the British Library on request

The right of George P. Pelecanos to be identified as the
author of this work has been asserted by him in
accordance with the Copyright, Designs and Patents
Act 1988

The author is grateful for permission to include the following
previously copyrighted material:
Excerpt from 'Back to the World' written by Curtis Mayfield.
Reprinted by permission of Curtis Mayfield, Curtom Classics,
Inc. and Ichiban Records, Inc.

First published in 1998 by Serpent's Tail,
4 Blackstock Mews, London N4
website: www.serpentstail.com

First published in this 5-star edition in 2000

Printed in Great Britain by Mackays of Chatham plc,
Chatham, Kent

10 9 8 7 6 5 4 3 2 1

In these city streets — Everywhere
You got to be careful
Where you move your feet, and how you part your hair
Do you really think God could ever forgive, this life we live
Back in the world, back in the world

— Curtis Mayfield
"Back to the World"

KING SUCKERMAN

ONE

Wilton Cooper reached for the speaker, counterclockwised the volume. It sounded to him, with all that static and shit, like the brothers were talking Chinese. Like he was watching some chop-socky thing, *Five Fingers of Death* or something like that. Anyway, Cooper didn't need that tinny-ass box hanging on the window. He knew the dialogue by heart. He'd seen *Black Caesar*, what, five, six times already. Even had the original sound track on cassette tape. James Brown, doin' it to death. "Down and Out in New York City." "The Boss." And *all* that.

It wasn't *Black Caesar* that Cooper had come to see, anyhow. And it sure wasn't that peckerwood biker picture — *Angels the Hard Way* — no, *Angels Hard as They Come*, that's what it was — that had gone second on the triple bill. Cooper had come to check out that new one, *The Master Gunfighter*, with Tom Laughlin and Ron O'Neal. Billy Jack and Superfly, way out West. Yeah, that would be something to see. He'd been waiting on that one to open for a long time.

Wilton Cooper took a last swig of Near Beer, crushed the can, tossed it over his shoulder to the backseat. He placed the speaker back in its cradle, got out of his ride, walked past rows of cars to the darkened field behind the projection house. With all that liquid in him, he had a fierce need to drain his lizard, and he just couldn't abide waiting in the men's room line.

Cooper moaned a little as he let a long stream fly. He could see the screen, Fred Williamson walking out of Tiffany's just before being gut-shot by that Irishman dressed as a cop. He always liked this part, and then the wild chase scene through Manhattan, people on the street looking right into the camera, the director not bothering to edit or reshoot, maybe because he had no budget for it, or he just plain didn't give a shit. Cooper dug checking out the extras, trying not to look into the lens but not able to help themselves, doing it just the same. On a bigger-budget feature the producers never would have let that slide. Cooper thought it was cool, though, just the way it was.

He shook himself off, tucked his snake back in where it belonged.

He saw a white boy then, heading from the opposite end of the field in the direction of the projection bunker's rear door.

The boy had one of those ratty, blown-out Afros, big as Dr. J's. He wore lemon yellow bells, with a rayon print shirt tails out over the pants. The shirt was untucked because he had slipped a short-barreled rifle — or a sawed-off, Cooper couldn't tell which — down inside the pant leg along his right hip.

Cooper knew. He had been with stickup kids who had done it the same way, walking into liquor stores and banks. Point of fact, this boy he knew, Delaroy was his name, he had worn his shotgun *just* that way when the two of them had done that Gas-and-Go outside of Monroe, Louisiana. That was the last armed robbery Cooper had ever done, the one that got him his five-year bit in Angola. He was into different shit now.

Anyway, that was Louisiana, and this here was Fayetteville, North Kakilaki. Now what the fuck was this white boy going to do with that big gun?

Cooper watched him walk — strut, really — toward the cinder-block bunker. The kid's left hand was cupped at his side, and he kind of swung it on the down-step. As the kid passed below the light of the floodlamp, Cooper could see the four-inch heels on the boy's stacks. Those platforms, the Afro, and the kid's street-nigger strut: a white-boy, wanna-be-a-black-boy cracker. He had the walk down, a little too much with the hand action for Cooper's taste, but not bad. And the kid was cooler than a motherfucker, too, the way he went straight through the door without knocking, not even looking around before he did. Cooper wondered, What's going to happen next?

It took about a hot minute for him to find out. Cooper heard the muffled report of a long gun come from the projection bunker just as the redheaded phony cop fired his pistol into Fred Williamson on screen. So the kid had timed whatever he had done to go with the gunshots in the film. Maybe he had seen *Black Caesar* enough times to plan the whole thing out. Or maybe he wasn't into the movie and he just happened to work at the drive-in. Cooper was curious either way. He figured he'd hang back there in the dark a little bit. Wait until the white boy came out, ask him then.

When Bobby Roy Clagget walked into the projection bunker, the fat man didn't even turn around. Couldn't hear the door open and shut, what with the whir of the reels and the flutter of film running through the gate. Clagget stood there, watching the fat man's back, his rounded shoulders, red fireman's suspenders over a blue work shirt holding up a worn pair of jeans hanging flat on a no-ass frame.

Clagget pulled the sawed-off Remington up out of his pant leg by its stock. He racked the pump, pointed the .12-gauge at the fat man.

"You know what this is?" said Clagget. "You recognize that sound?"

The fat man turned around at Clagget's voice.

"Bobby Roy," said the fat man, a friendly smile right away, noticing the shotgun but not showing fear or surprise. Not showing Bobby Roy a bit of respect. "Who's coverin' the concessions?"

"I said, you recognize that sound?"

"What sound?"

Damn, he hadn't even heard the pump. This wasn't at all like the script he had written up in his head. Clagget went ahead with the dialogue anyway. There wasn't much else he could do.

"That there," said Clagget, "was the sound of your own death."

"Say what?" The fat man looked Clagget up and down. "Shoot, son, what y'all doin' with that hog's leg? You fixin' to take out some crows?"

Clagget looked over at the cot in the corner of the booth, where some sort of needlepoint the fat man had been working on lay on a pillow atop wrinkled sheets. Clagget had known nearly all projectionists to have their own funny hobbies — model-car making, Nam memorabilia, shit like that — and this one was no different than the rest.

Clagget's eyes went along the dust-specked shaft of light, through the rectangular window to the screen. Fred Williamson was crossing Fifth Avenue with the Tiffany presents in his hand. The bogus uniformed cop had begun to close in.

"Go lay down on that cot," said Clagget, "and put that pillow over your face."

"Huh?" The fat man chuckled. Clagget couldn't believe it. By God, he had actually laughed.

Black Caesar bumped into a man in a suit, a decoy for the cop. In another second or two would come the shot.

"Why you want me to lay down, Bobby Roy?"

"Never you mind that now," said Clagget. He stepped forward, gripped the Remington tight.

"Bobby Roy?" said the fat man.

And Clagget squeezed the trigger.

The fat man flew back, hit the cinder-blocks, took down a bulletin board hung there. Clagget pumped the shotgun — it felt good, doing that — and watched the fat man kind of flop around for a few seconds like a dry-docked perch. A jagged piece of bone jutted up from the center of the fat man's shredded shoulders. Clagget wondered idly where the man's head had gone.

He slipped the shotgun inside his pant leg. Walking to the door, he wiped what felt like a warm slug off his cheek, flung it to the side. He imagined Fred Williamson, shot now and staggering across the street. Bobby Roy Clagget began to sing the J. B. vocals that he knew were now filling the interior of every car on the lot: "Look at me, you know what you see?/See a baaaad mother. . . ."

Clagget issued a brief sigh. Killing the fat man, it hadn't been like he expected. No thrill, no fear, and no remorse. It was no different than killing an animal. Nothing more than that.

The pillow would have made a good natural silencer — he had seen Henry Fonda use one for just that purpose in *Once Upon a Time in the*

West — and it was too bad he couldn't have used it himself. The way it worked out, though, he just didn't have the time. Claggett opened the door, thinking about the pillow and not paying attention to anything else. That's when he saw the big black dude, standing just a few feet away on the edge of the field, a funny kind of grin on his face.

Cooper had to smile, seeing the skinny white boy up close, a pattern of blood and who knew what else sprayed onto the front of his cheap print shirt. What was that, Tarzan swinging on vines all over the shirt? Couldn't be.

"What's goin' on?" said Cooper, still smiling, no threat at all in his voice.

"What's happenin', blood?"

Blood. Shit, Cooper couldn't have been more right.

"Just out here relieving myself. Saw you go inside. Thought I'd greet you when you came out."

The white boy cocked his hip, maintaining that all-the-way cool. "Oh, yeah? Why's that?"

"Thought you might need a friend, is all." Cooper pointed his chin in the direction of the boy's chest. "You done fucked up that pretty shirt. From the blow-back and shit."

The white boy looked down at himself, showed real regret at the sight. "Damn. My finest one, too."

Cooper watched the boy run his hand under the shirt, thinking now about pulling the weapon.

Cooper said, "Uh-uh."

"What's that?"

"Don't be drawing that long gun out. Don't even try. I'd be on you so fast . . . Look here, little brother" — *little brother,* Cooper knew he'd like that — "I mean you no harm. For real."

The white boy squinted his eyes. "What you want then, man?"

"The name's Wilton Cooper. You?"

"Make it B. R. For Bobby Roy."

"B. R. Bobby Roy. All right, here it is. I already know you're brave, but, no disrespect intended, that don't make you smart in the bargain. Now, whatever you did in there —"

"I killed a man."

There it was. Like it didn't mean a *damn* thing.

"Okay. You work here, right?"

"Yeah."

"That's gonna make you suspect number one. And I bet you pumped out a shell in that booth, didn't you?"

"I did."

"I *know* you did. 'Cause it kind of put a period on the end of the sentence, if you know what I mean. So they're gonna be looking to talk to you, and soon after, they're gonna have an empty shotgun shell with your prints on it. . . ." Cooper let it sink in. "By the way, you got wheels?"

"Uh-uh."

"No ride. How were you fixin' to get away?"

"Walk out, I guess. Through them woods."

"And if you made it through those swampy woods — that is, if the copperheads didn't get you first — what were you going to do then? Hitch a ride out on the two-lane? Wait for the county sheriff to pass on by?"

Clagget's shoulders slumped. "I hear you. But what do you *want?*"

Cooper said, "Tell you what. You ride out with me; we'll talk about it then."

"I don't know. I need to think."

"While you're thinking on it, think of this: This picture's got one more reel to it, right?"

"Yeah. The Hammer's gotta go and get the crooked cop, the one who fucked him up when he was a kid. Then he goes back to Harlem, gets it himself from the kids in his own neighborhood —"

"I know the picture, man. You don't have to tell me, 'cause I *know*. The thing is, when this reel is over — oh, I'd say about two minutes from now — your manager or whoever is gonna be runnin' back here to find out why the screen's turned all white."

"I do believe you got a point." Clagget rubbed his face. "Okay. Maybe we better go."

"Good. Mind, you don't want to be walking around where everyone can see you like that."

"Pick me up, then. I'll wait right here."

"And I'll just be a minute. Swing on back around with my short."

Bobby Roy Clagget watched the black man head back toward the cars, wide of shoulder and walking proud. He was big, strong as Jim Brown. Not the uncomfortable Jim Brown from *100* Rifles. The bad mother*fucker* Brown from *Slaughter's Big Rip-Off*. Big and bad like that. Clagget wouldn't mind riding with a guy like Wilton Cooper, at least long enough to get out of town. While he was riding, see what this Cooper dude had in mind.

Cooper brought his ride — a 1970 Challenger convertible, red on red with a wide black hood stripe running between the NACA scoops — around to the side of the projection house. Clagget went to the passenger side, opened the door, pulled the shotgun free, slipped it back behind the seat, dropped into the bucket, and shut the door. He ran his hand along the wood-grained dash.

"Damn," said Clagget. "*Vanishing Point!*"

"Cleavon Little."

"You know your movies, Cooper?"

"I've seen a few."

"I'm into movies myself."

"I sensed that in you, B. R."

The big screen had gone blank. A white man in a starched white shirt sprinted toward the projection bunker as a cacophony of horns filled the night air.

"That your boss?"

"Yeah."

"Then we best be on our way."

It took a little while to get out of the drive-in. Some frustrated customers up ahead had decided to go on and leave. Cooper put the

Challenger into the back of the line, got comfortable in the bucket, let himself relax. He wasn't worried about the cops just yet. He was a patient man until things got real good and hot, and he could see that the kid was, too. Cooper reached into his shirt pocket, withdrew a Salem long.

"I could use one of those myself," said Clagget.

Cooper shook one free, struck a match, held the flame out for Clagget. In the light he saw the awful cranberry red acne patterned like vomit on the boy's cheeks. The acne ruined his looks, but other than that, like many backwoods white boys, Clagget seemed almost featureless. Just a boy, most likely, not yet twenty-one.

"Thanks, bro," said Clagget.

"Sure thing," said Cooper, and he put the match to his own smoke. They were moving now, almost out of the exit gate.

"Funny thing," said Clagget.

"What's that?"

"The fat man. He never knew it was coming. Not even up till the end. And even then, I don't believe he ever knew why."

"Why'd you croak him then, man?"

"He was always *lookin'* at me. Lookin' at me and smilin'. And as hard as I'd look back at him, he'd still be giving me this smile. It got to the point I knew I'd have to take that smile off his face for real."

"You killed him 'cause he smiled at you."

"I guess."

"You ever think, B. R. — and I'm just makin' conversation here — that the man was smilin' just to be friendly?"

"I don't know. You could be right." Clagget dragged on his smoke, shrugged, looked down at the cigarette between his thin fingers. "Ain't too much I can do about it now."

"You got that right, B. R. You surely do."

They were out of the drive-in and going west on the two-lane. A cop car screamed down the asphalt toward them.

"Let's put the top down, Wilton."

"Might want to wait a minute on that one. Let the sheriff get on past." Cooper steadied the wheel with his thighs, put his hands over his ears to shut out the siren as the cop car went by. He hated that sound. He watched the taillights fade, put his hands back on the wheel. "Well, there goes your ride, boy. The one I was describing to you earlier."

Clagget nodded. "I do thank you."

"Glad to help."

"What now?"

"We'll be out of here tonight. Pick up a couple of local boys I know, get you some clothes, get ourselves on the road."

"I never even been out of this state."

"You're fixin' to have yourself a little adventure now."

Clagget looked out the open window. "You know, Wilton, I never did take to work much."

"Neither did I."

"But I sure am gonna miss that drive-in. Free movies all the time."

"You'll get over it."

"I know it. I was waiting on this real special one, though, was gonna open next week."

"Which one was that?"

"*King Suckerman*."

"One about the pimp?"

"Uh-huh. But like no pimp there ever was."

"Rougher than *The Mack*?"

"Shit, yeah. *Way* rougher."

"Who's playin' the player?"

"Ron St. John."

Cooper nodded, pursed his lips. "Ron St. John is *bad*, too."

"Yeah."

"Don't worry, little brother. They got plenty of movie theaters where we're goin', I expect."

"Where's that?"

"Washington, D.C."

"Chocolate City?" said Clagget.

Cooper said, "Who don't know *that*."

TWO

arcus Clay pulled the Hendrix out of the rack, walked it from Soul to Rock, slid it back where it belonged, in the H bin, in the mix between Heart and Humble Pie. That slim boy Rasheed — Karras liked to call him Rasheed *X* — kept filing Hendrix in the Soul section of the store. Rasheed, with his picked-out 'Fro, red, black, and green knit cap, and back-to-Africa ideology, keeping the flame for racial purity. Clay understood what the young brother was trying to say, and he respected that, but this here was a business — *Clay's* business, to the point. What if some pink-eyed white boy with an upside-down American flag patch on the ass end of his jeans came in looking for a copy of *Axis: Bold as Love,* couldn't find it, and then, too stoned and too timid to ask one of the black clerks, walked out the door? For what, some kind of statement? Marcus Clay didn't play that. And anyway, Jimi? That boy *did* belong in Rock.

"Hey, Rasheed!"

"Yeah." Rasheed, not looking up, standing behind the counter, tagging LPs with the price gun, mouthing the words to Curtis Mayfield's "Back to the World" as it came at three-quarter volume through the house KLMs. That was the other thing about Rasheed: always playing the music too loud in the shop. At least he had Curtis on the platter, though. The boy had enough good sense for that.

"I'm not gonna tell you again about moving Hendrix into Soul. I'm getting tired —"

"I hear you, boss." Copping to it, but still not looking up.

"See that you *do* hear me, man."

"Solid."

"Just see that you do," said Clay, turning his back.

12

Rasheed said, "I guess you ain't heard *Band of Gypsys*, then."

There it was. Clay closed his eyes, breathed deep. He stared at the *Rufusized* poster on the wall, let his eyes linger on Chaka Khan — man, she was fine — to make himself relax. "I heard it. So what?"

"With Buddy Miles on the sticks? Jimi steps up and plays some serious funk, no question. 'Machine Gun' and *all* that. So now you gonna make the claim his catalog don't belong in Soul? Cause you know funk was where he was headed when —"

"What you think you are, man, the Amazing Kreskin, some bullshit like that? You gonna tell me now where a dead man was headed with his shit? I'm telling *you* that where he was *when* he died was rock, and that's where his shit's gonna get filed long as it's in my shop. Dig?"

"I dig, boss," Rasheed said, with his put-on white-boy enunciation. "I do dig your heavy vibratos."

The front door opened then, which was a good thing for Rasheed since right about then Clay had gone about as far with all that as he would go. It was Cheek, Clay's big-as-a-bear assistant manager, entering the store. Cheek, a half hour late and higher than a hippie. Despite his Sly Stone oval-lensed shades, Clay could see from his tentative steps that the boy was damn near cooked.

Cheek stopped, grinned, cocked an ear in the direction of the speakers, cupped his hands around an imaginary mike, went right into a Curtis falsetto. Truth was, Cheek's tone was too high, closer to Eddie Kendricks than it was to Mayfield. But Clay had to admit the boy was pretty good.

"You're late," said Clay.

Cheek stopped singing, removed his shades, wiped dry his buggy eyes. "Yeah, I know it. And I do apologize. But I was out late last night —"

"Gettin' some of that stanky-ass pussy," said Rasheed, "from that Hoss Cartwright–lookin' bitch of his over in Capitol Heights."

"Naw, man," said Cheek. "And shut your mouth about Sholinda, too, nigger." Cheek looked at Clay. "Guess where I was last night, Marcus."

"I suppose you're gonna tell me."

"Listening to some funk. Or should I say, listenin' to some *uncut* funk."

"You went to the P-Funk show?" said Rasheed.

"Damn sure did," said Cheek. "I'm talkin' about the Bomb."

"Dag, boy!" Rasheed shook his head. "I wanted to check that motherfucker out my *own* self!"

"Well, you missed it." Cheek paused, waited for Rasheed to lean forward. "Yeah, Cole Field House, man. Seven hours of festival-style throwin' down with the Funk Mob. Bobby Bennett emceed —"

"The Mighty Burner was there?"

"That's right. Introduced the opening act."

"Who was it?"

"The Brothers Johnson. Thunder Thumbs and Lightnin' Licks."

"*Fuck* the Brothers Johnson."

"Yeah, I know. They was there is all I'm sayin'. But Gary Shider came out next. Wearin' a diaper and shit. Then Bootsy with the Rubber Band, played the *fuck* out that bass of his and then let loose with the Horny Horns. Fred Wesley and Maceo. Right after that? Starchild, citizen of the universe. The niggers was trippin'! Doin' it in three-D. . . ."

"All right," said Clay, "we get it."

"We gonna turn . . . this mu-tha . . . out," sang Cheek.

"I said we get it. I'm goin' out for a couple of hours, so it's time you got to work."

"You ain't gonna be too late, are you?" said Cheek.

"Why?"

"Thought I'd check out this new one they got opening up at the Town."

"I won't be late," said Clay.

"What new one?" said Rasheed.

"*King Suckerman,*" said Cheek.

Rasheed looked up. "That the one about the pimp?"

"Not any old pimp. The baddest player ever was. 'The Man with the Master Plan Who Be Takin' It to the Man.' "

"*Who be.* That's what the ad says, huh? I bet some white man wrote that movie; produced it, too. Even wrote that line about 'the Man' that's gonna get you in the theater. Like by goin' to that movie, givin' up your cash money, you gonna get over on the Man yourself."

"So?"

"So it's you they gettin' over on, blood. Don't you know it's those Caucasian producers out in Hollywood makin' all the money off you head-scratchin' mugs, pushin' your dollars through the box-office window for the privilege of watchin' two hours of nothin'? Puttin' money back into the white machinery so that they can go right on back and do it again? And all the while they be gettin' richer, and you just stuck where you're at, not goin' anywhere at all."

"It's called havin' a little fun, Rasheed. Ain't you never heard of that?"

"You're just ignorant, that's all."

"Yeah, I'm ignorant. I'm good and ignorant, *bleed.* And while you readin' your Little Red Book tonight, I'll be out havin' a good-ass time at the movies. And then, inside my crib a little later on, while you're still recitin' your proverbs and shit, I'll be hittin' the fuck out of some good pussy. You can *believe* that."

"Sholinda?" said Rasheed.

"Got-damn right."

Rasheed and Cheek were still talking shit as Clay walked to the back room. He washed up and changed into a pair of shorts, put his Superstar-highs on his feet and laced them tight. He was back out front in a few, and now Rasheed and Cheek were arguing about some detail on the Pedro Bell cover of *America Eats Its Young.* Cheek had laid side two on the platter, and the instrumental that kicked things off, "A Joyful Process," had come on in. Clay liked that one; the comic-book stuff in their lyrics, that he could do without, but Clinton and those boys in Funkadelic, no question, they could play.

"I'll be back in a couple of hours," said Clay, raising his voice over the horns.

Cheek, shaped like a brown snowman with a full Teddy Pendergrass beard, looked up. "What time you want me to cut the register tape, Marcus?"

" 'Bout an hour from now should do it."

"Playin' a little ball today, boss?" said Rasheed.

"Yeah."

"With your Caucasian friend?"

"He's Greek."

"He looks plenty white to me."

"Claims there's a difference," said Clay. "Damn if I know what it is."

Clay looked back at them before he left the store, standing there, smiling like fools. He knew, soon as he left, they'd be in the stockroom, firing up some of Cheek's Mexican. It made no difference to him, long as they did their jobs. Way he saw it, if they rang a few sales, didn't burn the place to the ground, and kept their hands out of the till, he'd be coming out ahead.

Dimitri Karras watched Marcus Clay leave his store, emerge from under the Real Right Records awning, head down Connecticut toward R, where Karras held the ragtop maroon Karmann Ghia idling by the curb. Clay with his smooth, dark skin, a modified Afro and thick mustache, walking with that head-held-high way of his, a kind of bounce, really, not exaggerated but earned. Karras didn't blame him; if he had Clay's looks, shit, man, he'd be strutting, too.

Karras checked himself in the rearview: black hair falling in waves to his shoulders, a black handlebar mustache, deep brown eyes picking up the chocolate color of his pocket T. Not bad. Not a stone swordsman like Clay, but not bad. Yeah, Karras, when he smiled — and he was smiling now, giving it to the mirror full on — he could turn some heads.

"Easy, lover," said Clay, dropping into the shotgun seat. "Next thing you know, you'll be picking out a ring."

"I thought I had something in my teeth. I was just —"

"Uh-huh."

Karras pushed the short-stick into first, checked the sideview before pulling out. "Too hot for you, Marcus? I could put the top back up."

"Naw, leave it down. That way I don't have to fold myself up to get in and out of this motherfucker. Course, this toy fits you just fine. Big man like me, though . . ."

Karras headed up Connecticut. The VW lurched into second, causing Clay's head to bob involuntarily, like one of those spring-necked dogs set in the back windows of cars. Clay gave Karras a look.

"Poor man's Porsche," explained Karras with an apologetic shrug.

"And a Vega GT's a poor man's Vette."

"Some do claim that."

Karras cut right, headed down into Rock Creek, reached back behind the passenger seat, pulled free a leatherette box filled with eight-track tapes. Clay held the wheel steady while Karras flipped back the lid and looked through the box.

"What you puttin' in? 'Cause I don't even want to hear no Mo the Rooster."

"Mott the Hoople."

"Yeah, none of that. Put somethin' in there that's got some bottom, man."

Karras slipped a tape into the deck. "Robin Trower. *Bridge of Sighs.* Rightful heir to Mr. Hendrix —"

"I don't want to talk about Jimi, now. Okay?"

Karras found a joint in his shirt pocket, fired it up off the VW's lighter. He hit it, passed it over to Clay. They exited a long tunnel and went by the National Zoo.

"Nice taste," said Clay.

"The end of my Lumbo. I'm pickin' up an LB later on today."

"What you going through now?"

"I move about a pound, pound and a half a week, keep just enough for myself. It's a living, man, you know?"

"Educated man like you, you ought to find yourself a real job. A good one, too."

"Smoke a little weed, play some ball, listen to tunes . . . get some P now and then — I gotta look at it this way: How could my life get any better?"

"For you, maybe. Me, I like to work."

"I know you do, Marcus."

Karras took in a deep hit of the pot. He offered it to Clay, who hit it again, passed it back. Karras kissed it one last time, butted what was left, pushed the roach to the back of the ashtray.

Clay checked out the sneakers on Karras's feet. "Where'd you get those Clydes, Dimitri?"

"Up at Mitchell's, on Wisconsin."

"I ain't seen 'em in that neutral color, though. They look good like that."

"Mitchell's," repeated Karras.

"I'll have to tell Rasheed. He's been lookin' for just that shade."

"Rasheed *X*."

"That boy's all right. You two just need to sit down and talk."

"Right."

"So where we headed, anyway?"

"Candy Cane City, I guess. Always get a decent game up there."

Clay nodded, then found his head moving to the gravelly Bill Lordan vocals, Trower's blues guitar working against a thick slab of bass. The Columbian was talking to him now, pushing him to find things in the music he might have otherwise overlooked. "This *is* a bad jam, you know it?"

Karras nodded. " 'The Fool and Me.' "

"Your boy Trower, he can play."

"Yeah," said Karras. "Trower's bad."

Clay put on his shades; Karras put on his. The Karmann Ghia moved through the warm summer air beneath a cooling canopy of trees.

THREE

Eddie Marchetti opened up the *Post*, checked out the TV Highlights chart for the day, went down the grid to four o'clock. The menu showed Money Movie Seven, the one where Johnny Batchelder gave away small-time dollars at the commercial break. It was Yul Brynner week, and today they were running *Taras Bulba*. Tony Curtis as Yul Brynner's son — what were they, five, six years apart in age? Right. Marchetti had seen it, and it wouldn't get any better a second time. Over on 9 was Dinah Shore: Ethel Merman, Frankie Valli, and Jimmie Walker, the skinny *titsune* with exactly one joke in his repertoire. No, thanks. He could watch *Robert Young, Family Doctor* on channel 4, but that was nothing but the old *Marcus Welby, M.D.* in syndication, and he had seen all of those on the first go-round. Anyhow, those geezer shows — *Welby, Barnaby Jones,* like that — Marchetti could only take so much of those.

Dinah was just about to start. Marchetti pointed the remote in the direction of the nineteen-inch Sony across the room, cut the power. He dropped the remote in the center drawer of the varnished desk in front of him. He swiveled in his chair, looked out the big picture window to the street.

A million-dollar view! A 'dozer pushing gravel into a mountain of it, and past the mountain of stones some kind of tepee-shaped silo. Beyond the fenced-in lot that housed the miniquarry was a big windowless structure of brick, a dead building by day but a fag club by night. Huge, sweaty dance floor, dick shots projected on the walls, angled mirrors in the johns so the tail-gunners could check out your equipment while you were trying to take a leak, disco music so loud you couldn't even taste the liquor in your drink. Fuck all that. Before

Marchetti's cousin Arturo had gone back to North Jersey, just after he had set Eddie up down in D.C., the two of them had checked the place out, Arturo Marchetti claiming that it would be easy pickings for a couple of swingin' dicks like them, on account of in a fag joint there wasn't any competition for the broads. But none of the women had wanted to dance with them, which left Eddie and Arturo standing there, sipping their drinks like a couple of mo-mos, looking at slide shows of bright-eyed, toothy guys with lizards hanging down to their knees. Eddie wanted to leave, but Arturo, he wanted to stay, ride the night out. For all Eddie knew, maybe Arturo was half queer. And the bitches, the ones that wouldn't dance with Eddie? He figured they must have been faggids themselves.

So the view, it sucked the high hard one. When the family had asked him to leave Jersey, set up a little business out of town — they were only trying to get rid of him, he knew — they had promised to put him in a nice office in a beautiful part of town. First and Potomac, they said, and when he heard the address it sounded so goddamn right. Like it caught a breeze off the river and shit. Well, it was a few blocks from the water, but not that you could tell, and when the odd breeze did come through, it stank of sulfur and diesel. So here he sat, in a moldy cinder-block building in a hot, treeless, dead-ass warehouse district in Southeast D.C. The absolute shithole part of town.

Eddie would show them, though. He'd stick it out. He'd make something happen down here and then he'd go back to his sweet hometown like the fattest motherfucker who ever rode in on four wheels. He would do that if he ever did one thing.

"Come here, baby," said Marchetti, spreading his arms out wide.

Vivian looked up from her place on the wine leather couch across the room. She tapped some ash onto her jeans from the joint dangling between her long thin fingers and returned her gaze to the paperback resting in her lap. Keeping her eyes on the page, she rubbed at the ashes until they had disappeared into the denim.

"Hey, Viv!" said Marchetti, more jovial now. "Come on over here, give Eddie Spags a hug." The kids used to call him Eddie Spaghetti back in Jersey, on account of he was a guido and he did love his pasta. Then Eddie Spags for short, which stuck. Marchetti liked the sound of it. Like it was right out of *The Valachi Papers* or some shit like that, though Eddie knew down deep that the Marchettis were strictly small-time players, double zeros on the back of a uniform. He and his relatives were about as connected as an amputated leg.

Vivian, still not looking up, said, "How about this, Eddie? How about you get up out of that chair, walk across the room, give *me* a hug? How about that?"

Eddie said, "Forget it," though he wished right away he hadn't spoken so quick. A hug, you never knew, if you forced it just a little, it could turn into something else.

Eddie opened the center drawer of his desk, brushed aside the snub-nosed .38 that lay there, grabbed the remote. Christ, if his own girlfriend was more interested in getting high and reading some make-believe story than paying a little attention to him, he might as well watch a little tube. It felt like a morgue in there, anyway, without the sound of the Sony.

Eddie switched on the set, sighed at the snow running across Dinah Shore's face.

"Hey, Clarenze!" he yelled, loud as he could. And Vivian looked up.

Clarence Tate was listening to Eugene Record's tenor, the harmonica drifting in behind the vocal, when he heard the sound of Eddie's voice. "Oh, Girl," that was one of the prettiest records the Chi-Lites had ever cut, and Tate had been sitting way back in the other side of the warehouse, just getting into the tortured beauty of the song, doing nothing but minding his own self. It would be just like Eddie to bust on Tate's groove at a time like that.

Tate got out of his chair, pulled the eight-track from the Capehart compact system, went through the doorway, headed on down the hall.

He passed rows of television sets still in their cartons, stereo systems, compacts and components, some boxed, some not. They'd have to move these right quick. Tate had hooked himself up with a delivery man — cat by the name of Bernard — who drove a truck for the big electronics distributor up in Baltimore. Bernard's company supplied all of D.C.'s electronics retailers — Luskin's-Dalmo, George's, Nutty Nathan's, and others — with their goods, and Bernard had a deal with one of the warehousemen, who'd load up Bernard's truck with a couple of extra pieces on every run. Tate figured it wouldn't be long before either that boy Bernard or the warehouseman would be caught, because that's the way things always ended for small-time boosters like them. So he thought it'd be a good idea to maximize the profit potential while the getting was still good. *Profit potential* — he'd been reading books lately on how to run a hard-goods operation. Course, the books never said a damn thing about *fencing* hard goods. But he figured the basic principles, they had to be about the same.

Didn't Eddie know you had to turn the inventory so you could take in more goods? Didn't he know nothin' about cash flow? No, he didn't expect that Eddie did. Tate would have to bring up the issue with him soon. Sit down with Eddie, counsel him a little, make up one of those business plans.

That is, if he could keep the fat man focused. The thing that bothered Tate was, Eddie was all over the place, throwing all the balls up in the air at the same time, trying to make that big score. He could do all right if he just kept to moving hard goods in and out of the warehouse. But uh-uh, the man had to be going in ten different directions at once, selling herb, pounds at a time, and now cocaine, brokering a deal between those Southern boys on their way into town and the Howard County bikers. Eddie, he had no idea what it meant to play with bad motherfuckers like that.

Clarence didn't know why he worried about it anyway. He had never meant to take on all this responsibility. It started when he had gone and answered that *Washington Post* ad, the one Eddie had placed for an "executive assistant," the description vague but with phrases thrown in like "sky's the limit, self starter," bullshit hustle like that. He figured he'd take the job for a short while, a transition thing, buy a few things extra for his little girl. Here he was a year later, still wet-nursing the Italian, running the show, *strategizing*, himself. Didn't *that* beat all?

Clarence Tate pushed on the door at the end of the hall, entered the main office. There sat Eddie Spags, eyes kind of glazed, watching the Sony. Who was that, that fool Jimmie Walker, talking all that fast, stupid shit on the screen? And the girl, Vivian, stoned and bored, sitting across the room with her legs tucked underneath her, taking that free ride from Eddie, not even giving it up anymore, just hanging around. One thing he did know: If she was his, Tate would never let her get away with that. Fine as she was, too.

"You call me, Eddie?"

"Yeah. It's snowin' on the Dinah Shore set, Clarenze."

Clarenze. Saying it like he thought the niggers would. Course, no brother had ever called him Clar*enze*. But Tate knew it would be a waste of time to try and explain it to him. What Eddie knew about the black man was what he picked up off the straight-up bullshit he saw on TV. The man was that kind of thick.

"I'll get up on the roof, jiggle the antenna."

"Thanks."

"And Eddie."

"Yeah."

"What's the schedule lookin' like for the rest of the day?"

"You know," said Marchetti. "Little bit of this and that. Got that guy Cooper coming into town sometime today. Wants to talk about the coke deal with those biker fellows I know."

"And you know Cooper from?"

"He works for a guy by the name of Carlos. Used to be a busboy in my old man's restaurant back in North Bergen. Went down to Miami a few years back and got himself into some more lucrative shit. Wears shiny suits now with long-collared shirts underneath." Marchetti winked at Tate. "We keep in touch."

"Okay." Tate sighed. "What else we lookin' at?"

"Greek boy by the name of Karras is coming by. Wants an LB."

"You know this Karras?"

"Loopy vouched for him."

"I thought you only sold herb to Loopy."

"That's right, but Loopy went out of town on a vaykay. He set me up with Karras so there wouldn't be any coitus interruptus on my dope trade. Just this one time." Marchetti chuckled. "Hey, Viv, you hear that? Coitus interruptus on the dope trade?"

"I heard you, Eddie."

"And how you know," said Tate, "that this Karras cat isn't a narc?"

"Because, like I said, Loopy vouched for him."

"Can't argue with that," said Tate. "Man named Loopy tells you something, you gotta believe it."

"And anyway," said Marchetti, "any fool knows, you ask someone, 'Are you a narc?' they have to answer true if they are, otherwise it ain't a clean bust."

"Okay, Eddie," said Tate. "Sounds like you got it all figured out."

"Why you wanna know what's on our plate, Clarenze?"

"Thought I'd cut out early. Was hoping to check out this movie tonight, just opened up."

"What movie?"

"*King Suckerman*," said Tate.

Vivian looked up. "That the one about the pimp?"

"Sure is," said Tate.

Marchetti said, "Like Rooster on *Baretta,* right?"

"Not exactly," said Tate.

Tate heard the slam of a car door, then another. He walked behind Marchetti's desk, stood before the big window, looked down to the street. A big Jim Brown–lookin' brother, two others darker than midnight, and a skinny white boy with a fucked-up face were moving away from a red-on-red ragtop Challenger. Tate could see from two floors up, the white boy had some kind of hog's leg stuck down in his pants.

"Eddie," said Tate. "This Cooper cat, he say how you'd know him when he showed up?"

Marchetti blinked his eyes. "Said he'd be rolling into town in a red Mopar. Why?"

"He's here," said Tate.

"Oh, yeah?" said Eddie.

"Uh-huh," said Tate. "Brought a few associates with him, too."

FOUR

Dimitri Karras put a bounce pass in to Marcus Clay; the shirts converged. Clay got it right back out to Karras at the top of the key, and Karras took the J. The ball hit the hole clean, kissed the bottom of the net.

"String music," said Karras.

"Game," said Clay.

The shirts went off the court, their heads down, hands on hips. One of them went to the portable eight-track on the sideline, changed the tape, put in *Gratitude*, turned up the V.

The skins — Karras, Clay, Kenny Lane, and Bill Valis — got in a loose circle, gave each other skin, caught their breath, waited for the shirts to come back out for the rubber match. Clay had played against Kenny Lane when Lane was a forward at Western in '65. Billy Valis was the young boy of the group, heavyset, but a guy who could drive and move underneath in unexpected ways. Valis wore an easy smile and a red bandanna, pirate-style, over his longish black hair. He loved to play ball, thought he was Earl Monroe.

The shirts came back out. The game began, and the shirts took an early lead. They had a guy named Heironymous — his teammates called him Hero — who had gone All-Met for Spingarn, and Heironymous was lighting it up from the outside, just handling Kenny Lane. Clay switched with Lane and noticed that Hero made a funny kind of grimace before he went up. Soon he had him shut down.

Karras took the ball out, shot it inside to Valis, who drove the lane. Valis went up, committed himself, turned around in midair, put some English on the ball as he spun it off the backboard and into the net.

"The Monroe Doctrine," said Valis to his defender.

"Damn," said his defender.

"Cover him, then," said Heironymous. "Motherfucker's a whirling dervish and shit."

One of the shirts took a corner shot. The ball bounced straight up off the back of the rim. Clay went up, pinned the rebound to the backboard, stayed in the air, threw it twenty feet out to Karras, who quick-released the jumper, sank the pill. Karras took the next shot from the same spot, hit it. The defender checked it to Karras, who took it back, hit it again. Valis let out a whoop.

"Respect yourself," said Karras to his defender, a stocky guy from Northeast.

"Staple Singers," said Clay, crossing the court to give Karras a low five.

Heironymous turned to the one defending Karras. "You gon' let Gail Goodrich take those all day?"

Karras took the ball out, dribbled back outside the key, made like he was going to take it, put it in to Clay, who was slanting inside. Clay came off a Valis pick, drove the lane, reversed the layup.

Heironymous and his crew came back with three in a row. Lane sank a double pump, and Valis corkscrewed one in right behind it. That tied things up.

Karras's defender drove right by him, put one up. Clay skied, rejected the shot. The ball went out to Karras. He went up listening to Phillip Bailey's falsetto on "Reasons." The ball caught only net. Karras watched it swish, the sun warming his face as the EWF horns kicked in. Karras knew, right then, that he'd never get a nine-to-five, that he'd play ball and get high as long as he could, and that he fucking loved D.C. His shot had ended the game.

The shirts did fifty push-ups in front of the skins. Valis said goodbye to his teammates and walked across the bridge, over the creek to his lime green '69 Dart. Heironymous stood up, took off his shirt, toweled himself off. He walked over to Karras and Clay.

"Game, Gail," said Heironymous with a slight nod of his chin.

"Thanks," said Karras.

Karras drifted. Heironymous shook Clay's hand — fist to fist, then finger grip — and snapped his fingers one time. They talked about the Suns-Celtics series, concluded in six a few weeks back. Black D.C. had been for the Suns, because they were for anyone playing the Celts, and as a bonus incentive the Suns' forward, Curtis Perry, had come out of Washington. It had been a good series, the subject of morning conversation all over town while it lasted; Game Five, with its triple OT, had been a certified NBA classic.

"Way to get up," said Heironymous before he walked away.

"Yeah, good game," said Clay. "You take it light, hear?"

Heironymous shrugged. "Everything is everything."

Clay found his shirt on the grass, went back to the Karmann Ghia, got into the passenger seat. Karras turned the ignition, backed out onto Beach Drive, drove toward town.

"Could use a shower," said Clay.

"You can get one at my crib before you go back to the shop."

" 'Preciate it. That would just about do me right."

"I need to make a stop, though, pick up that herb."

"Drop me off first, hear?"

"Come *with* me, man."

"Uh-uh. I don't need to be gettin' into that."

"What, you got no problem with smoking my weed, but you don't want to see where it comes from?"

"Aw, come on, Dimitri."

"What could happen, anyway?"

"All right, man," said Clay. "You made your point. But let's be quick about it, hear? I told Cheek I'd be back in time for him to make his show."

"Thanks, Marcus. Didn't feel like driving down to Southeast by myself."

Clay got down in the seat, closed his eyes, let the wind and sun dry his face. "Good ball today."

"Yeah, it was pretty nice."

"You had, what, two from that same spot?"

"Three."

"Should have been wearin' a Lakers jersey out there."

"Don't start with that Goodrich shit. Hero sees a white boy who can drill it from the outside, all of the sudden he's callin' him Gail. Shows a lack of imagination on his part, if you ask me. 'Cause you *know* my game is closer to Clyde Frazier's."

Clay grinned. "Guess Hero didn't notice those shoes of yours."

"Have to point them out to him," said Karras, "next time we do some hoop."

Clarence Tate sat on the edge of Marchetti's desk, let his leg swing kind of casual as Cooper and his boys walked into the room. This Cooper dude, it was clear as daylight he was the leader of the crew: It was in the way he walked, out front but not in any kind of hurry, kind of regal-like. And his clothes, too, pressed jeans hooked up with a maroon shirt, a nice wash-'n'-wear job gaping at the buttons from the pull of his running-back chest. A slick boy, that's what this Cooper was, a slick, survivin' motherfucker, the kind of dude who walks out of the prison yard every day on his own two feet. Cooper had the look of a smart con, and Tate knew that look, had been acquainted with plenty of boys just like this one back in the Petworth neighborhood off 13th Street, where he had come up.

The two dark-skinned brothers — not just black brothers, but brothers for *real* — it was obvious that one of them had done a couple of bits himself: hard and cut, not just in the body but in the face as well, like a sculptor had made him in a studio. The second, narrow-assed brother, with his big, open mouth, a hint of a goatee like a badly shaved pussy on his weak, dimpled chin, he wouldn't have lasted in the joint but a few weeks. But different as they looked, Tate could see straight off that they were kin. It was how they moved together, attached, almost, not because they wanted to be but because they had to be. Not like partners but like blood. A couple of stone Bamas on their first trip north to D.C.

And then the white boy. A light blue rayon shirt patterned with navy blue seashells, coffee-stained white bells, a wide black belt, and cheap black stacks with four-inch heels, a white line curlicued across the vamp. Chili mac—lookin' face. Small, stupid eyes. Trying to do some kind of pimp walk into the room, the downstroke kind of walk they tried to pass off as fly on TV. Doing it awkward, even for him, on account of the long gun slid down inside the hip of the bells. Tate couldn't figure out where this white boy fit in.

Slick said, "Afternoon. Wilton Cooper." He reached across the desk to where Marchetti had stood out of his chair.

"Mr. Cooper." Marchetti imprisoned Cooper's thumb, gave Cooper his idea of the soul shake. Tate saw a glimmer of amusement in Cooper's eyes. "Eddie Marchetti. They call me Eddie Spags."

"Eddie Spags. That right."

" 'Ey." Marchetti shrugged, spread his hands. "Got to jive to stay alive, right?"

Tate tried not to wince. Cooper looked at Tate out the side of his eyes. "And you are?"

"Clarence Tate."

Tate got off the desk, stood to his full height, noticed with some relief that he was at eye level with Cooper. They shook hands.

Tate put his ass back on the edge of the desk. Cooper pulled a folding metal chair over in front of the desk, had a seat, crossed one leg over the other, rubbed one hand along his muscled thigh. He looked back at the fine Oriental girl who sat legs-up on the wine-colored couch against the wall. She leaned forward a little, like she was interested in hearing what would be said next.

Cooper made a hand-sweep around the room, where the ones who had come in behind him stood, the brothers together, the white boy alone, all of them awkward, like rejects at a dance floor's edge.

"My boys," said Cooper. "Like you to meet the Thomas brothers, Ronald and Russell. Ronald, I met him in Angola. We kind of partnered up down there for a while, watched each other's backs. I like to call him Mandingo, with affection, understand, though I don't recommend that *you* do. His brother, Russell, he came along for the ride. Picked them up down in North Kakilaki, right from their uncle's farm."

Tate looked at the hard, chiseled features on the one called Mandingo — he *was* a Rafer Johnson–lookin' brother — watched him shake a Kool from the bottom of the pack where he had torn open a hole. Opening the pack from the bottom, that was just like a tobacco-road Bama — like the ad said, you could take Salem out of the country, but you couldn't take the country out of Salem.

"Gimme one of them double-O's," said Russell, the unfortunate one. Ronald Thomas handed his brother the deck. The two of them said something to one another and both of them laughed.

"Here goes my friend Bobby Roy Clagget," said Cooper. "Young man from Carolina way himself. Had the good fortune to meet him down there, thought he might like to come along for the ride."

As if on cue, Clagget pulled the sawed-off from his pant leg, curled his finger inside the trigger guard, let the shotgun hang down along his side.

"You can call him B. R.," said Cooper, "if you'd like."

"Nice to meet you gentlemen," said Marchetti. "All of you."

Vivian chuckled. She was stoned and she couldn't help but laugh. The one called Cooper, alone, he was dangerous for sure, but together as a group, even with the gun, she just couldn't take them in a serious way. They were pathetic, really. The idiot brothers and especially the skinny white one, with his ratty, shoulder-length Afro, the bad-dream *Soul Train* threads, disco-country with the ruined face.

Marchetti shot Vivian an annoyed look. Cooper looked back at her and smiled. He didn't mind her laughter. He and his boys, they *were* a funny sight. He knew it, and he didn't mind. You could laugh at them if you wanted, the way you could laugh at the big cats in the lion house. From *outside* the cage.

"Why the gun?" said Tate to Cooper carefully, like this whole scene wasn't digging a tunnel right through his gut. "You fixin' to knock us over?"

"Don't mind B. R.," said Cooper. "He means you no harm. The shotgun, in a funny kind of way, it's his friend."

"Sure," said Marchetti. "We're all on the same page. Clarenze here, he's the worrier of my staff. Needs to get down a little. Boogie. Know what I mean, Wilton? Can I call you Wilton?"

Cooper rolled his eyes toward Tate. "I'm a little confused. Your boss here called you Clarenze. Thought you said your name was Clarence."

"It is," said Tate.

"Just wanted to make sure I wasn't losing my mind."

"So," said Marchetti, "how's my buddy Carlos doin'?"

Wilton Cooper said, "Carlos is good. Stylin', too. Looks about a million miles away from when you knew him. What was he, a busboy in your daddy's place?"

"That's right."

"Well, he ain't no busboy now. Likes the warmer climate, too. More natural for him. But you know how it is, you improve your station in life, all you're doin' sometimes is tradin' in one set of troubles for another."

"Things aren't going so good for my friend Carlos down there?"

"Don't misunderstand me, now. Things are all right. But the goods Carlos trades in, well, the competition in South Florida, it can get a little fierce. And you get locked in to certain distribution channels, all of the sudden they start owning you."

Got to keep the vendors on their toes, thought Tate. Competition beats negotiation every time.

"So," said Cooper, "Carlos was talkin' to you, and you claimed you could hook him up with a sweet deal on a few keys of 'caine. Something we could take back home, step on a little, make a nice profit. At the same time, let our suppliers know in a subtle way that we can always buy somewhere else, but out of town, not in our own backyard, so we don't be startin' no wars down there and shit."

"That's exactly what I told him. I have a source —"

"A source," said Cooper.

"That's right," said Marchetti. "A biker I know. Guy by the name of Larry."

"Larry."

"Uh-huh. Him and his gang — well, I don't know if you can call them a gang, exactly, but they all ride bikes — they're staying out in a little house on some farmland in a place called Marriottsville, up near Baltimore. Larry and his friends, they deal in quantity."

"You know this."

"I struck up a friendship with Larry and his lady — Larry calls her his lady — in a bar here in D.C. Right on Capitol Hill. Same bar I took Viv over there away from, the place where she was serving drinks, getting her ass patted all day by the customers. Right, Viv?"

"Yeah, Eddie," said Vivian. "You swept me off my feet."

"So I tell Larry what I do. 'I buy and sell things for a living,' I say. And Larry says, 'I got something you can buy, bro, and you can turn around and sell it for a whole lot more.' And I'm like, 'Oh, yeah?' "

"Why didn't you, then?" said Cooper.

"What I do here," said Marchetti, "I buy hard goods, move them around for a profit."

"You're a fence."

"Yeah. And I move a little reefer, too. Viv likes to smoke it now and again, so it keeps us in a private stash. But cocaine? Shit, Wilton, I gotta be honest with you, I'm playing an away game there. I wouldn't know what to do with it if it was sitting in my lap."

"Start by gettin' it out your lap," said Russell, "and up your got-damn nose."

"Got *that* shit right," said Ronald, cooler than a corpse, giving soft skin to Russell without even moving his eyes.

"So you got to talking to Carlos," said Cooper.

"Thought we could work something out."

"You be the broker," said Cooper.

"For the standard ten points," said Marchetti.

"And that would bring us up to today."

"Right. The way Carlos put it, he'd send you up here, you show me you got the money so I don't embarrass myself, and I put you up with

Larry. You make the buy, I get my twenty G's, you go home, everyone's happy. How's that sound?"

"Solid as a motherfucker, Eddie."

"So," said Marchetti with a nervous smile. "The money."

"What," said Cooper, "you thought I'd forget about that?"

Tate looked over at the white boy, hip cocked, his finger grazing the back of the shotgun's trigger.

Cooper arched his back, dug into his front pocket, grunted. "Be glad when these tight jeans go out of style. Here we are." He pulled free a roll of bills, leaned forward, dropped the bills on Marchetti's desk. "Twenty grand. How's that look to you, Spags?"

Eddie Marchetti smiled, picked up the money. He looked at it briefly, like he didn't need to count it, counted it quickly in his head. Tate got off the desk at the sound of a car door, went to the window behind Marchetti's desk.

"Black dude and a white dude, Eddie, comin' to the door."

"White dude look like a Greek?" said Marchetti, his eyes still on the bills.

"How should I know, man?"

"It's that Karras guy, most likely, come to pick up his dope."

"Should I tell him to come back later?" said Tate.

"Hey, Wilton," said Marchetti, "you don't mind I do a little business real quick, do ya?"

"No," said Cooper, "I don't mind."

"Go ahead, Clarenze," said Marchetti. "Buzz the Greek in."

FIVE

U p this way, I guess," said Karras. Clay followed him up a darkened concrete-and-steel stairwell.

"You mean you've never been here before?"

"This isn't my usual distributor."

"So you don't even know who you're dealing with."

"Technically, yeah. But my distributor, guy named Loopy, he's going on vacation, he offered to hook me up with his man, just this one week."

"Loopy."

"Yeah. Don't worry, Loopy's cool."

"Name like Loopy, he don't sound all that cool to me."

Karras opened the heavy door at the top of the landing. He and Clay walked into a large room with a concrete floor, where several men stood and sat around and one young woman reclined on a wine leather couch. One of those standing, a skinny white kid with a face full of acne, held a sawed-off shotgun at his side.

Karras and Clay had a look at the group, all of whom had turned to look at them. Clay knew then he should not have come along. His friend had asked him to, and because Karras *was* his friend, Clay had done it. But he shouldn't have come, just the same. He only wanted to run his business, live a quiet kind of life. He had seen all the guns he would ever want to see. And here he was, facing a roomful of country knuckleheads and a teenage peckerwood with his finger curled around the hot trigger of doom. Clay knew there was nothing more dangerous than a young boy with a loaded gun. The young, they just didn't understand death.

"Who's Eddie Marchetti?" said Karras in a gregarious, confident tone, stepping across the room, a friendly smile on his face. He'd talked his way out of tighter situations than this: squarehead cops and jealous boyfriends and barroom bad-asses and all the rest. Clay walked with him.

"That's me," said Marchetti, dropping the money on his desk. "You Dimitri Karras?"

"That's right. This is my friend Marcus Clay."

Clay nodded, noticed the tall brother, the one with the gentle eyes who sat on the edge of the desk, give him a second look at the sound of his name.

"Dimitri and Marcus," said Marchetti, giving it *his* smile, just one of the boys. "Sounds like a couple of gladiators."

"Look more like Christopher Salt and Charlie Pepper to me," said Clagget. "Right, Wilton?"

"What's that?" said Marchetti.

"*Salt and Pepper,*" said Cooper. "Peter Lawford and Sammy Davis Jr. Nineteen sixty-eight. Am I right, B. R.?"

"That's right," said Clagget. "But what was the sequel?"

"*One More Time*?"

"Damn," said Clagget. "Most people get snagged on that one."

Clay turned his head briefly, checked out the two Bamas who were arguing about something behind his back.

"Loopy said you could hook me up," said Karras to Marchetti, hoping to get the transaction in gear.

"Sure. You're looking for what, an LB?"

"A pound ought to do it."

"Premium Lumbo," said Marchetti.

"Sounds good."

"Four bills, for you. You get what, fifty an OZ, you make a nice four-hundred-dollar profit."

"Sounds fair," said Karras with another smile. If this Marchetti wanted to brag like he knew the business, make himself look bigger in front of his guests, that was all right with him. "So let's do it."

"Clarenze," said Marchetti, "go get that bag out of the back."

Tate got off the desk, began to walk through the door to the hall, stopped, turned around to look at Clay. "Marcus Clay. I hear that right?"

"Right," said Clay.

"You played for Cardoza. Y'all won the Interhigh title in what, nineteen sixty-four?"

"Uh-huh."

"Clarenze," said Marchetti, "go get the weed."

"In a second." Tate put one finger up in the air. If Eddie would've asked, he would have told him that he, Tate, that is, was simply trying to get to know the men who had entered the office. Trying to *qualify* the customer. But Eddie never would have thought to ask.

Tate said, "I remember that championship game against Dunbar. Aaron Webster had the winning bucket, got a pass inside from that tiny-ass guard you had, what was his name?"

"Phil Scott."

"Yeah, that boy could play. *You* could sky, too. Saw you jump from the foul line once all the way to the bucket, just like Connie Hawkins."

"You played, too, didn't you?"

Tate nodded. "Clarence Tate. I was a forward for Roosevelt then. Sixth man."

"You played with Harvey Sebree, right?"

"Sebree and Ronald Graham." Tate looked over at Karras. "You look familiar, too, man."

"Wilson," muttered Karras.

"Guard, right?"

"Yep."

"The Wilson Tigers." Tate grinned. "Losingest basketball team in high school history. Even made *Sports Illustrated* and shit. What were y'all, oh and seventy-three?"

"Something like that, I guess. I don't remember."

"And that's why you're white to*day,*" offered Russell Thomas.

Marchetti said, "Clarenze, go get the weed."

"Hold on a second, Eddie," said Tate, and he looked at Clay. "Funny. I ain't seen you around D.C. in all these years gone by. Not in the Jellef league, nothin' like that. Where you been, man?"

"I was out of town for a few years," said Clay.

Wilton Cooper sized up Clay. *Out of town* ... Vietnam. Which meant the tall cool brother with the easy walk knew how to handle a gun. The way he was built, Trouble Man looked like he could use his hands to fuck some niggers *up,* too.

"Out of town?" said Tate.

"Overseas."

"And I didn't happen to catch what you said you were doin' now."

"I *didn't* say."

Cooper laughed.

"We wouldn't mind hangin' around with you guys" — Karras drew four one-hundred-dollar bills from his wallet, slapped them against his palm — "but we gotta get on our way."

"The weed," said Marchetti.

Tate looked at Clay a moment longer, pushed on the door, went through.

Cooper pulled his Salems from his shirt pocket, drew one for himself, tossed the pack over to Clagget, who caught it with his free hand. Cooper gave himself a light, lit a cigarette for Clagget, who walked over slow and cocky, off the same match.

"Guess you two basketball players are wonderin' who we are," said Cooper, examining the cigarette between his fingers.

Clay turned to the side a little. That way he could keep the two dark-skinned brothers in his sight.

"I'll tell you anyway," said Cooper, " 'cause I got the feeling, despite the way you're actin', all ice-cool and shit, you want to know. We come up to D.C. to do a little business, see. But I figure, we finish our business straight away or not, we gonna stick around a little bit. You all got this Bicentennial celebration up here next week, they claimin' it's gonna be the biggest party in the history of the Yoonited States. Thought it might be somethin' for us to see."

"Got some freaks up here, too," said Ronald Thomas.

"Ain't that cold?" said Russell Thomas.

"*Talk* about it," said Ronald.

"You and your boy," said Cooper, "you gonna check it out? Bet you two know all the spots."

Clay didn't answer. He wondered what was keeping Tate.

"You too good to talk to me, brother?" said Cooper to Clay.

Clay glanced at Karras, now checking out the Chinese freak on the couch. She was checking him out, too. Karras, even in a situation like this, always looking to get some play. Someone needed to talk a little sense to that boy.

"I see you've noticed Vivian," said Marchetti, good naturedly enough but with an edge. Karras saw a hardness in Marchetti's eyes, but a surface hardness, with only insecurity beneath the veneer.

Vivian smiled at Karras.

"She's beautiful, isn't she?" said Marchetti, raising his voice some. "You gotta admit, she's a mover."

"She's a mover," repeated Karras, because it made him think of the song. "Big Star."

"*Radio City*," said Vivian, naming the LP, which made Karras smile. A hot-looking chick like this, hip and into good tunes, sitting in a dark warehouse in Southeast with a meatball like Eddie Spags. Why?

"Chill, man," said Clay in a soft way.

Marchetti wiped sweat off his forehead. With the AC on, it was colder than a nun's snatch in there, and still he was sweating. It was the Greek and his little Chinese girlfriend, the one who never even fucked him, it was those two and the way they were flirting in front of him — in front of everyone — it was the two of them and the way they were disrespecting him that was making him sweat.

"Hey, Viv, honey," said Marchetti, but she didn't answer.

Clarence Tate came back into the room with a brown paper grocery bag in his hand. He walked it over to Karras, who exchanged it for the four hundred dollars.

Tate folded the money. "You want to weigh it, make sure? I got a scale in the back."

Karras hefted the bag, shook his head. "I don't need to scale it out. It's got good weight."

Tate said, "Solid." He walked back to the desk, where Clagget now stood, dragging on his cigarette.

"Let's go, man," said Clay.

"Vivian," said Marchetti. "Get me a beer out of the fridge, bring it over to Daddy, will you?"

"Get it yourself, Ed —"

"I said bring it here!"

Marchetti's voice left an echo in the room. Cooper put his cigarette between his lips, stifled a grin. His eyes moved from the Italian to the girl.

"All right, Eddie," said Vivian, uncoiling off the couch and walking, back straight and with a bounce, to the compact refrigerator in the corner of the room.

Dimitri Karras took her in: not just hip and hot and tune savvy. Long legs, a rack, and a nice package in the back, too.

"Hey, Mitri," said Clay. "Didn't you hear me, man? I said let's go."

Both of them turned, but Marchetti, standing out of his seat now, said, "Wait a sec, fellas, I want you to see something here. After all, Karras, you been lookin' at it the whole time. You might as well stay another minute, have a look at it all."

Vivian was moving across the room with quick, even steps, the can of beer in her hand. She pulled the ring off the top of the can and tossed it back over her shoulder.

"Aw, look at her," said Marchetti, "she's all upset."

"Let's do it, boy," said Clay.

"Karras," said Marchetti. "You ever see a Chinese broad with such a beautiful set of tits?"

No, thought Karras, I haven't. But why'd you have to go and disrespect her like that?

Vivian reached the desk, made a quick, sharp jerk of her wrist. The can in her hand shot off a short arc of beer. The beer splashed across Eddie Marchetti's face.

Clagget flicked his Salem against the cinder-block wall.

Marchetti said, "Bitch." He backhanded Vivian at the jawline. There was the dull clap of flesh on flesh, and Vivian went down before the desk.

Later, Karras couldn't remember crossing the room. It was like he was by the door one moment and around Marchetti's desk the next. With the pound of pot still in his left hand, he punched the fat little Italian in the eye with a short right, followed through with the punch. Marchetti went back over his own chair, did a half somersault to the concrete floor.

Clay had moved with Karras and now he pulled on the back of Karras's T-shirt. Then he turned at the sound of the shotgun's pump. The white boy with the fucked-up face was walking toward them, gun up and pointed, now just two feet away. No one else, not the dark-skinned brothers or the slick brother or Clarence Tate, had moved an inch.

It was slow motion from there but quick in its own way, the way heat time had always been for Clay. He straightened his arm, dropped it a little, came up with a snake-strike, knocked the short barrel of the shotgun to the side, grabbed as he did, and pulled the gun free. He had one hand on the pump then and the other on the stock, and the white boy stood in front of him with nothing in his own hands but air. Clay swung the stock of the shotgun sharply, smashed it into the white boy's mouth. Something cracked, and a couple of thin dice flew away from the kid's face in one direction while some blood and saliva sailed off in the other. The kid went down. Clay pumped out the shells that had been loaded into the shotgun. He tossed the shotgun across the room.

"Whoooeee," said Wilton Cooper, one leg crossed over the other, the cigarette still in place.

Clay heard Karras say, "C'mon, you're coming with us," and when he turned his head in the direction of the voice he saw Karras helping the Chinese girl to her feet.

Marchetti had gotten to his knees. He reached up toward the desk drawer.

"Don't, Eddie," said Tate, who hadn't gone forward at all, had not even moved his hands. "Just don't. Let it lie."

Marchetti sat back.

Clay, adrenalized, picked the stack of money up off the desk. He clumsily folded it into two rolls, put one roll in each pocket of his shorts. He couldn't have said, at that moment, why he had done a dumb thing like that. He felt it was owed him, and that was all.

"Now you gonna rob us, too," said Cooper. "That right, Trouble Man?"

"Teach you country motherfuckers a lesson," said Clay, not believing his own cocky words, regretting them as they came from his mouth.

Clay backed away to the door, past Ronald and Russell Thomas and their hard stares. Karras and the girl were already there.

"I expect we're gonna see you boys again," said Cooper.

"I expect you will," said Clay.

Clay, Karras, and Vivian went through the door. The ones in the office listened to their rapid footsteps echo in the stairwell.

Tate helped Marchetti to his feet.

"Wilton," said Clagget. He was on his knees, blood seeping through the fingers of the hand covering his mouth, dripping down into a small puddle pooled before him on the floor.

"I know, B. R. We gonna get you somewhere, fix your ass up."

"My mouth," said Clagget, working to sound out the word completely. His front teeth were gone.

"Trouble Man took you to school," said Cooper. "We gonna talk about that later."

Tate got Marchetti into his chair, then went to the window. He watched the three of them jog across the street, Clay and the girl climbing into the open-air VW while the Greek stashed the bag under the hood, which on that fool car was the trunk. Tate couldn't make out the number on the D.C. plates. No matter. There couldn't be many cars like that one in town. Tate watched Karras get behind the wheel and he watched them drive away.

Cooper saw Marchetti rub at his swelling eye. "Might want to put somethin' on that."

"What the hell happened?" said Marchetti.

"That's always the question," said Cooper, "isn't it?"

"Gimme one of them double-O's," said Russell to his brother. Ronald drew two cigarettes from the torn hole in the bottom of the deck, handed one to Russell. Russell struck a match, lit his smoke, lit his brother's.

"Tell you one thing," said Russell. "Trouble Man ever even have a dream about fuckin' with me, he gonna find somethin' out. I'd steal that nigger right in the face. I'd *double* steal that motherfucker."

Ronald chuckled. "That nigger would fuck you up, boy."

"Don't be callin' me no boy," said Russell.

"Go ahead, man."

"You see a boy standin' here," said Russell, "suck his dick."

"Aw, go ahead," said Ronald.

Cooper dropped the end of his Salem to the floor, crushed it beneath his canvas jazz shoe. He looked at Marchetti, whose left eye had begun to darken.

"Shame about the money," said Cooper.

Marchetti squinted. "That was *your* money, Wilton."

"You're mistaken," said Cooper. "I gave it to you, remember? That was your commission for puttin' me up with that biker friend of yours. What was his name?"

"Larry."

"Larry, that's right. Course, I might be interested in gettin' that money back for you. Say, for a fifty percent finder's fee. Right after I do my deal with Larry."

"Fifty points," mumbled Marchetti. "Real generous of you, Wilton."

"We friends," said Cooper, "right?"

"Wilton," said Clagget, staggering a little, still dazed as he walked toward Cooper sitting in the chair.

"All right, boy," said Cooper. "We better go see about gettin' you cleaned up."

Cooper got up out of his chair. Tate tossed him a rag. Cooper took the rag and went to Clagget.

Clagget said, "I'm gonna kill that motherfucker, Wilton."

"I know you are," said Cooper. He blotted the rag on the blood splashed across the blue rayon of Bobby Roy Clagget's chest.

"I swear for God," said Clagget.

"Hush," said Cooper, shaking his head. "Look at you, man. You done gone and fucked up another pretty shirt."

SIX

Dimitri Karras downshifted, took H across North Capitol. He relaxed his shoulders, glad to be out of the warehouse district, glad as hell to be back in Northwest. Marcus Clay sat to his right, staring straight ahead, mumbling occasionally as the recently completed events replayed themselves in his mind. In the rearview Karras watched Vivian, sitting sideways between the front buckets, her long black hair fanning out in the wind, a slight crescent of purple and a small ring dent on the left side of her pronounced jaw where Eddie Marchetti had given her his hand.

"You okay?" said Karras, turning his head briefly to catch Vivian's eye.

"I'm fine," said Vivian. "Thanks, guys."

"Yeah, Marcus. Thanks."

"Sure thing, lover."

"Wasn't the first time Marcus saved my ass," explained Karras.

"You guys have done this before?"

"Don't make a practice of it. And we damn sure don't make a practice of it when it involves guns. But my friend Dimitri here, he seems to find his way into situations, usually have something to do with a lady." Clay side-glanced Karras. "I'm just the lucky one who happens to be around when it all rains down."

Vivian said, "That thing you did, taking away the kid's gun like that. You were in the service, right?"

"Uh-huh."

"Where'd you learn that move? Vietnam?"

"Thirteenth and Euclid," said Clay.

Karras smiled a little. He knew Marcus would never cop to anything about Vietnam. Karras had talked once with Al Adamson — Rasheed's older brother — who had served with Clay overseas, and had found out how deep into it Marcus had been. But, like just about every soldier Karras had ever known who had seen real action, Marcus preferred to bury it, keep it in the past or let it sleep in some unlit corner of his head. Clay never talked about Vietnam, and Karras never asked.

"Well," said Karras, "it's over now."

Clay exhaled heavily. "You think so, huh?"

"Sure, why not?"

"The girl, for one," said Clay. "That Eddie Spaghetti character, he's gonna want her back. You don't mind if I call you a girl, do you, baby?"

"No, I don't mind."

"And the money," said Clay. "*Especially* the money. I never should've took the goddamn money."

"I was wondering what you were doing there," said Karras.

"Lost my temper and shit. That's all it was. A boy holds a gun on you like that, it steals something from you, man. I just wanted to steal something back."

Karras smiled. "You gave 'em a little attitude with your words, too, Marcus. Talkin' about that country shit."

"They were some Macon County Line–lookin' motherfuckers," said Clay.

He and Karras laughed. They gave each other skin. Vivian put her head forward between the front seats. She kissed Clay behind the ear and gave Karras one on his cheek.

"Hey, baby, you don't have to do that," said Clay.

"I wanted to," said Vivian.

Karras turned onto New York Avenue, headed west across town. "How old are you, anyway?" he said, his eyes in the rearview.

"How old are *you*?" said Vivian coyly. Karras noticed a dimple tucked along the laugh line of her right cheek.

"Twenty-seven."

"How about you, Marcus?"

"Same."

"I'm nineteen," said Vivian.

"Nineteen?" said Clay. "And here I was askin' if it was all right to call you girl."

"You're a gentleman," said Vivian, "that's all."

"Hey," said Karras, "what about me?"

"You," said Vivian, with some play in her voice. "I'm not so sure about you."

"After what I did?"

"I'm *still* not sure."

"Stupid," said Clay.

"Lighten up, man," said Karras.

"It was plain stupid, takin' that jack."

"So give it back."

"I plan on it," said Clay, "soon as everything cools down. Have to think on how to do it without causin' any more trouble. Maybe contact that Clarence Tate. He seems sensible enough."

Karras squinted. "We should be all right for a few days. They don't know anything about me except my name. And I'm not in the book."

"Neither am I."

"Which ought to buy us a little time."

Clay shook his head. "Stupid, though. Just plain stupid."

"Hey, where we going, anyway?" said Vivian.

"My apartment. Marcus needs a shower, and I could use one, too."

"I could use a little smoke," said Vivian. "I had a nice buzz goin' before you guys came to the party. All that trouble back there, it made me crash."

"Plenty of herb in the trunk," said Clay, pointing to the hood of the VW. "Where the engine is on a real car."

Clarence Tate looked out the window, watched the Challenger move down the block, cut right, disappear. Two blocks away, he could still hear the rumble of the engine.

"What a day," said Marchetti.

"Yeah," said Tate.

"I mean, was this a day or what?"

"It was a day, Eddie."

Marchetti fumbled through his desk, brought out the remote. He stared at it for a moment, held it in one hand while he gingerly touched the fingers of the other to his swollen eye.

"Did I deserve this?" said Marchetti.

"Yeah, you deserved it all right. You shouldn't have hit Vivian in front of those two. I mean, you shouldn't have gone and hit her *period*, understand what I'm sayin'? But hittin' her in front of those two is what started all the trouble."

"And then the kid with the gun. What the hell was he thinkin' of?"

"Just a dumb kid," said Tate. "You mix with those kinds, Eddie, I been tellin' you for the longest time, you're gonna get yourself into a world of trouble."

Marchetti waved his hand. "All right, all right."

"Then you go and give those boys a Baggie of cocaine before they leave. Like they need that freeze to get up. Bunch of finger-on-the-trigger motherfuckers to begin with."

"It was a gift, from Larry. I figured they'd want to sample what they were going to purchase. Anyway, what was I going to do with it? You know I don't use that shit. Hell, give me a nice highball to start, a plate of red sauce over linguine, a little antipast, a carafe of the house red to wash it down, that's the only high I need."

"Ray Charles can see that, Eddie."

"What, you think I'm too fat?"

"I ain't say that, man."

"But you think it, right?"

"You're askin' for the truth, you could lose a couple of ounces here and there."

Marchetti looked down at his gut. "If I was a little leaner . . . lean and loose, like that Greek . . . Vivian would've stayed more interested, is that what you're sayin'?"

"Hard to tell. You might have paid her a little more attention. You might have done that. And hittin' her like you did, that was straight-up wrong."

"I'd talk to her," said Marchetti, "if she was here right now. Tell her I was sorry for what I did."

"Maybe you'll get your chance."

"The thing is, I could've made her stay. If you had let me go for the short-nose, I could've backed those two off."

"You oughta be thankin' me. I've seen that Marcus Clay on a basketball court. Boy can get from A to B like quicksilver, man. He would've been *on* you. Lucky you got a local man like me, knowin' all the local boys myself. This here ain't your town, Eddie. You could get hurt, bein' a stranger here like you are."

"Maybe so. But I see those two again, they're gonna pay."

"Way those country boys were talkin'," said Tate, "you're gonna have to get in line."

Marchetti punched the power button on the remote and the Sony flickered on across the room. The news was on, Gordon and Max on channel 9. Another salt-and-pepper team, but these guys were pretty good. Not that you could see for shit, with the snow falling across the tube.

"Before all this started," said Marchetti, "you were gonna fix the antenna, remember?"

"Let me get to it," said Tate.

"Or do I need a new set?"

"We got ten Sonys in the back, Eddie, KV-1920s, just like this one. They're all gonna get the same reception, with all this metal and concrete. Anyhow, you need to stop worryin' about the snow on your set and start thinkin' about how we're gonna move those goods back there, boss."

"All right, all right, I'll think. In the meantime, go jiggle the antenna. *Harry-O*'s on tonight, and I don't wanna be distracted."

Tate grinned. "What, you gonna watch *Harry-O* over *Barnaby Jones*?"

"Quit fuckin' with me, Clarenze. You know I can't take that *Barnaby Jones*. What's Ebsen, like eighty years old? You ever known a bad guy who's gonna back down from Buddy Ebsen? Bad dude holding a gun on Buddy Ebsen, Ebsen going, 'Excuse me, could you hold off on that gun for a second, I got a little problem with my pacemaker.' " Marchetti clutched his chest, laughed, got hyped on his own pantomime. He pointed excitedly at Tate. "Or how about this? 'Excuse me a second, Mr. Bad-News, but could you put the piece down for a minute? I forgot to take my Geritol this morning. . . .' Ain't gonna happen. I *hate* those geezer shows."

"I know you do, Eddie."

"Started with the cripple shows, *Ironside* and then *Longstreet* — the one about the blind detective, like a blind detective could do shit. Now what do you got? You got old and you got old and crippled. Like *Cannon*, with his tuba theme music. He's old and he's a fat fuck in the bargain. What the hell's *he* gonna do, huh?"

"You askin' me a question?"

"I'll take *Harry-O* and *Bronk* any day over those geezer-crip shows. With those guys, at least they can walk down the street without a Seeing Eye dog or someone holding onto their arm, you know what I mean?" Marchetti waited. "You like David Janssen, Clarenze?"

"He's all right. Man don't smile much."

"I bet he gets a load of pussy, though."

"Man gets all that play, you think he'd smile every now and again."

"He smiles. Well, it's more like one of them facial tics, really."

"I better get up on that roof."

"Okay, Clarenze. You go ahead and fix me up."

Clarence Tate sighed. It didn't pay to kid Eddie Spags about his program choices, not unless you had all day to talk it out. Man was serious about his TV.

Tate left Marchetti sitting there, his head rested in his palm, and went through the door into the back hall. He walked by the Sonys and then some Litton microwave ovens and a stack of Webcor table radios — he'd have to talk to Bernard about dropping off the

Mickey Mouse bullshit like that — and some twenty-five-inch Philco "consolette" color TVs and a couple of complete Sansui systems that he wouldn't have minded owning himself. It hurt him, seeing all that inventory just gathering dust like that. He couldn't get it through Eddie's head that they had to move this shit out and move it quick.

Tate would have loved to have gotten out himself. Ex-cons and dead-eyed Bamas and pimply-ass, shotgun-carrying white boys; hot goods and cocaine — he didn't *need* all that in his life. He just wanted a decent job, a few extra dollars so he could see clear to some kind of better life. Not just for him, either. For his sweet little Denice, too.

SEVEN

Dimitri Karras swung the Ghia into a space in front of 1841 R Street, cut the engine.

"Here we are," said Karras.

Vivian had a look at the building: a former mansion with a peeling stucco facade, now four floors housing three units per floor, a small yard out front patched with brown where a fat gray cat with huge ears lay on the grass watching a cluster of gnats hover in the air.

"You live here?" said Vivian.

"Trauma Arms," said Clay.

Karras said, "Come on."

Karras got the grocery bag from the trunk. The three of them went into the building. The resident manager, Duncan Hazlewood — six four, broad of shoulder and chest, bearded, Hemingway with acrylic-stained khakis — was carrying a canvas from his studio and through the hall toward his front door. Hazlewood was an artist, a dropout advertising conceptualist turned painter, now into a period of black-and-white pen-and-ink drawings. His girlfriend, Libby Howland, held the door for him.

"Duncan," said Karras.

Hazlewood eyed the group. "Having a party?"

"We'll let you know."

"See that you do, damnit. Wouldn't want to miss out on it if you did."

They went up the stairs. A white man's raised voice, followed by the sheepish voice of a black man, emerged from behind a closed apartment door. Karras and Clay exchanged looks. The white man was Irvine Nichols, a drama and arts editor at the *Washington Post*. Nichols favored young black men, and he alternately loved them and berated them. For some reason these black men made their way to Nichols's apartment in prodigious numbers.

"Sounds like discipline time on the plantation," said Clay.

"He's a hard boss," said Karras, "but a fair one. Been askin' about you, too, Marcus."

"Knock that bullshit off, man."

Vivian stopped to stare at the door, but Karras and Clay were back on the stairs, heading up to the next level. She followed. Karras put a key to a locked door, opened the door, went through. Clay and Vivian went in behind him.

Karras's apartment went the depth of the building, front to back, with a big bay window facing R. The living area of painted wainscoting and plaster walls was wide and uncluttered, with high ceilings and painted, exposed beams. A Pullman kitchen, harvest gold enamel on steel, was fitted against the wall. Past the kitchen a narrow hall led to a single bedroom and bath.

Vivian took in the bare-bones look: an oak dining table with four hard-seat chairs; a brown couch with sagging cushions; a bentwood rocker; a cable-spool table in front of the couch, a tall blue plastic bong atop the table; a color television set, pushed to the corner of the room; two large floor speakers, wires exposed, placed on either side of the bay window; and, occupying an entire wall, unfinished bookshelves holding an amp, preamp, turntable, scores of paperback and hardback novels, and what seemed like hundreds of records. A ceiling fan moved warm air and dust around the room.

"Spartan," said Vivian.

"How'd you know?" said Karras.

"She ain't talkin' about where your people come from, man," said Clay. "She's sayin' you could use a little decorating advice."

"Oh."

"Let me get my shower," said Clay, and he quick-stepped toward the back of the place.

Karras dropped the bag of dope on the cable-spool table. He gestured to the bag. "Have a seat. Do a hit if you want; knock yourself out."

Vivian looked at the dirty water settled in the bong's tube, the poker stuck in the bowl. She could smell the bong water from where she stood. "You got any papers?"

"I'll get you some."

Karras went back to his room, listened to the ache of the pipes from the bathroom where Clay showered. He found a pack of Tops on his dresser and then straightened the sheets on his mattress, which lay frameless on the floor, before he left the room.

Vivian was breaking up a bud when he came back to the living room. The bud felt sticky between her fingers — a good sign — and its pungent scent filled the room.

"This looks pretty sweet," she said.

Karras gave her the papers. "Your boyfriend always get good dope?"

"Eddie? He wouldn't know Hawaiian from backyard ragweed grown from Mexican seeds. But, yeah, he buys good stuff. Why'd you think I was hanging out?"

"Was going to ask you about that."

"That was part of it. The other part was I had nowhere else to go." Vivian crumpled up the paper, tossed it impatiently to the side. "You better do this. I'm used to EZ-Widers."

"Okay." Karras had a seat next to her on the couch. He licked the glued end of one paper, attached it to another, made a neat fold in the second. He dropped the crushed-up bud into the fold, put the whole deal between the thumb and forefinger of both hands, began to roll a tight number. "What's your full name, anyway?"

"Vivian Lee."

"Right. Your parents *Gone with the Wind* fans?"

"My parents barely even speak English. I don't think they've ever seen a movie in their lives."

"Where'd you grow up?"

"Rockville."

"Your parents there now?"

"Last time I checked."

"They know where *you* are?"

"I haven't talked with them in a while."

"Bet they're worried."

"I guess."

"But you're not worried. You're —"

"Just hanging out."

"Here." Karras handed her the fat, tight joint. He found a book of matches in the pocket of his Levis, dropped it on the table. Vivian leaned across the table. She wore a T-shirt that ended a few inches above the belt loops of her jeans, exposing her flat belly. The T-shirt had blue horizontal stripes, and the lines of the fabric were stretched out where they ran across her breasts. Her breasts were large and hard and pushed straight out in the shirt.

Karras swallowed. "Wanna listen to some music?"

Vivian shook some of her long black hair off her shoulder. She lit the joint, exhaled. "What've you got?"

"Everything."

"Okay."

Karras got up off the couch, walked to the bookshelves, where his records were arranged alphabetically and spine out, making a subtle dick adjustment as he walked. "You like Captain Beefheart?"

"Which one?" said Vivian.

"I got *Spotlight Kid.* Let's see, and I got *Clear Spot.*"

"*Clear Spot*'s cool."

"You got it."

Karras placed the vinyl on his Dual 1228, dropped the needle of the Shure carefully onto the third track. He adjusted the V of the Marantz tube amp that powered the system, listened to the gentle guitar intro and then the bongos coming through the big Bose 501s spaced a wall apart on the other side of the room. Karras had bought the 501s from a jazz-loving salesman named Gregg at the old Sun Radio on Connecticut and Albermarle. Those speakers were his pride.

Clay walked into the room, tucking a short-sleeved button-down into a clean pair of jeans. He always kept some clothes at Karras's place, close as it was to the shop. Don Van Vliet's growl kicked in on the first verse of "Too Much Time."

"Captain Planet," said Clay, giving the eye to Karras.

"What, you gotta give me shit now? You *know* this is bad. Should've been the single of the year, if Reprise had known what to do with it."

Clay found his foot moving to the Memphis-style horns against the backbeat, the female vocalists behind the lead on the chorus, Van Vliet's warped blues vision. "He's doin' that Stax-Volt thing right there."

"Right."

"Sounds like he's got a few sisters singin' backup, too."

"The Blackberries."

"Okay, Dimitri. Your Captain Planet's down."

"You guys want any of this?" Vivian held out the fatty.

Karras took a hit, offered it to Clay, who shook his head. Karras handed it back to Vivian.

"You smoke cigarettes, right?" said Karras.

"Marlboros," said Vivian.

"Soft or hard?"

"Soft."

"I'm going to go out, get a few things. We could use some milk for coffee, shit like that. You can crash here tonight, okay?"

"Sure."

Karras saw Clay issue a small smile.

"Here's the setup," said Karras. "The guy with the beard on the first floor, Duncan, he's the guy to go to if you got a problem. On this floor you got a Secret Service guy who's never around, and a guy named David who's some solar-heat-and-cool architect. He's in and out."

"Okay."

"A lady named Janice lives downstairs. She lives with her boy, Lucas. Both of them are cool."

"All right."

"There's a few bums down in the boiler room, they sleep on cardboard there, they shouldn't bother you. If they do, again, you go to Duncan. He's a big man; he won't let anyone give you any shit."

Vivian smiled, stoned now. "Good weed," she said.

"That cat you saw outside? The house cat, Dumbo."

" 'Cause of the big ears," said Vivian.

"And now," said Clay, "you got the whole story of the Trauma Arms. C'mon, Dimitri, I gotta get into the shop."

"Help yourself to everything," said Karras.

Vivian giggled, tapped ash onto her jeans, bobbed her head to the music.

"There's an ashtray over there by the sink." Karras looked back at her once before he and Clay went out the door.

Out on R, Karras looked up at his open windows. Vivian had kicked up the volume on the stereo, and the music pumped out to the street. He and Clay walked toward Connecticut.

"You got your hands full there, boy."

"I'm only going to let her stay until she gets on her feet."

"Or till you get her on her back."

"Until she finds a place, I mean."

"Where's she gonna go? She's just one of those hippie chicks, 'bout five years too late. Hangin' out. Don't *want* to go nowhere, 'cept from one high to the next."

"I'll figure something out."

Clay smiled. "Shit, man, you al*ready* got it all figured out."

"Come on, man. She's nineteen."

"Would stop me, if we were talkin' about me. But we're talkin' about you."

"Marcus —"

"You gonna let that get away from you? Young Asian girl with a fine set of titties like that?"

"What," said Karras. "You think they're nice?"

They reached Connecticut and R, stopped on the corner. Karras put his hands in the pockets of his jeans, looked up at his friend.

"You holdin' the money?"

"Yeah. Gonna keep it in the shop for a few days, let things cool down."

"And then?"

"Like I said. Give it back."

Karras shifted his feet. "Funny how all that shit happened today. Not funny, but, you know . . . I was just buyin' a pound of dope, man, and all of the sudden everything flew apart."

"It's the city, man." Clay shrugged. "Life's just a trip and a half, Dimitri. You know that."

"No question."

"Anyway, let me get on into the shop. Promised Cheek the night off. Boy wants to see some movie just opened up. *King Suckerman,* some bullshit like that."

"One about the pimp?"

"Uh-huh."

Karras shook Clay's hand, some funky-ass double-buck shake the two of them had worked out themselves.

"Thanks for standing with me back there, Marcus. I do appreciate it."

"Right. You take it light, hear?"

"Yeah," said Karras. "You, too."

Wilton Cooper liked to sit low in the driver's seat, his elbow up on the window ledge, fingers barely brushing the steering wheel at twelve o'clock, amber-tinted shades over his eyes, driving the speed limit or below it like he wasn't in any special kind of hurry, no pressing place to be, nobody to tell him he had to be anywhere anytime quick.

The company he was keeping at the present time, it was just plain difficult to look one hundred percent down with them around, but Cooper was doing the best he could. He had B. R. in the passenger seat next to him, doped up on the couple of codeines they had given him back at D.C. General's ER. B. R. Clagget was ugly to begin with — Cooper would have to tell him some time, in a real gentle kind of way, to try laying off the fried foods — and now all his front teeth had been knocked out, which only added to the fright.

And then there were the two silly-ass, country-ass niggers in the backseat, who were hitting the cocaine from the Baggie that Eddie Spaghetti had given them back in Southeast, hitting it right in plain view, the top down on the Dodge, as they drove across town.

"Hey, Mandingo," said Cooper, "y'all keep that shit down back there, hear?"

Ronald lowered the bag. Russell reached over, dipped his long-nailed pinkie into the Baggie, leaned forward, put a chunky little mound up into his right nostril, hit it hard.

Russell reared back like he had been slapped in the head. "Whoo!" He shook his head like a dog, pulled something from his nostril. "What the fuck is *this*?"

Ronald laughed. "That's rice, nigger!"

"Rice? What the fuck's that Eye-talian motherfucker doin' puttin' rice in my 'caine?"

"Keeps the freeze from goin' away in all this humidity and shit. Don't you know nothin', boy?"

"You see a boy," said Russell, "kick his ass."

Cooper slapped in a Buddy Miles cassette — *More Miles per Gallon* — and kicked it up. He looked over at Clagget, whose head was kind of tilted to the side.

"You all right, B. R?"

Clagget blinked his eyes. "I'm okay, blood. Where's my gun?"

"In the trunk with the money. With all the other guns, too. You tellin' me you don't remember puttin' that shotgun there yourself?"

"It's those pills they gave me. I don't like feelin' like this."

"I don't like it, either. I don't fuck no way with no kinda drugs myself. You know I don't even drink. Man's got to be clearheaded in this life if he wants the good things."

"I feel the same way."

"Just one of the things I like about you, B. R."

From the backseat Russell sang, "Rockin' and a-rollin' on the streets of Hollywood." And Ronald joined him on the second line of the chorus: "Rockin' and a-rollin', don't know if I could." They touched hands.

Russell looked out the window, said with excitement, "Hey, check out that El D!" There was a nice baby blue El Dorado riding right beside them. "I'm gonna get me one of those, Ronald, soon as we get our money. Damn sure am."

"Shit, Russell, you be lucky to get you a Buick, maybe. 'Cause you know you ain't nothin' but a deuce-and-a-quarter-ridin' motherfucker."

"Leastways I'll be ridin' in somethin', man. While you walkin' down the highway scratchin' the bugs out your nappy hair."

Ronald said, "Go ahead."

Clagget leaned over, spoke softly near Cooper's ear. "Those two coming with us?"

"Uh-uh. They got a cousin over in Northeast. Cuz don't know it yet, but those fools are stayin' with her. Gonna keep that bag of ice with us, too. Don't want those two to be gettin' into trouble behind that shit. I'll let 'em get back into it when I want trouble to happen, understand?"

"What about you and me?"

"You and me are gonna get us a room over on New York Avenue, headin' toward the county line. That okay by you?"

"Sounds good, blood."

"And I got a surprise for you, man. We goin' to a show tonight. While they were fixin' your shit back there, I saw in the newspaper that a certain movie was openin' tonight."

"*King Suckerman*?"

"Uh-huh. You and me, we're goin' to the nine-thirty show."

"Dag! I been waitin' for that one!"

"I know you have, B. R."

"Thanks, Wilton!"

"You stick with me, little brother. I'm gonna take care of your ass real good."

"Listen to this shit, boss," said Rasheed. He turned up the volume on the system. Fiery guitar blossomed through the house KLMs.

"Who is this?" said Clay.

"Group called El Chicano, on the Shadybrook label, out of L.A. This brown guitarist, he's got a sound like 'Los, don't he?"

"He does sound a little like Santana, man, I'll give you that."

"Which only proves my point. It's only men of color who can get that feeling out of a guitar."

"Maybe so. But you know, the best guitarist I ever saw was white. John McLaughlin, man. Was three rows back when he played the Warner with the Mahavishnu Orchestra. Touring behind *Visions of the Emerald Beyond*. Had that twelve-string of his, and I swear to you, man, it was like the Lord himself had his fingers on the frets. And you know, I've seen damn near all of the great ones. B. B. and Muddy and all those blues boys. Saw Hendrix at the Ambassador, too. But nobody, not even Jimi, played like Johnny McLaughlin played that night."

"It's the color experience, Marcus, that's what gets the feeling out of the instrument. Look at the blues!"

"I hear you, Rasheed. And I agree. But I'm only tellin' you what I saw with my own eyes. *My* experience, dig?"

"It's like the white man took the blues, co-opted that shit for himself. Rolling Stones, Led Zeppelin, and all that. And now you got those dumb-ass movies, like the one Cheek was in such a hurry to go off and see tonight. Those white producers tryin' to exploit *our* culture, showin' us what *our* ghetto thing is all about. And us, givin' them our money like stone suckers. It's bullshit, man. You don't understand."

"It's *you* that . . . Look: You got to get beyond that shit, young brother. 'Cause out in the world, it's only gonna cripple your ass. Be aware of your history and what was done to us, and don't ever forget. Keep your black aesthetic and be proud of it. But get rid of the bitterness, man. It ain't gonna do you no good."

"I hear you, man."

"You do?"

"Yeah, I do."

Clay sighed, pointed his chin to the front of the shop. "Go on and lock the front door. I want to show you something before you go."

Rasheed Adamson went to the door, locked it with the keys Marcus Clay had given him upon his promotion. He looked out the window at the dusk fallen on the avenue, checked his watch. He went back behind the counter. Clay was down on his knees, pushing aside the throw rug that covered the removable panel over the small hole he had cut in the wood floor, a hole just big enough to accommodate a cash box. Clay kept a hundred and change in the register overnight, just enough to make a burglar think that a hundred and change was all he kept in the shop; the real money he kept in the cash box beneath the floor.

"Get on down here, boy," said Clay.

Now they were both sitting on the floor, below counter level, out of sight of any pedestrians window-shopping on Connecticut. Clay opened the steel box. He reached into each of his pant pockets, withdrew two rolls of large-denomination bills.

Rasheed looked at the money. He fingered the macrame red, black, and green Africa cutout that hung around his neck on a leather string. "You got some serious change there, boss."

"Goddamn right it's serious. You're lookin' at twenty grand."

"For real?"

"Square business."

"Where'd you get it?"

"This here is trouble money, Rasheed. Me and Karras got ourselves into some shit today. Truth be told, this money isn't exactly mine."

"Karras, huh? I told you about hangin' out with that Caucasian friend of yours."

"Dimitri got us into it, that's a fact. But it was me who fucked up and got cocky, took what wasn't mine."

"What you fixin' to do with it?"

"Sit on it a few days, let things chill. Let the boys I took it from cool off, then give it back."

"Leave it here?"

Clay's brow wrinkled in thought. "Half." He counted out ten thousand, placed it in the cash box. He put the other ten back in his pocket. "Case we get knocked over, some shit like that, I won't lose it all. I'll keep the rest over at my crib."

"Why you tellin' me?"

"Straight up? 'Cause I trust you, man."

"Thanks."

"You're a good boy, Rasheed. A little thickheaded about some things, but you're good. I know you won't give me up."

Rasheed's grin went from ear to ear. Serious as he was, and with the facade of toughness Rasheed felt he always needed to wear, it wasn't often Clay saw him smile. For a moment, he looked like the kid he was.

Rasheed said, "Count on it, blood."

Clay said, "You know I will."

They shook hands. Clay put the cash box in the hole, replaced the panel, covered the panel with the throw rug. When he stood, Rasheed was glancing at his wristwatch again as he headed for the door.

"You lock up behind me, boss?" he said over his shoulder.

"Sure. What's your hurry?"

"I got a meeting, man, across town. An empowerment seminar. See you tomorrow, hear?"

Rasheed unlocked the door, went out, walked south on the avenue. Marcus Clay watched him go as he put his key to the lock.

Clay grinned, seeing the quickness in Rasheed's step as he turned the corner at R. He knew Rasheed wasn't going to sit in on any seminar. Rasheed, with all his talk and ideology, he was just like any young man, looking to have a little fun. Rasheed, he was going downtown to check out that movie, just opened at the Town. The one everybody was talking about.

The one about the pimp.

EIGHT

Jimmy Castle watched from the backseat as Dewey Schmidt slapped in his eight-track of *Not Fragile*. From the passenger seat, Jerry Baluzy turned to his friend Dewey, who sat behind the wheel, and rocked his head back and forth at the twin guitar kick-in, his motion slopping beer from the can of Bud he held in his hand. Bachman-Turner Overdrive was Dewey and Jerry's favorite group.

"Aw, come on, man," said Jimmy, who was totally not into BTO. "Not this again."

"Not fragiiiile," sang Dewey and Jerry together, giving it their best gravelly try. They laughed and slapped each other five. Dewey grabbed the beer can lodged between his thighs and took a long swig, closing his eyes momentarily as he drank. The Pontiac swerved a little, and the driver of an AMC Rebel to the right of them honked his horn. Dewey flipped the guy off before accelerating and cutting into the right lane.

"Hey, Dewey," said Jimmy, "why don't you give this shit a rest?"

Dewey nudged Jerry, said to Jimmy, "Whaddaya wanna listen to, Toothpick? Gong? Kraftwerk? Some bullshit like that?"

Dewey called Jimmy Toothpick just to piss him off. Jimmy wasn't just thin. He was skinny, and in a scary kind of way.

"Anything," said Jimmy.

"How about Ritchie Blackmore's Rainbow?" said Dewey.

Jimmy had a pull off his beer while he thought it over. "Leave this on," he said. "I guess this is all right."

Jerry grabbed the bag from the glove box and the pipe from under the seat. The pipe was Dewey's, a corncob number he had purchased from a retarded middle-aged clerk at People's Drug in Wheaton Plaza. On the pipe's body Dewey had wood-burned a sketch of a snake with a tongue in the shape of a cross. Dewey was known around Einstein High as Schmidt the Snake, a name he had invented himself. Though he talked a big game about his lovemaking technique, quoting liberally from the porno mags spread around his bedroom in the garden apartment he shared with his widowed mom, Dewey Schmidt had seen very little action in his seventeen years on earth — one shockingly quick blow job from a hooker on his sixteenth birthday and one messy cherry-bust with a short-term girlfriend named Laurie Lynn — but somehow the moniker had stuck.

Dewey punched the gas, going south on 14th. The '68 Firebird sounded faster than it was — a stock 350 sat beneath the hood — courtesy of the dual exhaust and Glas-pac Dewey had added after he bought the car. They neared Thomas Circle, and Dewey put his head out the window to yell at a black woman with blond hair who wore a short, tight leather skirt.

"Hey, sugar, you datin' tonight?" he called.

"Pull over," said the whore halfheartedly, her eyes blank, her smile as long lasting as a street-bought watch, but Dewey just laughed and kept driving.

"Hey, Jerry," said Dewey, "what's your mother doin' downtown?"

"Your father," said Jerry.

"Your baby sister," said Jimmy, because he was expected to say something.

"Fuck you, bitch," said Dewey. He wiped some beer off his chin.

Jerry filled the pipe, gave it a light. He passed the reefer over to Dewey, who hit it hard.

Jimmy looked out the window at the lights and the movement and the life on the street. Like Jerry and Dewey, he was a Maryland boy who came from Montgomery Hills — *Monkey* Hills to the locals — a community in Silver Spring just a couple of miles over the District line. Their infrequent trips into D.C. always made Jimmy's pulse race, partly from the thrill of the new and partly from fear. Whatever the reason, he liked the way driving into the city made him feel.

"Here," said Dewey, trying to hold the smoke in as he spoke. He passed the pipe over his shoulder to Jimmy.

Jimmy drew hard on the pipe, watched the embers flare in the bowl. He coughed out a lungful, sending a horizontal mushroom cloud of smoke toward the front. Dewey and Jerry had rolled their windows up to "keep in the high," and a thick gray curtain had settled in the car. Jimmy was hot, sweating through his favorite long-sleeved shirt, a cowboy-style job with fake pearl buttons he had purchased at the Slack Shack. Jimmy wore long sleeves even in the summer; he was embarrassed about his girlishly thin arms.

"What, are you Bogartin' that shit back there?" said Dewey. Jimmy handed him the pipe.

Dewey cut over to 13th. Jimmy watched Jerry Baluzy, who was staring at Dewey hitting the pipe. Jerry's eyes were at half-mast, pink and glassy; his thick-lipped mouth was open, too. Jimmy smiled.

"Hit that motherfucker," said Jerry, blinking heavily and jerking his chin in the direction of the pipe.

"Hit 'er in the shitter," said Dewey.

All of them laughed.

"But you're not getting any," said Jerry.

"That's not what your mama says," said Dewey.

"Huh," said Jerry, issuing a short, honking guffaw. He looked stupidly at Dewey. "You gotta suck it, maaaan!"

"Suck this," said Dewey.

The chorus came back in on the song. Dewey and Jerry put their heads together, sang, "Not fragiiile." Jimmy had one of those smiles on his face he couldn't unglue. He was ripped and with his boys. The BTO tape, it sounded pretty good.

Dewey parked on 13th, slanted it a little off the curb so the Firebird caught the light coming down from the street lamp just right. Dewey had just waxed the car in Sligo Creek Park that afternoon, and he had Armor Alled the vinyl roof as well. The olive green finish had a nice buff glow to it in the yellowish light, and the chrome-reverse Cregar wheels shone flawlessly. Dewey had even SOSed the raised white letters on the wide-track tires. The air shocks he had installed made the car sit up in the back, gave it a look like an animal poised to strike; Dewey thought so, anyway. A blue-and-orange Hi-Jackers sticker, a cartoon rabbit with tires for back legs burning rubber in the street, had been affixed to the top right corner of the back window.

"Bad ride," said Dewey, stroking his weak Charles Bronson mustache, looking back one time at the Firebird as they moved away.

"The Green Ghost," said Jerry, who had given Dewey's car its name but did not own a car himself.

On the sidewalk, Jimmy Castle got down on one knee, raised his jeans at the cuff, retrieved his pack of Marlboros from inside his sock, where he always stashed it before walking past his mother and father when leaving the house. He struck a match, lit a 'Boro, caught up with Dewey and Jerry. He went behind them, trying to walk normally. When Jimmy got high, he had a kind of awkward bounce in his step; it was a stoner's walk, and he felt it, but when he concentrated against it, the bounce only became more pronounced. He wore tanned leather shoes with wedge heels, and they made him a bit unsteady on his feet.

Jimmy watched Dewey and Jerry walking with confidence ahead as they neared New York Avenue. Dewey had a dumbell set in his bedroom, and when he wasn't jacking off to *Swank* or drawing his replica CO_2 .357 in the full-length mirror, he used it regularly. With each backswing of his arms, Dewey's triceps became defined, his straight black hair jerking with the action. Jerry was not so muscular, but he had naturally wide shoulders, and he was tall. He was kind of ugly, though, with a knot of blackheads on his thick nose and black frizzy hair that was nearly matted in several spots. Jerry was some kind of Arab, Lebanese or Turkish or some shit like that, Jimmy wasn't sure which. Still, despite the fact that Dewey was borderline redneck and Jerry was both red in the neck area and ugly, Jimmy wouldn't have minded being either one of those guys for a day or so, just to see what it felt like to be normal sized. And then he thought, studying their bodies, What am I doing, admiring a couple of guys like that for? Or any guy, for that matter? What am

I, some kind of faggot or something? And then Jimmy thought, like he often did when these things entered his head, I wish I hadn't of smoked so much weed.

They neared the Town theater, its marquee brightly lit and a crowd around its box-office window. The ticket line went halfway down the block. Jimmy dragged hard on his smoke, flicked it out into the street. As he neared the line it seemed that he, Dewey, and Jerry were the only white faces in the crowd. Then he saw a skinny white kid with a ratty Afro standing at the head of the line next to a big dude who looked a little like Jim Brown. But the skinny white kid with the bad face was definitely it; the rest of the patrons were all black.

At the back of the line, Dewey tapped the shoulder of the guy ahead of him, a tall black man who appeared to be alone.

"Say," said Dewey, "you got the time, blood?"

The man turned around, looked Dewey up and down. "Blood? Who you callin' blood? The name's Clarence Tate."

"Okay, Clarence."

"Clarence nothin'. It's 'sir' to you."

Jimmy felt that pulsing thing again, racing through his blood.

The Town theater was huge, bigger by a mile than any of the neighborhood KB theaters or the Roth's in Silver Spring, and though it wasn't a beautiful marble palace like the RKO Keith's on 15th and G, it was still plenty awesome. Jimmy Castle's dad had taken him to his first adult movie, *The Dirty Dozen,* at the Town when Jimmy was like eight years old. When Jimmy became a teenager, about the time he started smoking pot with his friends, he had grown apart from his father, and it seemed like they would never again be pals like they were when Jimmy was a kid. But the Town, it still brought a special feeling to him when he entered its lobby, and Jimmy figured that feeling had something to do with the way it had been with his dad.

The auditorium was nearly full. They had run a couple of trailers, one for a Fred Williamson picture called *Death Journey* ("Fred Williamson is Jesse Crowder — one mean cat!") and another for a

Raquel Welch – Bill Cosby movie named *Mother, Jugs & Speed*. Dewey hooted every time the trailer showed Welch bursting out of her shirt, but Jimmy knew better than to waste his money on a Raquel Welch flick, since Welch never showed bare tit in any movie, and he had been taken enough times already to not make the same mistake again. Finally the houselights came down all the way, and the main feature began.

Scratchy guitar and chicken-fried vocals came out over the main titles, with Tower of Power – style horn bursts punctuating the chorus, the singer talking about "King Suckermaaaan, runnin' down the master plaaaan, takin' it right to the Maaaan." Some young D.C. ladies, Interhigh girls, groups of two and three, got out into the main aisle of the auditorium and began doing the bump spontaneously to the title tune. Jerry Baluzy stood up to watch until the deep voice of a brother behind them instructed him to sit his "narrow ass the fuck on down." Jimmy had a chill, watching the girls dance. The way they were into it, *deep* into it and proud, was straight-up beautiful to him.

Wilton Cooper and Bobby Roy Clagget sat quietly during the show. Clagget because he was getting an education, and Cooper because he was relaxing, checking the whole thing out. Cooper had never pimped, but he had known plenty of players in his time, both in the joint and out, so he knew what it was to be in the life for real.

The movie started out like most of the films Cooper and Clagget had seen in drive-ins and B houses the last few years. The injustice of Ghetto Life specifically and Amerika in general had turned a basically good brother toward a life of crime. In that arena, evil competitors and a couple of bad white cops pressured the antihero for a piece of his action and caused the brother to take violent matters into his own hands. Usually the brother got out of the life in the last reel, but not before exacting his bloody revenge.

King Suckerman started out exactly that way, though from the beginning the audience sensed that there was something unsettling going on in the film. For one thing, Ron St. John, who played the title role, he was one stone ugly motherfucker, scarred in the face and narrow of shoulder and chest. Cooper had liked *The Mack,* thought it was more authentic than most, but in truth Max Julien as the pimp had always bothered him. Julien could be tough, but with his smooth skin, too-easy smile, and deep dimples, he was just way too pretty to be believable as the hard man a pimp had to be. You needed someone rougher in the face and body to make the story true. But Ron St. John? He went all the way in the other direction.

Ugly as he was, though, Ron St. John was cool. Cool *and* bad. No one could fuck with King Suckerman, 'cause the man feared no one and had *all* the bitches in his stable.

In the second act, the pimp took a wire hanger to one of his women, a girl named Diandra who had done a little too much blow, gotten cocky behind it, sassed him in front of the others, and then refused to get out of bed and go to work. King Suckerman gave her a backful of open welts, then kicked her in the face repeatedly as she cowered on the floor. She went out the door crying hysterically, begging her pimp to give her one more chance. She peddled her pussy like that, bloodied and chip-toothed and with torn clothes, all night in the street.

When that scene played, the auditorium had gone dead quiet. Even the smart-mouthed brothers who usually talked shit throughout the show, yelled at the screen and laughed at their own jokes, had shut their mouths. And then it got worse. King Suckerman let himself get framed by the two bad white cops, got convicted by an all-white jury, was let down by an indifferent white PD. And King Suckerman went to jail. The last shot of the movie had King Suckerman in his cell, wasting away from tertiary syphilis. The camera zoomed into his eyes, the hollow eyes of any scared old man lying alone in the terminal ward, waiting for death. A freeze-frame appeared then, and a slower, bluesier version of the title song ran over the end credits. By then most of the patrons had walked out of the auditorium without comment.

"That was boolshit," said a man who had stayed, just a few rows back from Cooper and Clagget.

Clagget turned to Cooper. "Was it bullshit, Wilton?"

"Little brother?" said Cooper. "That there was the real deal."

Jimmy Castle, Dewey Schmidt, and Jerry Baluzy walked quickly to the Firebird. The tone of the movie had killed their high from the very beginning, and they had crashed halfway into the flick. None of the patrons they saw out on the street, the ones who had been joking and enthusiastic while standing in the ticket line, looked happy or friendly now. Jimmy caught a couple of unprovoked hard looks. And then a black kid their age went out of his way to bump his shoulder against Dewey's. Dewey stared at the young man for a second, if only to avoid losing face with his boys. But he quickly looked away.

"What," said the young man. "You want some go?"

"Naw, that's all right," said Dewey in an unconcerned way, but still moving toward the car.

"I ain't think so, bitch."

Dewey let that slide. Jimmy and Jerry followed behind him, looking down at their feet. They hurriedly got themselves into the car.

Dewey fired the ignition, pulled away from the curb. He headed the Firebird north toward the Maryland line. Jerry filled a bowl and lit it, passed it around. In a few minutes they had gotten their heads up again, but not to where they had been earlier in the night. Dewey pushed a Grand Funk eight-track into the deck. "We're an American Band" came from the wedge speakers mounted on the rear deck. Jimmy thought of complaining; the song was just a U.S. rip-off of "Smoke on the Water," and basically it blew. But he knew Dewey was pissed, being stood down in front of them by the black kid like that. Jimmy kept his mouth shut.

"That was pretty good," said Jerry, talking about the movie.

"Who was that actor played the pimp?" said Dewey.

"Ron St. John," said Jerry.

"Ugly sumbitch," said Dewey. "Had some soup-spoon lips on him, too."

"That was one Leeroy-lookin' dude," agreed Jerry.

"Fuckin' niggers," said Dewey. "Right, Toothpick?"

Jimmy Castle didn't answer. He hung out with this one kid at Einstein every so often, a black kid named Keith. They cut fourth period together about once a week, got high in the nearby woods. Jimmy thought Keith was a pretty nice guy.

Cheek first saw Rasheed as he exited the theater lobby after the show. Cheek recognized his red, black, and green knit cap and that quick walk of Rasheed's straight off. He grinned, followed Rasheed out the doors and into the night. He walked behind him for a bit, then tapped him on the shoulder as they passed into the darkened end of the street.

Rasheed turned warily, his eyes wide. He relaxed when he saw Cheek, tried to recover his composure.

Cheek smiled. "What you doin' down here, man?"

"Gettin' up on a meeting down this way."

Cheek laughed. "You a lyin' motherfucker, nigger. I saw your thin ass walking out the theater."

"Shit."

"Gettin' up on a meeting. Yeah."

"I was curious is all."

"That's all right, blood. Curious is cool."

Rasheed touched a finger to his lips. "It wasn't what I expected, you know?"

"Me either, man. That's the truth. They laid that shit out and ran it down."

"You *know* that picture's not gonna do any business."

"Oh, yeah?"

" 'Cause it tells the truth. And the brothers out here, they don't want to know about the truth."

"Hey, Rasheed: Lighten up with that shit, okay?" Cheek checked out the watch on his fat wrist.

"Where you off to, man?"

"See my girl."

"Sholinda?"

"Got-damn right."

"She is big, man."

"Don't be doggin' my girl, now."

"I ain't doggin' her, man. Just makin' a statement is all. Matter of fact, she's just the right size" — Rasheed grinned — "for a Rerun-lookin' motherfucker like you."

Cheek threw a soft right, pulled it at the last second. Rasheed ducked the punch, did a spin kick he had seen Bruce do in *The Chinese Connection*. Cheek stepped away from it, put up his hands. Cheek and Rasheed laughed.

"Come on, man," said Cheek. "I'll drive you home. While we're on the move, pick up some good-ass barbecue first, place they got up around my way."

"You know I don't eat no pork, Cheek. A pig ain't nothin' but a filthy-ass animal and shit."

"Oh, you'll eat *this*, Rasheed. And afterwards? You'll be lickin' your motherfuckin' fingers, too."

Cheek knocked Rasheed's cap slightly askew. Rasheed straightened it on his head just right. The two friends walked in the warm summer air to Cheek's car: a '67 Belvedere, white over blue, with nice, clean lines.

NINE

Dimitri Karras wandered around Dupont Circle in the early evening. In the fountain area at the center of the circle he did a little business, got the word out that he was holding some good weed. He sold a few OZs like that, just mentioning it to a couple of guys he knew, and told those guys when and where they could cop their bags.

Karras crossed in front of traffic, went down to Bialek's, Marcus Clay's main competitor, the wood-floored record and book store on the west side of Connecticut near N. He found an Atomic Rooster LP there that he had been looking for, and a hard-to-find David Sancious LP called *Transformation (The Speed of Love)*, but he replaced them in their bins after a few moments of thought. He'd check with Marcus first, see if Real Right Records could order them in.

He went over to P Street, walked into a small consignment shop, bought a few things for Vivian Lee: a second pair of Levis, already worn in, and a halter top with a brown paisley design. He picked up a red-and-white striped tube top on the way to the register, threw that in the stack as well. Marcus would have said he was buying all the easy-to-get-off, no-brassiere-wearing shirts he could find. Karras was glad that Marcus wasn't there to give him shit; he thought the girl would look good in those shirts, and he thought she'd be comfortable in them, that was all.

Karras stopped last at the Fairfax Market on P, picked up some essentials: milk, cereal, cigarettes, beer. Karras rarely ate at his crib. He bought some chick shampoo — well, the bottle was pink, anyway — and a bar of scented soap. The geeze at the counter rang him up, and Karras walked back to the Trauma Arms in what had suddenly become darkness.

Duncan Hazlewood stopped him in the foyer of 1841. "Well, what about that party?"

"I'll let you know, Duncan."

Hazlewood's eyes registered mischief. "See that you do, damnit."

Karras went up the stairs. He transferred his bags to one hand, turned the knob on his apartment door.

Vivian Lee sat on the couch, watching *Barney Miller* with the sound off while listening to Todd Rundgren's *Something/Anything* on the stereo at the same time. A lot of stoners liked to pass their time like that, but the confusion was not to Karras's taste. He couldn't deal with it, high or straight.

Vivian turned her head, smiled. She yelled over the music, "You got my cigs?"

"Here." He tossed her the Marlboro softs and a blue book of D.C. Vending matches with the message "Thank You for Your Patronage" printed on its face. She lit herself a smoke.

Karras put away the groceries, dropped the bag of clothing on the couch next to Vivian. "I got you a few things." And: "I'm gonna take a shower."

He went to his bedroom, stripped, wrapped a towel around his waist, and walked through the hall. He stopped, saw Vivian facing the window trying on the halter top, watched the wash of muscle over her rib cage as she reached behind her to tie the knot.

"It fits!" she yelled over her shoulder.

Karras had a cool shower. Thinking of Vivian, the way her body had looked as she tied the halter, it was all he could do to get himself soaped up and rinsed off without reaching down to yank his meat.

"I'm going out," said Karras, standing over her as he tucked a clean Hawaiian shirt into his jeans. She was rolling a joint with the Tops papers and having a time of it, too. Karras put his feet up on the cable-spool table, one after the other. He rolled up the cuffs, cigarette style, on his Levis.

"Don't you wanna hang out?" said Vivian.

Goddamn right I want to hang out. It's my place and there's a mattress in the back and you're young and fucking beautiful.

"Nah," said Karras. "I'm meeting a friend for a beer."

"Okay," said Vivian with a shrug.

"Okay."

Wilton Cooper stopped the Challenger in front of a DGA store in Northeast, cut the engine.

"Be right back," said Cooper to Clagget.

Cooper went into the grocery-variety market, picked up a six of Near Beer and a jar of Vaseline and took both to the counter. He waited behind an old lady who was pulling pennies from her change purse with arthritic hands. He pulled a paperback off the rack to the right of the counter and placed the book on top of the six. The old lady fussed over her things for a moment and walked away. Cooper asked the clerk to add a couple of decks of Salem longs to the rest of his purchases. Cooper paid, the clerk bagged the shit, and Cooper left the store.

Cooper dropped himself into the driver's bucket, reached into the bag. He tossed the paperback over to Clagget.

"Got you a present, little brother."

Clagget read the title, smiling a little as he said the name. "*Pimp*."

"By Iceberg Slim."

"What is it, Wilton?"

"That there's the Book. The Bible of the Street. Most of what you saw in that movie tonight, they took that shit straight from Ice, man. Read that and you'll know what's really goin' on."

"Thanks, Wilton."

"Don't mention it."

Bobby Roy Clagget rubbed his thumb along the book's cover. "Where we goin' now?"

"Back to the motel. That okay by you?"

"Sure."

"Thought we'd kick back some, B. R."

"Sounds good."

Cooper pulled the ring off a can of Near Beer. "Yeah, you and me, we gonna relax, have us a little fun."

Karras walked straight to Benbow's, his neighborhood joint, on Connecticut below the Janus theater near 18th. He wasn't particularly thirsty, and he had made no plans to meet a friend, but he felt he had to get out of the apartment and away from Vivian. He entered and had a seat at the bar. The tender, a guy named Don, drew a mug of draft and placed it on a coaster in front of Karras. Don looked like he had quaffed a few that evening himself.

Karras raised his glass. "Thanks."

Don pulled an open bottle of Bud from the ice chest, winked, and drank. "To you, Dimitri."

Benbow's called itself a restaurant, though Karras had rarely seen the patrons there partaking in its alleged cuisine. It was a narrow place with a bar, dartboards, a juke, and a couple of heads. When Karras wanted breakfast, he got it at the Jefferson Coffee Shop on 19th between M and N, and sometimes at the lunch counter at Schwartze's drugstore nearby, but he often took his morning java at Benbow's. Occasionally he'd go in and make a cup of instant himself, as Don was frequently sleeping one off on top of the bar.

Karras wasn't much of a drinker. He sipped his draft and listened to the Hues Corporation doing "Rock the Boat" from the juke.

"Hey, Dimitri."

Karras turned his head at the voice and the tap on his shoulder. Donna DiConstanza, a secretary who worked at the Machinists building on Connecticut and N, stood by his side. She had a feathery Farrah Fawcett-Majors thing happening with her reddish hair and a wide smile showing crooked, yellowing teeth. Donna wore flared Lee jeans and one of those gauzy, brightly colored shirts out of Pakistan that shrank to nothing the first time you put them in the dryer. She had a pair of red Dr. Scholl's sandals on her feet. Karras had done her, standing up against the sidewalk side of a parked van back on R street, about six months back. It was a cold night, both of them high and with their pants down at two in the morning, Donna's ass against the frosty metal door of some stranger's Econoline, and it had been quick.

"Hey, Donna."

"Where you been, stranger?"

"Here and there." Karras with the cool, mysterious response, giving her the fifty-dollar grin despite himself.

"Buy me one?"

Better not.

Karras gave her an eye sweep. She looked a little like Bonnie Raitt on the cover of *Home Plate*. Not as pretty, but sexy in a high-mileage kind of way. He felt something move, sluglike, in his jeans.

"Sure," said Karras. "Have a seat."

He bought her a whiskey sour. He drank his beer and she had her cocktail and they ordered another round the same way. A drunk the regulars alternately called Poppy or Popeye — like the cartoon character: The old guy had a toothless, rubbery mouth — came over to talk to them, and Karras ended up buying him one as well.

"I'm from Mars, man," said Poppy.

Poppy drifted, and the conversation between Donna and Karras went to dope.

"So," said Donna. "You holding?"

Karras patted the breast pocket of his Hawaiian shirt and smiled. He retrieved the joint slyly and palmed it over to Donna.

Donna said, "Be right back."

She got off her bar stool and went to the ladies' room. Karras ordered another round, and by the time Don served it, Donna had returned. She had the sourish smell of marijuana on her clothes and in her hair, and she had to grab the bar to get into her seat. She drew a Benson & Hedges from the pack set next to her rocks glass. Karras gave her a light.

"Thanks."

"No problem."

"Good weed, Dimitri."

"Always."

"Here." She passed him what remained of the joint.

Karras walked past the back of the bar and along a short hallway, went through a door labeled Gents. The head was tiny, with a butt-littered wall urinal, sink, and clouded mirror. Karras pissed in the urinal, cranked open a casement window above it as he drained. Benbow's management had run a small but decent speaker from the juke to the head, and the long version of the O'Jays' "For the Love of Money," with its insistent, classic bass line, was now coming through. Karras put his back against the door, watched himself in the mirror and grooved on the O'Jays as he smoked down the joint. He extinguished what remained with his thumb and forefinger, dropped the roach back in his shirt.

Back at the bar, Donna was looking a little more drunk and a lot more beautiful in that Bonnie kind of way than she had before. Karras stumbled a little getting onto his stool.

"Whoa," he said.

"Yeah," said Donna.

The two of them laughed.

In a couple of minutes Karras crossed into that zone he always got to when he put reefer on top of a few glasses of beer. He seemed to be floating, rather than sitting, on a stool without legs. The singles on the jukebox, the ones he would never listen to on the radio, sounded damn good. And nothing he said to Donna sounded wrong.

Donna leaned her head on Karras's shoulder, looked up at him with her waxed green eyes.

"So, Dimitri."

"What?"

"Wanna fuck?"

"Okay."

He watched her walk along the bar and into the hallway, watched her stop at the door marked Gents and make a clumsy toss of her feathered hair, her eyes moving broadly and suggestively in the direction of the door. Then she had gone through the door, and Karras got off his stool, excited and kind of sad for both of them at the same time.

He tried not to look at Don, who was attempting to catch his eye from behind the bar.

Karras entered the bathroom. He and Donna began to kiss furiously at once. He ran his hands up into her shirt and felt her small hard breasts. She unbuttoned her jeans, pulled them down around her ankles, turned, faced the mirror, bent forward, gripped the sink. Karras took a dirty bar of soap off the sink's platform, wet it under the tap, lathered up his right hand. Someone knocked on the door and laughed. Karras slid his soapy hand beneath Donna's ass, lubricated her sex. He dropped his own jeans, soaping his cock quickly as Donna stood on her tiptoes to let him in.

"Uh," said Donna.

"All right," said Karras. He caught his reflection in the mirror, a long-haired, handlebar-mustached, city desperado with a Cheshire grin.

They got down to it. Their bodies moved to the sounds of Rhythm Heritage doing "Theme from 'S.W.A.T.'" from the small speaker overhead.

Eddie Marchetti watched the last few minutes, the part those QM Production shows called "the epilogue," of *Streets of San Francisco*. The show was a repeat, the one where some high school kid is accused of killing his teacher. Marchetti hadn't cared for it much the first time he caught it, back in the fall. With Karl Malden in his raincoat all the time and lugging around a nose that looked like it had been stuffed with a ten-dollar roll of quarters, *Streets* was just another geezer show to Eddie. Well, half a geezer show, anyway. It had Kirk Douglas's kid in it, at least, a young upstart with longish hair and sideburns, as Malden's partner.

Harry-O would be on in about five.

Marchetti looked around the darkened warehouse. He scratched his balls through his double-knit slacks. Clarence had gone home to see to his little daughter, and Vivian . . . well, who knew where Vivian had gone, or if she would ever be back. The place was quiet without the two of them. He heard the television and the faint thump of bass from the disco-fag joint down the block, and nothing else.

"Goddamn you, Eddie," Marchetti said aloud. And to himself: I shoulda been nicer to the girl.

Clarence Tate looked to his right. Denice, his little girl, breathed evenly, one little chocolate hand moving arrhythmically to some tune playing in her head. She stared at the patterns in the wallpapered ceiling, her eyelids dropping slowly, coming open, dropping back down. Almost there.

At least he had gotten home from that pimp movie in time to put her to bed.

Tate closed the book he had been reading to Denice: *The Best Time of Day.* The book was about a little brother named William who has a full kid's schedule — at the community center, at his grandparents', taking an afternoon nap, shit like that — and then sits around with his folks at night, after his daddy comes home from work. Denice loved that one the best of all her books. Tate kind of liked it, too.

Tate got off the bed carefully, turned on Denice's portable record player, put the kiddie tonearm on the album he perpetually left on the platter, Gil Scott-Heron's *Winter in America.* "Your Daddy Loves You," one of the most beautiful songs Clarence Tate had ever heard, started in, just the vibes at first and then Gil's rich, deep vocals. As he did every night, Tate began to sing along.

When the song ended, Tate shut off the phonograph, turned out the light. He stayed in the room a few minutes longer, sitting in a chair he had drawn to the edge of the bed. He watched Denice sleep.

Marcus Clay drove his '72 Riviera with the boat-tail rear through Adams Morgan, sitting low in the bucket, the AC cooling his face. He pushed in a homemade cassette he had labeled "Superjam, Part 1." The sounds of Creative Source's "Who Is He and What Is He to You" began to pulse through the car. The band was doing one of those long, insinuating instrumental intros like the Temps had pioneered on "Papa Was a Rolling Stone," the same kind of dramatic, intricate production. Marcus figured Creative Source to be a studio concoction, not really a cohesive group, but regardless of the fact that they would probably have little longevity, this was one of those tunes, like William DeVaughn's landmark single "Be Thankful for What You Got," that justified an entire career. The song was just all the way bad.

Marcus stopped at Heller's Bakery on Mt. Pleasant Street and picked up a couple of those Boston creams that Elaine liked so much. Elaine worked as a secretary by day, was doing law school by night. On her two nights off, she liked to cook a nice dinner for the two of them. He knew she'd be doing that now.

He drove over to Brown, a small street on the edge of Mount Pleasant just west of 16th, and parked in front of his row house. He shot the shit with a neighbor of his, a Puerto Rican named Pepe, out on the sidewalk before taking the concrete steps up to his house.

Entering his front door, he smelled the fried chicken Elaine Taylor had prepared for dinner. The living room stereo was softly putting out some planetary jazz, Miles Davis's Jack Johnson tribute. Elaine loved her Miles. He went to the kitchen, saw her standing there over the gas stove moving some greens around in a lightly oiled frying pan.

"Hey, girlfriend," said Clay.

"Baby," said Elaine. "What's going on?"

"You." He handed her the Boston creams.

"Mmm, Marcus."

"Little something for dessert."

"Come here."

They embraced, kissed softly. Elaine was a tall woman, six feet without heels, athletic, dark skinned, smooth, proud, beautiful. She looked into his eyes.

"What's wrong, Marcus? What's troubling you?"

"Nothin', baby. Everything's cool."

"Uh-huh." She stood back, looked at him fully. "Pour yourself a glass of wine, go have a seat in that old chair of yours. We'll have some dinner first, relax. Maybe talk later on. Okay?"

"Right."

They ate, smoked a little herb, went upstairs to bed. They rubbed each other down with heated oils, made love slowly in a room lit by votive candles. Afterward, Clay told Elaine about his day.

"What're you going to do about all this, Marcus?"

"Figure out a way to make things right." Clay stared at the flame shadows licking at the ceiling. "The thing is, I don't need this right now. I'm trying to build a business, stay on the track."

"You need to stay away from those influences," said Elaine. "I been tellin' you . . ."

"I know. But see, it was me that did the damage today. Thing is, I never should've gone with him in the first place."

"It's nothing against Dimitri. I know you care about him, and you know I do, too. It's just —"

"What?"

"Dimitri's in a big hurry to get nowhere quick. I hate to put it that plain, but there it is."

"You're right," said Clay. "But he's my friend."

"What about you?" said Elaine. "What about me?"

Clay rolled onto his side, slipped an arm beneath Elaine, wrapped the other around her shoulder. He pulled her to him tight.

Dimitri Karras stumbled up the stairs. The big gray house cat, Dumbo, tore down a flight from out of who knew where, disappeared. Karras made it to the next landing, listened to Irvine Nichols from behind his door, lecturing one of his young black lovers about being late. Karras took the next set of stairs.

He used his key to enter his apartment. Vivian lay on the couch facedown, one arm off and touching the floor, her breath heavy and stale and souring the air. The lamps and overheads had been turned off; only the blue glow of the television tube lit the room. Karras stood for a couple of minutes, watching the end of an old *Mannix*. God, it was late. He went to the girl, turned her face so that her nose and mouth were off the cushion, put his palm on her back. She had sweat into her shirt. He killed the power on the TV.

In the closeness of his bathroom, Karras could smell the cigarettes, booze, and reefer in his clothes. He stripped and clumsily kicked his jeans and Hawaiian shirt toward a straw hamper that sat against the wall. Looking in the mirror, he placed his fingers beneath his nose, took in the lingering fish smell of Donna's box.

"You old bastard," said Karras roguishly, but he couldn't even bring himself to smile. Maybe he'd get Marcus on the phone, tell him about his stand-up fuck in the head at Benbow's, have a few laughs about it, then go into that bit about his guilt, how he'd felt sad after he'd pulled out, looking at the jiz shot trail down good-time Donna's leg. How he really was only looking for that one good girl out there, that one he'd never been able to find. But Marcus would be asleep now, next to Elaine. And Marcus, Karras saw it more often now in his face, he was getting tired of listening to that song. The truth was, Karras could barely stand to listen to it himself.

Karras washed, went to bed. In the dark of his room he remembered that his mother had phoned earlier in the week. Before passing to sleep, he made a promise to himself that he would visit her soon.

Bobby Roy Clagget lay facedown on the bed, his head turned toward the window. Reflected light from the motel pool below played across the brownish curtains that covered the window facing the street. Over a song coming from the nightstand's clock radio he could hear the movement of tractor trailers along New York Avenue, the industrial-corridor artery that led in and out of town. He felt Wilton Cooper's callused palm and fingers, slick with some sort of grease, rub his naked thighs and then knead his bare behind.

Cooper sang along to the tune coming from the radio: "Are you man enough, big and baaad enough?" The Four Tops had seen their best days, Cooper knew. But this cut was kickin', and Levi Stubbs, you could always count on him to be bad. Cooper took a long swig of his Near Beer, put the can down on the stained green carpet by the bed.

Clagget swallowed hard. Ugly and skinny as he was, he had never had a woman, had never expected to have one. What Wilton was doing to him, he had not considered it himself. Strangely, Wilton's touch, it didn't feel all that wrong. After all, Wilton was family, like an older brother, or an uncle, someone like that.

Or a father. That was something else Clagget had never had.

There was his own father, not even a memory, gone before he had even gotten up on his own two feet. And then there was the stepfather with the sour-mash breath who beat him near bloody every goddamn night, until Bobby Roy had to hurt someone, anyone, or anything else, had to give some of that pain back. But Clagget had been too thin and weak to put a hurting on any of the farm boys who called him names in his hometown. Animals, now — animals were something else. Animals were easy. Clagget started with chickens, pulverizing them with buckshot and sometimes cutting them slowly at the base of their skinny necks with the buck knife he always kept whetting-stone sharp. Then barnyard kittens, so many of them always around they would never be missed. You could get one to like you real easy, so that it crawled right into your lap. While it was purring, just a hard, sure push of your thumbnail into the soft spot right behind its ear. Or shove the buck straight up into its chest while the kitten squirmed in your hand, the warm blood splashing across your fingers.

Warm. Like the warmth of being held by a father.

Clagget winced as Cooper's finger slipped inside him.

"Wilton," whispered Clagget.

"Hush," said Cooper. "Just gettin' friendly, is all."

The song ended, and the station's jock went into a commercial about a place called the Style Shop. The Style Shop, the Style Shop, the Style Shop . . . he must have repeated it a half dozen times.

Clagget said, "Wilton?"

"Yes, little brother?"

"What are we doing here?"

Wilton's voice was silk. "Oh, a little bit of this and that. Gonna go out to that farm tomorrow, pick up that cocaine from those biker boys. Gonna need your help there, B. R. Give you a chance to realize the promise I seen in you back at the drive-in."

"And then?"

"Get the money back from Trouble Man, I guess. After that, hang out, enjoy that Bicentennial thing they got planned up here. Then take the 'caine back to Carlos, keep all the money, Carlos's drug money and the money we get back from Trouble Man, for ourselves. Carlos, as far as we are from Miami, he won't know a thing. How's that sound to you?"

Clagget concentrated on the brown curtain, the blue reflection rippling against the fabric. A thick black bug crawled across the curtain, its antennae wiggling in the light.

"B. R.?" said Cooper. "I asked you how that sounds."

"Sounds good, Wilton." Clagget swallowed. "Sounds good."

Wilton Cooper undid his belt buckle as he stood away from the bed. He looked at the skinny boy lying there, the bare-twig arms, the acned buttocks and back. Well, the boy sure wasn't no prize. But he was his for the trip, and he was steady with a gun.

Cooper stepped out of his drawers. It wasn't like he was anybody's sissy, nothing like that. Uh-uh. And he would cut any man who dared call him a punk. He had learned something in prison, though, and once you learned it you never went back: There wasn't no pussy in the world tighter than the brown eye on a young boy. You could take that motherfucker to the bank and draw interest on it, every goddamn time.

TEN

Ronald Thomas shook a Kool out from the bottom of the deck. He sat on the stoop, watched his brother Russell approach a couple of fine young girls who stood on the street corner, talking and laughing and telling stories. Russell looked back at his brother, smiled as he put a little down-strut into his walk. Ronald lit his smoke.

Russell couldn't talk to the ladies, had never even been close to having the rap down, but he was one of those dudes who believed he could. Ronald couldn't think of a time Russell had gotten any play his own self. It was always Ronald, hooking Russell up on a double, a girlfriend of one of Ronald's freaks, situations like that. Nothing but mercy-pussy for young Russell, on account of he was one sorry-looking motherfucker for real. Their uncle even had him going on one of those special buses for a while back in grade school, this bus where all the kids wore helmets and shit, had drool going down their chins, falling onto raggedy-ass bibs that were always gray and wet. Russell dropped out of school sometime after that, partly 'cause he couldn't keep up and partly from shame. Soon after, Ronald dropped out with him.

They grew up on their uncle's farm, worked it hard. Hotter than the devil's living room down in Carolina, and the heat made you hornier than a motherfucker, too. It made Russell that way, for sure. More than one time Ronald had caught Russell on the treeline side of the barn, stump-breaking some mule. Once, a few kids from a neighboring farm caught Russell doing just that, and Ronald had to fuck a couple of them up just to save some kind of dignity for the family name. It seemed that Ronald was always looking after Russell, except for during those hard bits Ronald had to do later on. The first armed robbery stretch in Delaware, in that prison they had up there on 113, and then in Angola, where Ronald had met Wilton Cooper. But once he got out, Ronald went right back to wet-nursing his younger brother. *Someone* had to look after Russell, foolish as he was.

"What's goin' on, baby?" said Russell to the girl leaning her forearm on the corner mailbox, a short, tight thing wearing hoop earrings and filling a jean skirt with her bubble ass.

"Nothin' much," she said, glancing warily at her girlfriend, who was older, taller, wearing a short-sleeved jumper and cork-wedge heels.

Russell stood near the girl in the hoop earrings, appraised her carefully. "Uh-huh. Mmm-huh." He stroked his spare goatee, nodded his head. "Yeah. You are *fine*, too."

Ronald blew a smoke ring, watched his brother move closer to the short girl, watched the short girl kind of back away. The tall one looked over at Ronald, gave him a little smile. It had always been easy for him.

"My Nubian princess," said Russell, going straight into his tired rap.

"What you talkin' about, fool?" said the girl. "You don't *even* know me."

"What'samatter, baby?" said Russell. "You got a George?"

"Whether I got a George or not, you know it ain't none of your business." She once-overed Russell's green patterned-knit slacks. "So you best get your Cavalier Men's Shop–lookin' ass the fuck on out of here 'fore my older brother comes around, sees you botherin' us, hear?"

"Shit, baby, it's cool." Russell made a parting-of-the-waves motion with his hands. "You change your mind, me and my brother are stayin' with our cuz, just up the way."

Russell walked slowly back to Ronald on the stoop. He put out his hand. "Gimme one of them double-O's," he said.

Ronald shook a Kool out for Russell, gave him a light. Right about then, the red Challenger came around the corner and moved down the block.

"There's Cooper," said Ronald.

"Yeah," said Russell. "Good thing for Shorty he showed up, too.

'Cause I was fixin' to go back over there, talk her into a date. And you *know* I would've torn that shit up."

"Yeah, she was into you, Russell."

"Damn sure was. Said I was cavalier and shit."

"Go ahead, boy."

"Who you callin' boy?"

"Go ahead."

"You see a boy, give him five dollars."

"Aw, go ahead."

The Thomas brothers folded themselves into the backseat of the Challenger. Wilton Cooper drove to a surplus store on F Street, downtown. He bought a lightweight hunting vest for Bobby Roy Clagget and threw it in the trunk with the guns and ammunition they had brought up from the South. He went to a record store and bought some new cassette tapes, stopped at a 7-Eleven for cigarettes, gassed up on New York Avenue. In the bathroom of the service station he patted his Afro in the mirror, made certain that he was looking clean.

They drove out of D.C., cut off of the BW Parkway, crossed over to 95 and headed north. Cooper slid an Edwin Birdsong cassette into the box, something called *What's Your Sign?*, and he put it up loud enough so that no one even thought about trying to speak. Ronald Thomas could tell that Cooper just wanted to drive, smoke his Salem longs down to the filter, think. Every so often he'd see the white boy lean real close to Cooper, whisper something in his ear, so close that it looked like the white boy had become Cooper's bitch. Not that Ronald would even think about cracking on Cooper about being a sissy, even in fun. He knew Cooper could fuck a nigger up if that's what he had a mind to do; he'd seen Cooper strike quicker than a woodpile snake in the yard so many times before. If Cooper wanted the white boy to be his girl, shit, man, it was cool by Ronald.

Around a place called Columbia, Cooper tossed the Baggie of cocaine over his shoulder, told Russell and Ronald to knock themselves out. The Thomas brothers used their fingernails to hit the coke, laughing and giving each other skin after each go-round. Ronald thought the freeze was pretty good, not stepped on too hard, with a fast rush to it and a nice drip back in the throat. Russell seemed to be enjoying it, too; he was talking shit now, *much* shit, even for Russell, his mouth overloading his asshole. The two of them couldn't light their cigarettes fast enough. Cooper had put a Jimmy Castor Bunch cassette into the deck, kept the volume cranked. Ronald and Russell sang along to a bad jam called "Supersound."

Cooper checked Eddie Spaghetti's directions, turned off 95 at an exit marked Marriottsville. A couple of miles past small farms and wooded land and Cooper made another turn into an unmarked, graveled one-lane that led into a forest of oak and pine. A half mile into the woods, Cooper killed the music, coasted a hundred feet, cut the engine on the Dodge.

"All right," said Cooper, "everybody out."

They got out of the car and followed Cooper back to the trunk. Cooper turned the key and popped open the lid. B. R. Clagget reached in, put the hunting vest on over his rayon shirt. He pulled free the sawed-off, thumbed in a couple of double-aught shells. He took another half dozen rounds and fitted them through the loops of his vest.

"We goin' in showin' like that?" said Ronald.

"The Miami way," said Cooper.

Ronald Thomas shrugged, looked over at Russell, slack-jawed. Ronald took the short-barreled .357 he favored from the trunk, broke the cylinder, spun it, saw the copper casings snug in their homes. He wrist-snapped the cylinder shut, put the pistol barrel-down behind the waistband of his slacks. Russell withdrew his .38, clumsily aped his brother's action, fitted the S&W inside his patterned double knits.

Cooper dressed holsters over each shoulder of his maroon polo shirt. He thumb-checked the top round on each of the magazines of his twin Colts, slapped in the magazines, racked the receivers on both guns. He holstered the .45s. He reached into the trunk, brought out Carlos's briefcase filled with banded stacks of cash money.

Cooper nodded at Ronald, tossed him the keys. Ronald caught the ring, swung it on his finger. Cooper looked up at the sun, directly overhead. He wiped sweat off his brow.

"After these woods clear," said Cooper, "there's supposed to be a house in a field. You drive us out halfway, Ronald, drop us off."

"Right," said Ronald.

"What about me?" said Russell.

"You stay with your brother. When it starts, he'll tell you what to do."

"Wilton?" said Clagget.

"You're comin' with me."

"Thanks!"

"All right, then," said Cooper. "Let's take it to the bridge."

They got back into the Challenger. Ronald Thomas situated himself behind the wheel, turned the ignition. He headed for the white light sheeted at the break in the trees.

Larry Spence popped the ring on a can of National Bohemian, threw back a foamy swig, let some gas pass through his mouth. He had another sip of the warm beer, his first of the day. Rocking back on the heels of his engineer boots, he looked out the window of the bungalow. Out in the field, Poor Boy, his shirt off, his jeans hung low, a Prussian helmet covering his head, sat on his heels, polishing the chrome on his hog. A half dozen bikes stood nearby in an orderly row, gleaming in the sun.

"Nice day to get in the wind," said Larry.

"Huh?" said Albert, who sat on the couch, cleaning pot on the cover of *Pronounced Leh-Nerd Skin-Nerd.*

"He said it's a good day to ride," said Charlie, wearing a Tijuana Pussy Posse T-shirt and sitting next to Albert.

"Oh," said Albert. "It *is* a good day." Albert was high and happy.

Larry stared out the window. "Why don't somebody put some fuckin' music on," he said.

"Put some on," said Charlie to Albert.

"I'm gettin' the seeds and stems out of the shit," said Albert.

"I'll put some on, then," said Charlie.

Charlie took his can of Natty Bo off the table in front of him and went to the stereo, where the albums were set face out in a peach crate. Charlie flipped past a couple of Dead albums, a New Riders of the Purple Sage, and a scratched London-label Stones that had no cover. He stopped at a double near the back of the crate.

"*Steppenwolf Live* all right?" said Charlie.

"Put it on," said Larry.

Charlie put on side four, his favorite, which kicked off with "Hey Lawdy Mama." He shook his kinky black hair, played some air guitar with the hand that did not hold a beer as Deborah, Larry's woman, came into the room.

Deborah stood near six feet and wore hip-hugger jeans with one snap on the fly and a leather headband tied around her long, straight chestnut hair. The headband made her look faintly Indian, that and her deep tan and high cheekbones. The long nipples of her thin, conical breasts pressed out against her shorty T. She flipped her hair off her shoulder, revealing one feather earring. Deborah had just done a line of uncut snow back in the kitchen; she rubbed its residue onto her gums, then licked her finger clean.

"What the fuck's happening, Larry?" she said.

"Waitin' on those buyers," said Larry, turning around to look at his woman. Larry scratched at his beard. He had another swig of beer, tossing his head back for a long one. His jean vest parted to expose his barrel chest and a great white belly covered with hair. Larry belched.

Albert did a bong hit, passed the bong over to Charlie, seated now on the couch. Albert shook a Marlboro red out of his box, gave himself a light. Charlie filled the bowl of the bong.

"You know these guys?" said Deborah.

"Remember that fat guy from Jersey, we met him in that bar in D.C., the dude bought us all those beers?"

"Yeah?"

"He knows 'em."

"That supposed to mean something?" said Deborah.

"Shit, Deb, it's a beautiful day. Why you gotta be so negative and shit?"

"Yeah," said Albert, "you're killing my high."

"Just shut the fuck up, Albert," said Deborah.

"You gonna let your lady harsh me out like that, bro?" said Albert. Albert blinked his close-set eyes and shook a curtain of greasy brown hair out of his face.

Larry didn't answer. He crossed the room, gave Deborah a kiss, calmed her down. It was more to protect Albert than it was Deborah. Larry had seen Deborah kick Albert's ass one night at a keg party out by the fire in the middle of the field. Albert claimed it was the barrel acid on top of the 714s that night that had thrown off his timing. But Larry knew it was his lady's fierce will to come out on top. Hell, she even had to fuck him the same way — always on top. Deborah, she was one tough lady.

"Hey," he whispered in her ear. "Let's work on some peaceful vibes around here today, okay?"

"Okay, Larry," she said. "Okay."

Charlie used a poker to force the rest of the hit through the bong's bowl. He put the bong on the lacquered wood table and walked to the front window. He looked out into the yard.

A red muscle car appeared over the hill near the tree line, came slowly down the gravel road. Poor Boy stopped polishing his bike, stared at the car as it stopped fifty yards from the house. Charlie gave a stoned chuckle as he squinted through the streaked window, seeing the Afros inside the car.

"Hey, Larry," said Charlie, saying it loud enough so Larry could hear over the John Kay vocals and dirty guitar filling the room.

"Yeah," said Larry.

"Buncha boofers in a cage just pulled up and stopped in the middle of the yard."

"What kind of a cage, Slo Ride?" said Larry.

"Dodge," said Charlie, who was called Slo Ride by his bros. "Red ragtop with black hood stripes."

"That's the way Eddie described it," said Larry. "That's them."

Charlie watched the doors open, watched two figures emerge from the backseat. Charlie pushed a block of hair back behind his ear.

"Goddamn," said Charlie.

"What?" said Larry.

"Two of 'em are walking toward the house. One's packing double automatics and a suitcase and the other's holding a sawed-off. They ain't trying to hide it, neither."

Albert stood up from his seat on the couch. He stabbed his smoke into the tire ashtray that sat on the table. "What the fuck's going on, Larry?"

Larry picked at his beard. "Hell if I know. The way they do it down in Florida, I guess."

"I'll get the guns," said Deborah, anticipation and excitement in her voice.

"Right." Larry nodded rapidly. "And you go with her, Albert. Then go out the back door and get yourself against the side of the house."

Albert and Deborah went back to the bedroom, came back quickly with guns and ammunition stacked like firewood in their arms. They dumped the guns on the couch.

"C'mon, Slo Ride," said Larry. But Charlie hadn't moved. He was smiling at the two who were now nearing the bungalow.

"What're you waitin' on, Slo Ride?" said Larry.

"Just lookin' at our visitors, is all."

"Yeah? Whaddaya see?"

"A bad-lookin' nigger and a white boy who walks like a nigger. I'm tellin' you, you ought to see it. It's funnier than shit."

"Never mind that," said Larry. "Get your ass over here, now."

Deborah slapped a magazine into the house M16 she had picked up off the couch. She switched the selector to full auto, cocked her hip, struck an SLA pose.

"How do I look, baby?" said Deborah.

"Just like Patty," said Larry, a hint of pride in his voice.

Deborah said, "Bring 'em on."

Larry could only look at her and smile.

Ronald Thomas leaned over toward the passenger seat, snorted a neat white mound off the crook of Russell's hand. He felt the burn in his sinuses and almost right after, the medicinal drip in the back of his throat. The freeze was nice, but it made him want to do something: get out of the car, fuck someone up, talk to some bitches . . . do *something*. He heard Russell take some more blow up into his nose.

"Got-*damn,* boy, this shit is right!" Russell put out his hand. "Gimme one of them double-O's, man."

Ronald shook two Kools out from the bottom of the deck. He pushed in the dash lighter. He smiled a little, watching Cooper and that B. R. boy walking toward the house, putting something extra in their strides, Clagget having a time of it, trying to put a city black man's down-step to it on those four-inch-high stacks of his. The two of them stopped at the shirtless biker cat who had been polishing his hog when they first drove up. Then Cooper got up on the front porch, stepped right in, just opened the screen door without knocking, went inside. B. R. Clagget stayed out in the yard, talking with the shirtless biker with the German army–looking helmet on his head.

"Right here," said Russell, holding out the hot lighter, Ronald leaning over, putting fire to his Kool.

Ronald heard a rumble, looked in the rearview. A big ugly sucker wearing goggles and sitting low to the ground on a big bike was approaching from behind on the gravel road, his long straight hair blowing back in the wind. The bike went around the Challenger, the rider giving Ronald and Russell a good hard look before he continued on to where the other bikes were parked in front of the house. Ronald smiled at the man and nodded even as he shifted in his seat.

"Ronald," said Russell.

"Be cool," said Ronald. "Man's just comin' back to his crib."

Ronald watched the big guy get off his bike, go over to where Clagget and the shirtless cat with the helmet were having their talk. Right about then, Ronald saw some movement on the side of the house: A thin white dude with a gun in his hand had himself pressed against the cedar shake siding, was moving slowly to the front. Ronald saw him put the gun back behind his jeans, try to get loose and natural as he pushed himself away from the house. Slick.

So it was those three out in the yard, one of them packing. And Ronald could see the dark outline of a few bodies through the bay window of the house. Two, maybe three in there. If he had to peg it, Ronald made it six against three: Cooper, Clagget, and himself. He didn't count his younger brother; Ronald never counted on Russell in a pinch, simple as he was.

"See that shit?" said Russell.

"I see it." Ronald slipped the .357 out of his slacks and placed it on his lap. "Now, you listen to me, boy —"

"Who you callin' —"

"Just listen. Whatever goes down, I want you to sit your ass low in that seat, and I want you to stay there. Don't do nothin' *but* that, hear?"

"Yeah, I hear." Russell had pulled the .38 and was rubbing his thumb nervously against the checkered grip. He looked over at his brother. "Ronald?"

"Uh-huh?"

"This motherfucker's gonna *happen*, ain't it?"

"Gonna happen, all right."

A line of blood had dripped down from Russell's nose. He wiped the blood from his upper lip. "When, Ronald?"

"If I was gonna place a bet" — Ronald pushed the gearshift into first — "I'd say it was gonna happen right about now."

Bobby Roy Clagget swung the shotgun at his side, kind of threw his other arm out when he came up off the down-step. He had that free hand cupped like he was cupping a smoke. It felt good, walking next to Cooper. It wasn't just that moving next to Cooper made him feel safe; moving alongside Cooper made Clagget feel *bad*, too.

It was hot out in the sun. Maryland in the summer, it was as hot and still as Carolina in July. Walking across the field toward the house, with the bugs buzzing in his ears, the sweat making the rayon shirt underneath the hunting vest stick to his back, Clagget had a feeling that he was a boy again, his stepfather yelling at him from the house as he walked along the plow lines of his mother's farm.

They came near the shirtless guy polishing his bike. The guy had stood up and was watching them approach with a wary but cool eye. Clagget checked out the bikes sitting in the row: small-saddled, customized Harleys, all of them, their forks stretched and raked, Twin and Big Twin Knucklehead engines, one newer model sporting the AMF logo, a Panhead on the end. Shirtless's bike was a Panhead as well. Growing up in the south, Clagget knew something about bikes; he had taken apart and put back together a street Yamaha his stepfather had won at cards just a few years back. He'd have something to talk about with the guy in the yard.

They stopped in front of the biker. Clagget noticed his very blue, almost Chinese eyes, and the twin SS stickers on the Prussian helmet pushed back on his head. An awful scrape ran from shoulder to elbow on the biker's right arm. The sound of a bluesy guitar came from the bungalow's screen door.

"How do," said Cooper, smiling broadly. "Larry around?"

"Inside," said the man. "You got —"

"An appointment? Sure do. And what's your name?"

"They call me Poor Boy."

"Tell you what, Poor Boy. I'm gonna go on in, have my meeting with Larry. Anyone else in there with him?"

Poor Boy looked at the .45s slung loosely under Cooper's arms. He looked at Clagget's shotgun. "Well . . . there's Deborah, Larry's lady. Dude named Charlie, goes by the name of Slo Ride. Another dude named Albert."

"This Albert got another name?"

"Uh-uh."

"Okay. So I'm gonna go on in. This here's my young friend B. R. He's gonna stay out here, keep you company. That sound good to you?"

"Sure," said Poor Boy, his hands fluttering nervously.

Without another word, Cooper stepped up onto the bungalow's porch, touching one of four pillars that held up the overhanging roof, and went to the screen door. Clagget watched him open the door, step inside without stopping to knock or even announce himself. Yeah, Cooper was one genuine bad-ass dude.

Clagget looked at Poor Boy's scraped arm. "Where'd you get the road rash?"

"Dropped my bike on Six Ninety-five."

"You didn't hardly scratch the bike."

"Saved it with my arm and leg. Leg's worse."

Clagget chin-nodded at Poor Boy's Harley. "It sure is nice."

"Thanks."

"Panhead, right? Got those fishtail pipes. Like Peter Fonda's Captain America."

"Huh?"

"*Easy Rider.*"

"Peter Fonda. That all you know? You know movies, but what you know about bikes?"

"Broke down a Yamaha once."

"Fuck a Yamaha."

"Bike's a bike."

Poor Boy said, "Rice rocket ain't no bike."

"If you say," said Clagget.

Poor Boy stared at the kid, the khaki hunting vest over the disco shirt, a ticktacktoe design, rust on yellow; rust-colored baggies, cuffed at the ends, breaking low on the stacks. Even with the shotgun in Disco Boy's hand, Poor Boy had to know.

"Say, man," said Poor Boy. "You mind if I ask you somethin'?"

"Go ahead."

"What's a natural-born white boy like you doin' hangin' out with a bunch of niggers?"

"Just fortunate, I guess."

Both of them turned at the sound of a monster bike coming down the gravel road. The rider was fat and uglier than a pig's ass, and he clutched the ape-hanger handlebars in the crucifix position as he went around the Challenger and blew in toward the house. He sat way low in the saddle and leaned back against the sissy bar with his feet high on the pegs. He came to a stop near Clagget and Poor Boy, cut the engine, got off the bike.

The guy towered over Clagget by a head, outweighed him by a hundred and fifty pounds. He wore black boots with heel-wrapped chains, fingerless gloves, and Red Baron—style goggles. His arms were tattooed wrist to shoulder, and there were teardrop tats coming down behind the goggle of his right eye.

The big biker looked Clagget over thoroughly. "What the fuck are you supposed to be?" he said.

Poor Boy chuckled. With the big guy around, he had gotten back some of his courage. "He's with some rugheads came to make a buy from Larry."

"That a fact."

"Name's B. R.," offered Clagget. "Didn't catch yours."

The big man hesitated. Disco had the shotgun — he'd play Disco's game.

"Lucer," said the big man.

"Loser?" said Clagget.

The big man sighed. "Not Loser. *Lucer*. Billy Lucer. It's my name."

Clagget looked at Lucer's bike. "Old Shovelhead, right?"

"Yeah."

"Boss tubes," said Clagget, pointing to the pipes on Lucer's bike. "You slash 'em like that your own self?"

"Yeah. Slash-cut 'em and turned 'em out."

"Ain't no wonder it's so loud."

"One of the loudest on the street."

"Yeah," said Clagget, "it sure is a nice sled."

"Thanks," said Lucer, squinting at Clagget, not sure if the skinny, toothless kid with the fucked-up face was putting him on.

"Yeah, I mean to tell you, it really is nice." Clagget took a few steps over to the bike. "You mind if I kick it over?"

Lucer looked at Poor Boy for a moment, then back to Clagget. "I guess it's all right."

Clagget smiled. He had seen this in a flick at the drive-in, *Angels Die Hard* or *The Savage Seven*, he couldn't remember which. He never thought he'd get the chance to do it himself.

"I do thank you," said Clagget.

"Hey," said Lucer, as Clagget lifted his right leg.

Clagget put his shoe to the flame-painted gas tank, kicked the bike over on its side. It hit the hard ground, bounced a few inches, kicked up a cloud of dust.

"You're fuckin' dead," growled Lucer, moving forward.

Clagget stepped back a couple of feet and swung the shotgun between the two men. "You boys know what this is?"

Poor Boy nodded stupidly, stumbled back a step. Lucer stopped dead in his tracks.

Clagget pumped the sawed-off, pointed the shotgun at the one called Poor Boy. "And you sure do know what that sound is, don't you?"

Poor Boy opened his mouth to speak. Before any words came out, they all heard the double clap of gunfire and then a woman's scream from inside the house.

When Wilton Cooper stepped into the living room of the bungalow, he saw three biker types spread out in a loose triangle, all of them holding guns. There was a fat man tapping the barrel of a .44 against his side and a kinky-haired stoner holding a revolver of undetermined caliber and a tall bitch cradling an M16. Fat Man stood in front of the couch, with Stoner standing to the side next to a wood table with smoking paraphernalia on it. The tall Pocahontas-looking freak — she was back in what would have been a dining room, near the kitchen — she had those bright, fearless eyes Cooper had known in certain stickup boys he had run with back in the years past. Of the group, she was the one to watch.

They were just standing there, waiting for Cooper to say something, he guessed. The stereo was cranking, the singer digging out the first verse of the song from somewhere deep in his throat: "You know I smoked a lot grass, Loooord I popped a lot of pills. . . ."

Cooper moved closer to the group, smiled. "How do?" he said.

"You Cooper?" said Larry.

"It is me," said Cooper.

"Larry," said Larry.

Cooper said, "Well, all right."

Larry nodded to the kinky-haired one with the uncertain eyes, wearing a T-shirt with a cartoon Mexican, some fool thing about pussy written on it. Like wearing that shirt was going to get him some play.

"This here's Slo Ride," said Larry.

"Pleased to know you," said Cooper.

Larry motioned his head behind him, managed to do it without taking his eyes off Cooper. "And my lady, Deborah."

"My pleasure, baby," said Cooper.

Deborah had moved back farther into the dining room. Smart girl. Cooper wondered where the fourth one had gone to; out in the yard, Poor Boy had said that a cat named Albert was in the house. Could be back in the kitchen, some shit like that, or maybe out back, moving around the bungalow. No matter. Cooper had faith in B. R., and he knew Ronald Thomas would be on it, too. Cooper would just put Albert out of his mind, deal with him if he had to when the time came.

"Goooddamn . . . the pusher," growled the singer from the speakers.

"Turn the music down," said Larry to Charlie. "I can't fuckin' think."

"That's okay," said Cooper. "Used to hear this tune all the time. Had a lot of boys, looked something like you, used to play this all the time, back at my alma mater."

"Yeah?" said Charlie. "Where's that?"

"Louisiana State."

"Angola?"

"The same."

"Had some bros in there myself."

"I figured you did." Cooper dropped the suitcase on the wood table.

"Well, anyway. What y'all say we do our business? Kind of in a hurry to get back to the city, if you know what I mean."

Cooper opened the suitcase, and Larry stepped over to have a look. His eyes widened: It was a shitload of cash money in there, rubber-banded and stacked. He picked up one of the bundles, flipped through it, made sure there wasn't blank paper behind the cover bill. He tossed the stack back into the case.

"Looks good," said Larry. He turned his head. "Hey, Deb, go ahead and bring out the shit."

Deborah booked.

Cooper stood there, smiling, rocking back on his heels, waiting for the Indian girl to come back with the blow. The solo had kicked in on the song, and the simple-ass mug they called Slo Ride was playing a little air guitar with his free hand. No attention span, thought Cooper, even when an ex-con, stone-nigger gunman was standing right before him. *Slo Ride.* Slow, hell. Motherfucker was standing still.

The girl came back in the room with a brown paper grocery bag, dropped it on the table next to the suitcase. She moved quickly back to the dining room, stood half in and half out of Cooper's sight, near the open kitchen door. Goddamn, thought Cooper, was she the only one in this group with a brain in her head?

Cooper opened the bag, reached inside. He pulled free one of the Baggies, felt its weight. The Baggie was cold, near frozen, with several grains of rice scattered throughout the snow.

"We kept it in the freezer," said Larry, seeing Cooper's perplexed expression, "so's it didn't disappear in this heat."

Cooper realized for the first time that he was sweating right through his shirt. "It is hot in here, too." Cooper dropped the blow back in the grocery bag. "Anyway, there's your money. Two hundred grand, just like Eddie Spags said."

"What," said Larry, "ain't you gonna check out the merchandise?"

"Don't use it myself, don't even want to try it for business reasons," said Cooper. "My boys took your sample for a test run, gave it a passing grade. Besides, if it ain't right, you know I'll be back."

Larry looked over at Slo Ride, shrugged.

Cooper said genially, "I'd go ahead and take the cash, put it in a safe place if I was you. Don't want to leave all those ducats lyin' around and shit."

Larry switched the .44 to his left hand, picked up the suitcase with his right, like Cooper knew he'd do. Yahoo, motherfucker — Mountain Dew.

"Larry," said Deborah, noticing Larry's mistake from way back in the room. But Larry couldn't hear her. The music had absorbed Deborah's voice.

Slo Ride squinted, scratched the barrel of his pistol along the side of his head. "Hey, Cooper."

"Yeah?"

"I'm just wonderin'. You left-handed or right?"

"Right."

"So when you pull them guns you got — when you get in a situation, I mean — which one you pull first?"

Larry looked up.

"Aw, that's easy, Slo Ride." Cooper laughed. He looked down at the .45s hanging beneath each arm. He moved his left hand to the right grip, the right hand to the left grip, like he was giving himself a hug.

"Larry!" screamed Deborah, and Larry turned his head.

"You just do this," said Cooper, still smiling. "Called a cross-draw."

Cooper pulled both guns from their holsters, squeezed both triggers at once, shot Larry twice in a close-pattern square in the chest. Cooper turned his head at the blow-back as Larry toppled ass over tits and seemed to disappear into the makeup of the room.

Cooper turned to the right. Slo Ride had dropped his gun, just dropped it like Cooper knew he would, and he was raising his shaking hands. Cooper blew the top of Slo Ride's head off with one clean shot. Slo Ride kind of sailed off to the side, an arc of brains and blood moving with him, like he was diving into a pool.

Deborah screamed, came into full view, fired the M16 into the living room.

Cooper hit the floor, chunks of upholstery flying off the couch around him, the bay window exploding behind his back. The woman was strafing the place now, giving it all, full clip, the wood splintering around him as Cooper held the .45s straight out while trying to fend off the ricochet rounds that were popping and pinging all over the house.

Over the sound of the gunfire and machine-gun guitar, Cooper heard the explosion of a shotgun outside the bungalow, then another, then felt the house shake as something ran straight into the porch.

There was a quiet. The Indian girl had stopped shooting. An empty magazine hit the floor, and a full one replaced it with a soft click. Cooper heard the girl's footsteps come across the hardwood floor.

"Little brother," said Cooper, whispering it to himself. "Get on it, boy."

The screen door swung on its hinges. B. R. Clagget appeared in the open frame.

As soon as B. R. Clagget heard the shots from inside the house and then the woman's scream, he shotgunned Poor Boy straight off his feet with a direct hit to the chest. Poor Boy flew back as if blown by a strong wind. He knocked down his bike and the Big Twin beside it before coming to rest.

Clagget swung the shotgun on Lucer, pumped in a shell, fired as Lucer tried to turn away. The blast took off Lucer's right arm at the bicep. Lucer screamed, still on his feet, blood ejaculating from the frayed meat stub dangling below his shirtsleeve.

Clagget stepped back. He drew a shell from his hunting vest, fumbled as he thumbed it into the Remington. Lucer tripped, fell down, managed to get back up on his feet by pushing himself up with the arm he still owned. Lucer turned three hundred and sixty degrees and began to run away.

Just then Clagget saw a greasy-haired guy moving quickly from around the side of the house. He saw the guy stop in front of the bungalow's porch, saw him pull a pistol, saw him fire it, saw smoke blow out of the barrel with each shot. He heard the rounds spark off the bike at his feet. Clagget suddenly realized the greasy-haired guy was firing the pistol at him. Oddly, Clagget knew he would not be hit. It was as if he were watching the whole thing up on a screen.

Clagget got the first shell into the shotgun. He managed to fit another one in the breech.

The rapid fire of an automatic rifle came from the bungalow just as the Challenger's four forty sprang to life. Its tires spat gravel, and the back end fishtailed as Ronald Thomas drove the Dodge straight for the gunman standing in front of the house. Clagget heard the greasy-haired guy issue a high-pitched, slide-whistle scream, watched his eyes widen like the eyes of an animal frozen in the road as the hood of the Challenger scooped him up and carried him right into the bungalow's porch. The porch and its roof collapsed on one side where the force of the collision snapped one of the pillars clean in half.

Ronald backed up the Dodge in the smoke and dust. He turned it around, drove across the field to where Lucer was running toward the trees. Lucer, running without an arm, lost his balance and right about then began to go into shock. As if in his own bad dream, the big ugly biker moved his legs but seemed to be making no progress at all. Clagget figured that Ronald would be there in a few hot seconds, take care of Lucer out in the field.

Clagget pumped a round into the Remington. He walked toward the house. He passed the greasy-haired biker who had shot at him, saw that the biker's legs had been pinned against the edge of the porch by the Challenger's bumper. One of his legs appeared to have been amputated below the knee, while the other hung by a few strands of tendon. His jeans, ripped at the knee and open there, exposed a smashed pink-and-white stew of muscle and bone. The man was conscious, his eyes glassy and fixed, his face a tight and unholy mask.

Clagget heard a single gunshot from behind him in the field. He walked on.

He stepped up on the porch, through the broken window saw a tall woman with a Vietnam-looking rifle walking toward the front of the living room. Clagget knew then that this was his movie, his and

Cooper's. As Cooper had done, Clagget opened the screen door, went right into the house.

The woman turned as he entered, swung the rifle in his direction. Clagget dove to the side, firing while still in the air. The recoil threw him back against the wall. As he hit, he watched the woman kind of fold in on her middle, saw a shower of blood and something else erupt simultaneously from her midsection and back.

Clagget heard a funny kind of drumming sound against the hardwood floor.

Cooper stood up slowly from behind the couch, his right gun arm extended. He walked to where the woman lay kicking at the floor. He put her down with a head shot. He holstered both of his guns.

"Lord have mercy, baby," said Cooper, talking softly to Deborah. "You was man enough for *all* these motherfuckers. You know it?"

"Wilton," said Clagget, getting to his feet.

"You all right?"

"Yeah."

"You did good, little brother. I knew you would."

Cooper went and picked up the suitcase where it sat in a smeared puddle of blood next to Larry Spence. Cooper wiped off the handle, gripped it tight. He went to the stereo, kicked the turntable savagely. The rip of a needle on vinyl and then silence hit the room.

"I always did hate that song," said Cooper. He turned to Clagget. "Get that grocery bag off the table, boy."

Clagget picked up the bag. They heard the crack of gunshots then, two barely spaced reports.

"Ronald?" said Cooper.

"Finishin' up, I expect."

Cooper nodded one time.

They left the house, stood on the slanting porch. It was quiet now, hot and still, like it had been when they arrived. Some gun smoke hovered out in the field. Near the tree line, Clagget could see the body of Lucer lying facedown, one hand palm up at his side.

Ronald was walking away from Albert, whom he had just finished.

He moved toward the Challenger, which was now parked near the bikes. Russell stood against the passenger door, smoking a cigarette, the .38 in his hand. Cooper didn't have to smell the barrel to know the gun hadn't been fired. Useless as he was, Russell came with Ronald, and that made carrying him more than worthwhile.

Cooper and Clagget stepped off the porch. There was blood on their clothing and a spray of it on Cooper's face. Cooper got down on one knee, checked out the Dodge's front end.

"*Damn*, Mandingo. You done fucked up my ride."

"Had to." Ronald shrugged, head-motioned toward Albert. "Anyway, I didn't fuck it up near as bad as I fucked up that boy's day."

"I heard *that*," said Cooper.

"*Busted* on his groove," said Russell.

Cooper got the grocery bag from Clagget, put it with the suitcase in the Challenger's trunk. He went to the driver's side of the car, reached inside, got his Salem longs from where they were wedged in the visor. He passed one to Clagget, lit his own, lit Clagget's. He took a deep drag, held the smoke in, let it out slow.

"We're rich, fellas," said Cooper.

Russell and Ronald gave each other skin.

"We goin' home now, Coop?" said Ronald.

"Not just yet," said Cooper. "Got a little business still, back in D.C."

Cooper, Clagget, and Ronald got the bodies into the house while Russell found some gasoline in the root cellar. They set fire to the bungalow. They stood in the field and watched the fire catch.

Cooper tugged on the sleeve of Clagget's shirt. "C'mon now. We best be on our way."

"Can't we stay and watch it, Wilton? It's beautiful!"

"I know it is," said Cooper. "But we got to be goin'. In another minute, that smoke's gonna get up over them trees."

ELEVEN

Dimitri Karras woke early on Friday morning, started some coffee, watched the rise and fall of Vivian Lee's back as she lay sleeping on the couch. The coffee perked, and Karras shook Vivian awake. She greeted him with stale breath and went to the bathroom to wash up and brush her teeth.

They took their coffee by the window in the morning sun. From his seat Karras could see Duncan Hazlewood and Libby Howland leave the Trauma Arms and walk toward Connecticut for their breakfast at Schwartze's.

"You get in late last night?" said Vivian.

"Yeah."

"I guess I fell asleep in front of the tube."

"You did."

"That reefer kinda knocked me out. You always get weed good as Eddie's, Dimitri?"

"Always," said Karras with a smile. The same response he had given Donna DiConstanza at Benbow's. Karras, even with the smell of Donna still on him from the night before, unable to stop himself from giving Vivian the same tired response.

Vivian's long black hair gleamed in the light. You can always look good in the morning when you're young, thought Karras. There had been heavy baggage under his eyes when he had had his first look at himself in the bathroom mirror that morning.

"I was looking through your bookshelf," said Vivian. "You've got quite a selection."

"Yeah, I'm hooked up."

"I like to read."

"It's one of those good habits."

"You've got a lot of interesting books."

"Some of those are from a class I taught out at College Park while I was getting my master's."

"In literature?"

"Yep."

"So you did some time in graduate school." Vivian pushed a strand of hair away from her eyes. "That what kept you out of the war?"

"Who said I stayed out?"

"You don't have the look. Like you've seen something that made you lose something else forever. You're too . . . I don't know. You look too *privileged*. Nothing's hit you yet."

"A moving target, sweetheart. That's me." Karras looked into his coffee cup. "You're pretty smart, Vivian. Pretty observant. For a nineteen year old —"

"I'm gonna be twenty next month."

"Okay. But you're still pretty smart."

"So that's it, right? You stayed in school to get the deferment."

"Yeah. I took it to the legal limit. My mother used a part of her insurance money, from when my father died, to keep me in school. By the time my number came up the draft was over. So, yeah, you're right. I've been privileged, I guess. Much more privileged than a lot of my friends."

"Were you against the war?"

"I never met anyone who was for it. But I can't say I went out in the streets or protested against it or anything like that. In the end, I was just against dying."

"I'm glad you didn't go."

"Thanks."

Vivian reached out, ran her finger along Karras's laugh line, touched his mouth. "You're kinda cute, Dimitri, you know it?"

"I'm cute, all right." Karras took her hand, placed it gently down on the table. "Let's get out of here, okay? I got a few things to do this morning. I need to get an early start."

*　*　*

Karras and Vivian left the apartment and walked south. The sidewalks were dense with people, tourists in for the big Sunday show. The papers, the TV news, all the stories were on the upcoming Bicentennial bash. The carpenters had been hammering down on the Mall for weeks now.

Karras was relieved when Vivian told him she wanted to spend the day hanging at the circle. He gave her his duplicate apartment key, left her with a girl she recognized at the fountain, told her he'd see her later, and got on his way.

Karras went down below the circle to the Jefferson Coffee Shop on 19th, entered the narrow city diner through a glass door tied open with heavy string. The open door told him that the Jefferson's air conditioner had gone down once again. He had a seat on an orange stool at the end of the counter next to a guy named Dale, the huge but gentle bouncer who worked the Brickskeller, a glorified beer garden on 22nd above P.

"Hey, Dale."

"Dimitri."

"How's it goin'?"

"Goin' good."

It was that time between breakfast and lunch when the lawyers, government types, and IBM repairmen were already hard at work, and the local restaurant workers were just starting their day. Moe and Terry, a couple of waiters from the Palm, the pricey steak-and-lobster house next door, sat in the middle of the counter, laughing about something that had happened at a four-top the night before.

Pete, the Greek who owned the place, walked down to Karras, set a cup of coffee in front of him, took his order, said, "Okay, young fella," went back to the grill, and cracked open a couple of eggs with one hand. Like Karras's old man, who had also been named Pete, the Jefferson's Pete was a veteran of the Philippine campaign of World War II. This Pete did not know Dimitri's father, but he had heard of him. Peter Karras had died under violent, mysterious circumstances in 1949. About his father Dimitri Karras knew little else.

Karras liked the Jefferson. They never broke the yolks on his easy overs, and as far as lunch deals went, the Royalburger with shoestring fries was one of the best combos in town. Pete, reserved in a friendly kind of way, had recently returned to the store after a long illness; his teenaged son had stepped up to run the place for the last six months while his father recovered. The son, a skinny, Camaro-driving, outgoing kid with shoulder-length curls, was in the back of the coffee shop, talking and joking with the dishwasher, a boy everyone called Butterball, and the grill-girl, another teenager from the Shaw part of town. She was keeping up with the conversation while singing along to Hot Chocolate's "You Sexy Thing," which was blasting from the house radio. In the Jefferson, the radio dial was always set on WOL, except for that period after lunch when Lula, the booth and counter waitress, was allowed her hour of gospel. Karras came here in the mornings for breakfast and a daily dose of Top 40 funk.

A leggy blond secretary came in for some carry-out, endured the burning eyes of all the men at the counter while she waited for her food. She left hurriedly. Dale and Karras discussed the Wayne Hays affair, an exchange prompted, of course, by the Liz Ray look-alike who had just left.

"Wayne Hayes," said Dale, shaking his head. "Man lost everything for a piece of tail. Can you believe it?"

Karras said, "I can."

Karras left three on two twenty-nine and stepped out of the Jefferson into the prenoon heat. He walked north, pointedly going around the circle rather than through it, stopping once or twice to talk to friends, passing girl-watching businessmen, stoners, cruising homosexuals, short-skirted secretaries, doe-faced chicken hawks eyeing little boys, the whole Dupont stew. A pimp-wagon Lincoln rolled up Connecticut, heavy wah-wah guitar and bass pounding from its open windows; a quick-footed, bearded Arnold and Porter messenger wearing a *Rock 'n' Roll Animal* T-shirt waved to Karras from across the avenue.

Karras stopped at Real Right Records above R, stepped into the store. They had a Graham Central Station tune, an epic instrumental workout called "The Jam," cranking through the house KLMs. Cheek was in the corner of the shop, talking to a P-Funk-loving regular, a kid named Mills with a major-league Afro, who had his own personal copy of *Standing on the Verge of Getting It On* cradled under his arm. Mills claimed to have Parliament's *Osmium* on the Invictus label in his private collection. Cheek had never actually seen it, though, and had repeatedly asked Mills to bring the proof into the store. Cheek and Mills had gotten past that now and were arguing about the meaning of a certain cut off *Maggot Brain*.

Rasheed stood behind the counter, gave Karras an eye sweep. Karras nodded, and Rasheed nodded back. He head-motioned Karras to the back room.

Marcus Clay sat doing the books at an old desk amongst general clutter and cartons of stock, squinting in the dim light. He looked up as Karras entered.

"Mitri."

"Marcus."

"What's goin' on?"

"Marvin Gaye."

"What you *doin'* today, man? Anything? Or you just wanderin' around?"

"Got a little business to take care of."

"Business, huh?"

"Yeah. After that, maybe go out and see my mom."

"Tell her I said hey."

"I will."

Clay rubbed his face, looked through the open door frame leading to the floor. "Damn, those boys are playin' that Larry Graham loud."

"*Ain't No Bout-a-Doubt It.*"

"You agree!"

"I'm sayin' that's the name of the LP."

"Whatever the name, it's still too goddamn loud."

"You got a record store here, Marcus."

"Now you're gonna tell me how to run my shop?"

"Just pointing it out." Karras had a seat on the edge of Clay's desk. "What's up, man? What's botherin' you?"

"The money and shit." Clay dropped his pencil on his desk. "Still haven't figured out what to do about that. Damn fool thing I did."

"You haven't heard from anyone yet, have you?"

"Not a damn thing yet."

"Then relax. We're all right."

Clay looked up. "Where's your girl?"

"Out."

"You —?"

"Uh-uh."

Clay grinned. "Showin' some *restraint*. Not like you, man."

Karras started to tell Clay about Donna DiConstanza and the Benbow's men's room the night before: how he'd gone out and just fucked someone, anyone, to keep himself from hitting on the teenage girl back at his crib.

"You know me, Marcus," said Karras. "Just trying to do right."

Clay, agitated and tight, stood up. "Goddamn, man, those boys just gotta turn that shit down!"

Karras followed Clay out to the floor. Clay went behind the counter as Rasheed stepped aside. Cheek and the Mills kid had kept up their intense discussion without missing a beat. Clay lowered the volume in the store.

"All right?" said Clay.

"Solid, boss," said Rasheed.

"Hey, Marcus," said Karras, who had stopped at the H bin of the store's Rock section. "When you gonna get around to moving Jimi into Soul?"

"What?" said Clay.

"What, haven't you ever listened to *Band of Gypsys*?" said Karras.

Rasheed laughed as Karras walked toward the door.

"Dimitri," said Clay. "We still got a game this evening?"

"Chevy Chase library," said Karras.

"I was thinkin', after that we could hook up at your place for a little thing. Listen to a few records, dance some." Clay's eyes smiled. "Me and Elaine, you and your . . . friend. You know?"

"Sounds good," said Karras. "Later, Marcus. Later, Rasheed. Y'all take it light."

Clay said, "You too."

Rasheed stood on the throw rug covering the cash box in the floor. "You hear what your boy said about Hendrix?"

"Yeah," said Clay, moving out from behind the counter. "Told you he was down."

"He knows his music is all. But down? I wouldn't go so far as all *that*."

Clay grinned a little as he walked away.

Karras went back to his place, scaled out some ounces, bagged them, rolled a joint for himself. He made a couple of phone calls, put some ball clothes together with the herb into a gym bag, and left his apartment. He put the top down on his Karmann Ghia, slapped his eight-track of *Johnny Winter And* into the deck, and pulled out of his spot. Down on Corcoran Street he hooked up with a guy named Robert Berk, passed him three ounces of weed, took back a hundred and fifty in cash.

Karras took a few hits of Columbian while driving north through Rock Creek Park. He went slowly by a group of city kids riding ten-speeds showing orange flags; the kids blew whistles at him as he passed, Karras watching them in the rearview. The reefer had taken, Winter singing the Winwood-Capaldi song "No Time to Live," Johnny's junk-ravaged vocals going out against his own lovely blues guitar.

Riding high in the park in his sporty ragtop, the wind blowing back his long hair, Dimitri Karras smiled.

TWELVE

Wilton Cooper stepped out of the shower, wrapped a towel around his waist. Coming out into the room, he cracked a cold Near Beer straight off. He had a long pull, had another, put the can down on the nightstand.

"Go ahead and have yours," he said to Bobby Roy Clagget, who stood naked before him. "I like it cold in the summertime, so there's plenty of hot water for you, if that's your pleasure."

"Thanks, Wilton."

"Go on, boy."

Cooper watched Clagget walk to the bathroom. From the backside the boy wasn't too bad. Scarier than a motherfucker, though, in the face. Cooper had noticed, on top of the pimples and his general ugliness, that now the boy had a line of white pus along his gums where his teeth had been. Infection, most likely, which meant a fever'd be setting in anytime soon. But like the brothers in lockup used to say, you ain't gonna fuck no face anyhow, and in the heinie-parts department the Clagget kid looked as fine as any young boy he'd seen. Yeah, Cooper, he figured he'd wait on getting dressed himself, just sit around in the coolness of the AC and sip his funny beer, let the boy come out from the shower and put him where he was born to be, facedown on the bed.

The kid, he had done all right out there at that farm, too, played it real good and cool. Cooper had known Clagget would be down when the time came. He'd seen it that first night, with his shotgun fitted in his pant leg, strutting across that field.

Cooper lit a Salem long.

He looked at the briefcase filled with money, the grocery bag filled with cocaine, the briefcase and the bag side by side in the corner of the room. Funny how neither one meant a damn thing to him. The money couldn't buy him anything better than he had right now, than he had felt that afternoon: the rush of just taking something you decided was yours, the head-up feeling in your stride afterward when you were walking away. *The ride* . . . It was all about the ride.

As far as the blow went, Cooper had already decided he wasn't going to bother driving Carlos's shit all the way down to South Florida. For what? To be some brown motherfucker's butt-boy again? Uh-uh, man, that shit was way done. Cooper was going to take this ride as far as it would go, 'cause it *felt* good. Course, he knew the way it was going to end, the same way it always ended for guys like him who had never had no chance and didn't give a good fuck if one came along. The point of it all was to walk like a motherfuckin' man; if you had to, go down like one, too.

Anyway, the whole thing was in motion, Cooper knew. They had been too careless, made too many mistakes. Even with the fire, which had covered some of their tracks, at least, the Baltimore cops or whoever would find and run the remaining Marriottsville evidence — shells, shot patterns, prints, tire impressions, all that — with the Feds, who'd match at least one item up with the Carolina shotgun kill. Somebody'd seen the Challenger leaving the drive-in that night, *somebody*'d seen Bobby Roy gettin' in the car. And Cooper's prints — Ronald Thomas's prints, for that matter — they were on the national network. Cooper figured it would be best if he and Bobby Roy moved over to the Thomas cousin's crib in Northeast, switched cars, maybe, though Cooper hated to give up his ride. Move around a little, buy some time.

The Clagget kid and the Thomas brothers, they didn't have to know none of that. He'd just go on ahead and keep it to himself.

B. R. Clagget came from the bathroom wearing only his briefs.

"Wilton?"

"Yeah."

"What we doin'?"

"Gonna go see Eddie Spaghetti."

"Now?"

"Little later on. In the meantime, come on over here and drop them drawers." Cooper stabbed out his cigarette. "Gonna give you something good, little brother, on account of how proud you made me today."

Dimitri Karras bought some yellow daisies at Boukas Florists on upper Connecticut, then drove west into AU Park. He stopped the Karmann Ghia in the shade of a large elm on 45th and Davenport. He had parked all his cars, from his first Bug to his '66 Nova to the Ghia, in the same oil-stained rectangle of street beneath that tree.

Karras was familiar with most of the old trees on the block. He knew the best climbing trees and those that bore fruit, and could tell you, even in the winter, which dogwoods would blossom pink and which would blossom white, and in whose yard grew the most interesting birch or the magnolia with the loveliest blooms. Beneath a weeping willow in old Mr. Montemorano's backyard, he had shown little Katie O'Donnell his thing and she had shown him hers; ten years later, at the age of fourteen, he had dry-humped his first girl behind the curtain of that very willow's branches. At eight he fell out of an oak in front of Ricky Young's house and broke his arm; at seventeen, sick from drink and unable to make it the half block to his mother's house, he had vomited spaghetti against the same tree. There was a history to the trees in the neighborhood where a guy grew up.

Eleni Karras stood behind the storm door, watched her son walk toward the Cape Cod where he had been raised. He needed a haircut, not that she'd bother bringing the subject up. And he always wore those same bluejeans, turned up once at the cuff. A twenty-seven-year-old man, wearing blue jeans all the time. If he had a good job, maybe he'd have to get some nicer clothes, start spending money, get into a little healthy debt, make him have to work harder. . . . Who was she kidding? She didn't even know what he did to pay the bills. "Little bit of this and that, Ma," he'd always say, then give her the millionaire's smile. Well, he always did have a nice smile. Admittedly, Dimitri had no visible means of support and little in the way of prospects, but with his kind of looks it still surprised her that no girl — a Greek girl would have been very nice — had scooped him up yet. Eleni knew a few *koritsakis* from good families he could talk to at Saint Sophia. That is, if he ever stepped foot in church.

Look at him, thought Eleni: He still walks with that happy bounce, like he did when he was a kid.

"Hey, Ma," said Dimitri, opening the door and giving his mother a kiss. He handed her the daisies, wrapped in sheer green paper.

"*Dimi, mou,*" said Eleni. "*Pos eise, pethi mou?*"

"I'm okay. How's my girl?"

"*Etsi ke etsi.*" Eleni made a flip of her hand. "I'm doin' all right."

Karras followed his mother to the kitchen. Walking behind her, he saw that she had put on a few more pounds. She had always had thick ankles, and over the years the rest of her had come up to speed.

They passed a photograph of his father, Peter Karras, and a frame filled with war medals hung in the hall. As a little boy, Karras used to study the photograph of the man he never knew, his father in his Marine Corps dress uniform, square-jawed and handsome, nearly blond, with a prominent mole beside his mouth. Sometimes, when his mother was off at work, Dimitri would take the photograph down from the wall, go to the bathroom mirror, hold the picture up next to his own face, try to find the resemblance between him and his old man. But there was no resemblance there. Dimitri Karras always favored his mother's side, and as time passed he got to where he liked the way he looked, and found that women liked it, too.

In the kitchen, Eleni put the flowers in a vase and set the vase in the center of the gray Formica-topped table. Karras took his usual seat.

"Thanks for the daisies, honey."

"It's okay."

"*Thelis ligo* rice pudding?"

"What, you made a pot?"

"This morning. You said you were coming by!"

"Sure."

Eleni served it to him in a glass dessert bowl. The pudding was still warm from the stove and thick with raisins. His mother had sprinkled some cinnamon on top as well.

"Mmm."

"*Entaxi, eine?*"

"It's better than *entaxi*, Ma. It's great!"

She poured him a cup of coffee and a cup for herself. Karras could stand a cup of coffee on a July afternoon on account of his mother kept the house so damned cold. What it was, she was addicted to the AC from working reception in a doctor's office for twenty-odd years. Old Doc Steinberg, he wanted it like ice in the place. Eleni got to like it after a while, though her coworker, Ida Mae Clay, could never take it and ended up wearing sweaters in to work year round. Karras almost smiled, thinking of Marcus's mother, standing there behind the sliding glass window, her fists balled on her hips — that was the way she stood when she was all fired up — bitching about the cold in the office for half her working life.

"How's Marcus doin'?" said Eleni.

"He's okay."

"His business good?"

"He's makin' it."

"You should go into some kind of business yourself."

"I'll get right on it, Ma."

"Sure, sure."

"Anyway . . . what else is on your mind?"

"Eh?"

"When you called you said someone from church wanted to talk with me about something."

"Oh, yeah. You remember Nick Stefanos?"

"The guy Pop worked for after the war, right? He had a grill down on Fourteenth Street —"

"He *still* has it. Fourteenth and R."

"So?"

"I'm not sure what he wants, exactly. Said something about a problem with his grandson. You know, Nick raised the boy himself."

"That's nice. But what's it got to do with me?"

"I don't know. I told Nick you'd go down to the grill and see him today —"

"Ma!"

"What, you too busy?"

"Me and Marcus have a game over at the library later on."

"Game, huh? Twenty-seven years old, you're playin' games." Eleni shook a thick finger at Karras. "Look, you don't have any idea what Nick Stefanos did for your father and me after the war. We were living in this little apartment in Chinatown — the three of us, you were just a baby still — and we were gettin' close to being evicted. Your dad had gotten this . . . he had gotten this *limp*, see. Back then they didn't have these programs they got now, and nobody wanted to hire a cripple —"

"All right, Ma, all right. You told me this story like fifty times."

"Nick Stefanos hired him. Nick took him in."

"I said all right."

"You go down and see Nick today. Okay?"

Right after I go and off an ounce of weed to a bunch of high school boys. Yeah, then I'll give some old guy advice on how to raise a kid.

"Okay," said Karras. "I'll go see Nick."

Eleni Karras leaned her back against the sink. Past her round shoulders Dimitri Karras watched a wren glide and light on the corner of the outside windowsill, where it was building a nest. His mother had always stood there in front of the sink, her arms crossed, talking to him about his day while he ate the food she had prepared; and birds had been building nests in that spot for twenty years. Karras smiled.

"What's so funny, *Dimitraki*? Eh?

"Nothin'. Just good to see you, that's all."

"Wanna little bit more pudding?"

"Sure, Ma. One more bowl."

Wilton Cooper sat on the edge of Eddie Marchetti's desk, rapped a rolled-up District of Columbia detail map against his thigh. B. R.

Clagget stood behind him, hip cocked, smoking a long white cigarette.

"So the deal went all right," said Marchetti, nervously moving his swivel chair back and forth behind the desk.

"Deal went real smooth," said Cooper.

"See, Clarenze? I told you, no problemo."

Clarence Tate, standing next to the office window, nodded shortly. He was watching the skinny white dude, thinking how pale and weak he looked. Tate had noticed the pus on the kid's gums, figured he was heading into a fever infection now. Cooper should've made sure the kid was treated right, if he had given a fuck. But Cooper, you could see it in his eyes, he didn't care if he ever saw the sun come up on another day. Why would he care if the kid he was riding with lived or died?

"You meet Larry's lady?" said Marchetti.

"Oh, yeah," said Cooper. "That was one wild freak."

"She makes quite an impression, right?"

"*Talk* about it," said Cooper. "She damn near blew me away!"

Cooper and Marchetti laughed. Tate watched Clagget's pig eyes move knowingly toward Cooper.

"So anyway," said Cooper, "been a pleasure doin' business with all a y'all, so far. Now I mean to clean things up, get that money back from Trouble Man."

"Sounds good," said Marchetti. "If you see my girl, maybe you could persuade her to come on back, too."

"Maybe so. Might just throw her in on the bargain."

Marchetti head-motioned Tate. "Clarenze, you were gonna ask around, see if you could dig up an address on that Clay character, or the Greek."

Tate had made some calls that morning, talked to a couple brothers he had kept in contact with who had played Interhigh ball in the midsixties and still played pickup around town. Tate told them he owed Marcus Clay a few bucks, that he was trying to locate Clay to pay him back. Both of them knew Clay, but the first guy he talked to didn't fall for that old game and said nothing further. The second brother, who was slow from a five-year love affair with a bottle of Tango, told Tate that Clay owned a record shop called Real Right on Connecticut above Dupont.

Marchetti said, "You turn up anything yet?"

Tate said, "Nothing yet."

Cooper smiled. "No matter." He unrolled the detail map, held it up so Tate could see. "It's a trip, man. With a phone book and one of these, you can find damn near anyone you want real easy. See, I remember that Karras dude talking about his high school — Wilson, if I recall. He did play for Wilson, didn't he, Clarence?"

"What the man said."

"So I looked up the high school on the map, then all the Karrases in the phone book who lived in that area. Wasn't *but* one. His folks, I'd guess. Thought I'd slide on over there, see what I could dig up on my own."

"That's a start, then," said Marchetti happily.

"Real slick, how you did that," said Tate.

"Oh, I'm on it, blood," said Cooper, sliding off the desk and standing straight. He reached into his shirt pocket, pulled free a slip of notepaper, tossed it onto Marchetti's desk. "Thought you might like to know where me and B. R. gonna be at the next few days. Decided we'd check out of our motel, stay close to the Thomas brothers, kind of double up in their cousin's place. More convenient and shit."

Marchetti looked at the scribbling on the paper. "You put your phone number on here. Good."

"Case you need to reach me. Mind, I don't think you ought to be giving out the number to anybody else. Might make me . . . *misunderstand* our relationship. Dig?"

"Solid, Wilton," said Marchetti.

"Yeah," said Cooper, winking at Tate. "Solid as a motherfucker, Spags." Cooper jerked his head in the direction of the door. "Let's go, B. R. Time you and me was headin' uptown."

A few minutes later, Tate tracked Cooper and Clagget from the window as they walked to the red Challenger out on the street.

"Hey, Eddie."

"What."

"You talk to your biker friend Larry today, see how *he* liked the way the deal went down?"

"I called him a couple of times, but I couldn't get through. The phone must be fucked or somethin'. Why?"

Tate studied the collapsed front end on the Dodge. "No reason."

"You worry too much, Clarenze."

"Cats like Cooper —"

"Look, you've got to deal with guys like Cooper once in a while if you want to score. I been around the block enough times to know Cooper's dangerous. But, hey: No balls, no glory, right?"

Right, thought Tate. And no brains, no headaches, either.

THIRTEEN

Dewey Schmidt shot off on the magazine photograph of a girl named Tracey who liked guys with muscles and candlelit dinners and long walks on the beach. He opened his eyes, shivered, looked down at his manhood as he gave himself a few more strokes to squeeze out the excess jam. Most guys felt a little blue after, but Dewey could go a couple of times a day easy without a bit of remorse. He really loved to jerk off.

Dewey closed the magazine, put it in the bottom of the stack. You had to rotate the *Swanks*, otherwise you'd ruin them fast. Dewey had his favorite magazine girls, but once you got a good ten-hut going, one naked chick was as good as the next, and by then Dewey had forgotten about Tracey anyhow and shifted his fantasy to Lindy, one of his Magnificent Seven at Einstein High. Dewey kept a list of seven girls tacked to his bulletin board next to his lobby card of Clint Eastwood from *Magnum Force*. The list changed frequently, Lindy having bumped a girl named Betty Dasch — Dewey called her Betty Gash — after Dewey had seen Lindy on the last day of school in her imitation leopard-skin shorts. It was those shorts, and what lay black and steaming beneath them, that had made Dewey dump Betty from the list and get dizzy in love over Lindy.

Dewey pulled his jeans up from down around his ankles, zipped his fly. He picked up a dumbbell, did curls with his right arm until the vein in his bicep popped up nice, repeated the action with his left. Looking in the full-length mirror that hung on the back of his bedroom door, he shook out his straight black hair.

"Schmidt the Snake," said Dewey, smiling rakishly as he ran a thumb along the cat hairs of his mustache.

Dewey went to the living room, left a note for his mom, a secretary at the Department of Transportation, in case she came home early. He slipped the note under a Harold Robbins paperback called *The Adventurers* that his mother had been reading for the last year. Going out the door, he pulled on the crotch of his jeans, separating it and his fishnet underwear from where his cock had begun to stick.

He took the steps down to the garden apartment parking lot. The Green Ghost was in its spot, ready to strike, slanted a little and shining in the sun.

Dewey Schmidt picked Jerry Baluzy up out front of Ferdinand's, the restaurant on Grandview Avenue in Wheaton where Jerry had a summer job busing tables at lunch. Jerry was waiting on the corner, playing with his matted, frizzy black hair. He wore shorts and a black T-shirt, with a pair of Chucks, once-black highs now gone gray, on his long feet. It was a hot day, and Dewey wished he could have worn shorts like Jerry instead of his heavy jeans. But Dewey thought shorts looked faggoty on a guy, so he only wore them around the apartment in front of his mom.

Jerry dropped into the passenger seat. "Dude."

"Jer. Nice shorts, man."

"Gimme a break, Dewey."

"Okay."

"Man, guess who was in the restaurant today."

"I dunno, who?"

"Fuckin' Roy Jefferson, man!" Jerry smiled, waiting for Dewey's response. He knew how much Dewey loved the Skins.

"Aw, shit, you shoulda called me! What'd he look like?"

"You know. Bad lookin' motherfucker with muttonchop 'burns. He smokes, though."

"He smokes?"

"Yeah. Kool one hundreds."

"Damn."

"But listen. About halfway through lunch, this blond chick comes over from another table, asks for Roy's autograph, next thing you know she's sittin' on his lap. Funny as fuck, man, this blond sittin' on Roy Jefferson's johnson. You know he was feelin' good and shit. He was smilin'. . . . I'm tellin' you, you shoulda seen those pearly whites."

"You know what they say about Roy Jefferson, don't you?"

"What?"

"Roy Jefferson don't like white *people,* but he sure does like them white *girls.*"

"Huh," honked Jerry.

They drove over to Jerry's Subs, a little dive on University Boulevard owned by a cool old Jewish guy named Max. Both of them had the roast beef sub with special sauce and raw onions, in their opinion the best sandwich in town. They talked to Max some, but kept it low, since there were some Northwood boys eating at the counter, and if they found out Dewey and Jerry were Einsteiners, you never knew, maybe the Northwood boys might follow them outside and try to kick their asses. It was like that up in Wheaton, with guys from different high schools all around.

Dewey and Jerry got back in the Firebird and drove up University. Out of the Wheaton business district, Jerry reached into the backseat and grabbed a light that spun around in a glass dome, like the cherry on top of a cop car, only yellow. Jerry's dad worked for a road construction company named F. O. Day, and earlier in the day Jerry had boosted it out of the bed of his father's F-150.

"Plug that shit in," said Dewey.

"Should we?" said Jerry.

Dewey said, "You're fuckin' A right."

Jerry pulled the cigarette lighter out of the dash, plugged the light's cord in the empty socket. He reached out the window, placed the bubble light with its magnetized base on the roof of the car. Dewey landed on the horn, punched the gas. He put some play in the wheel, swerved the Firebird like he had seen it done on TV when cops were responding to a call. A Ford Maverick up ahead pulled over to the side of the road and let them pass.

"Ha!" said Jerry.

Dewey pulled an imaginary microphone from the dash, leaned forward, spoke into his cupped hand. "One Adam twelve, one Adam twelve. We have a two eleven in progress . . . shhhhhhhhhhh."

Jerry rocked back and forth with laughter. A Tavares single came on the radio, and Dewey turned the volume way up. The chorus went, "It only takes a minute, girl,/To fall in love, to fall in love." Dewey and Jerry sang, "It only takes a minute, girl,/To get a nut, to get a nut. . . ."

Dewey and Jerry laughed, slapped each other five.

"Where we goin', man?" said Jerry.

"Pick up Toothpick," said Dewey.

The traffic parted for the Green Ghost.

Jimmy Castle crushed his cigarette in the tin ashtray he had lifted from Red Barn, blew his last lungful of smoke out the open window of his room. He had lit a cone of incense, which burned in the mouth of a ceramic frog, to cover any of the nicotine smell that remained. Not that his mother would be anywhere near his room for a while; Mom was upstairs in her bedroom doing her daily traction, and Jimmy's room was down two floors from hers in their split-level house.

Jimmy turned up the V on the Miida compact stereo he had purchased from a fast-talking salesman named Stehman up at the Luskin's-Dalmo in Wheaton. The Miida put out good sound. Jimmy had been listening to *Brain Salad Surgery* up until a few minutes ago, and now he had switched the mode button over to the radio, where WGTB was playing *The Lamb Lies Down on Broadway* today in its entirety. GTB played the most progressive shit, especially late at night. Jimmy would often lie in bed listening to the station well after his parents had fallen asleep. It was on those nights, when Jimmy was really tripping on some good THC, that he had been introduced to groups like Can and freaked-out bands like Gong, whose album *You* was his current favorite. "One Nation Underground" was the station's slogan; Jimmy had the bumper sticker Scotch-taped to the dust cover of his turntable.

Jimmy dug hanging out in his room. He still had his childhood dresser and still slept in the same single bed he had always slept in. On the wall was a fluorescent Ravi Shankar poster, handed down to him by his older brother, Noah, that had Ravi sitting cross-legged, playing sitar against what looked like a giant orange bumblebee. Next to the dresser sat an old cushioned chair on which he mostly threw his dirty clothes, and beside the chair was a wicker wastebasket that he kept by his bed on weekends in case he needed to lean over in the middle of the night and puke.

Over his bed hung a black light; Jimmy never used it when he was alone, since all his friends told him it would radiate his nuts and make him shoot blanks. But he turned it on when he could get a chick over the house to get high during school hours while his parents were at work. Not that this happened a lot — it had happened exactly twice, with two different girls. After they'd smoked a joint, Jimmy and the girl had gone to the bedroom to "check out some tunes," and Jimmy had turned on the black light, thrown his one Barry White record — *Stone Gon'* — on the platter, and made his move. Due to a hair-trigger problem, though, Jimmy had still not busted his cherry. On both occasions he had shot his load into his jeans as soon as he touched bare nipple, enduring the awful *pffft, pffft, pffft* sound of his jiz spurting over the elastic band of his briefs, the sound reddening his face. But Jimmy was determined to fuck a girl before his eighteenth birthday, and he would continue to try.

Jimmy dressed in jeans and a long-sleeved T. He would've liked to put on a pair of shorts, but he knew Dewey would call him a faggot if he did. He'd rather be hot than take a bunch of Dewey's shit.

Jimmy slipped his cigarette pack behind his sock, went upstairs, stood in the foyer. He could see his mom in her bedroom, facing the door, sitting in a chair in her paisley housedress and wearing a neck brace on a cord run through a pulley and balanced by a water-bottle weight on its other end.

"Bye, honey," she said, unable to turn her head. She had slipped on the stairs a year ago and fucked up her back real bad. "Have fun."

"Okay."

Dewey's horn sounded, and Jimmy Castle went outside.

Jimmy sat in the back of the Firebird as he always did, Jerry riding shotgun with Dewey driving. Dewey sat low in the seat, steering with the wrist of his right hand on top of the wheel. They drove down University toward Sligo Creek Park.

"I was lookin' at *Led Zeppelin Three* this morning," said Jerry, "before I went to work."

"What," said Dewey. "You were playin' with the cover again?"

"Naw, not the cover. I was lookin' at the album. This guy at school, Randolph Seman —"

"Randolph Seman? Go ahead, man. You *know* I'd change my name."

"Yeah, no shit. So Randy's this Zep freak, and he's telling me that they put messages in the vinyl. You know, that smooth place between where the last cut ends and the label begins?"

"So?"

"So he was right, man! It's etched in cursive, right there: 'Do What Thou Wilt,' it says. Whaddaya think that means?"

"Sounds British," offered Jimmy.

"He knows it sounds British, Toothpick," said Dewey. "He asked what it means. *I'll* tell you what that motherfucker means. Bet you Jimmy Page put that shit on there himself. Got something to do with the devil and shit."

"Like the *Houses of the Holy* cover," said Jerry, "with all those naked little girls climbing up that pyramid or whatever it is, trying to get to the top, and then you open up the cover and on the inside there's a guy holdin' up one of the girls over his head, gettin' ready to sacrifice her or somethin'. "

"Put a whole bunch of 'em on his dick first, prob'ly," said Dewey. "Like a shish kebab."

"No question," said Jerry.

He and Jerry gave each other skin.

" 'No Quarter' is bad," said Jimmy, but no one replied.

Dewey rifled through his eight-track box while Jerry pulled an amber-colored vial from his pocket.

"Where in the fuck's my Uriah Heep tape?" said Dewey.

"*Demons and Wizards*?" said Jerry.

"Yeah."

"I dunno," mumbled Jerry, who had borrowed the tape without asking and left it out in the sun. "Hey, let's check out some of this." He held up the vial.

Dewey found a Mahogany Rush tape and slapped it into the deck. "What's that, Jer, perfume?"

"Naw," said Jerry. "This dishwasher at work gave it to me, got it at some head shop on Route One out in College Park. Heart On, it's called. This dishwasher, he's one of those disco boys on the weekends, goes down to Last Hurrah and the Pier and places like that."

Dewey said, "He pull that out of some guy's tar pit?"

"He ain't no faggot, Dewey," said Jerry. "This guy gets more pussy than you ever had a dream about gettin'. Looks like Travolta and shit. He likes to dance, that's all. Anyway, he said this stuff is a rush."

Jerry unscrewed the top, put the vial under his nose, snorted in some fumes. His eyes widened, and he sat back in his seat. "Whew. You gotta try this shit, maaan."

Dewey hooked a right into the park. Jerry passed the vial back to Jimmy, who inhaled a deep hit of the amyl nitrite. Jimmy threw his head back, closed his eyes. He felt his heartbeat accelerate and then a pounding in his head. The pounding wouldn't stop. He thought his head might explode. For a moment he was scared.

"It is *too* fuckin' Hendrix," Jimmy heard Jerry say.

"Bullshit," said Dewey, who turned up the volume on "Child of the Novelty," the tape's title cut.

"I'm tellin' you, man," said Jerry, raising his voice over the music. "Frank Marino was in this car crash, dude. He never sang or played guitar or nothin' before. But after the crash he woke up out of his coma and just started playin'. They say the spirit of Hendrix entered his body —"

"Bull*shit*," said Dewey Schmidt.

Jimmy opened his eyes. The pounding had gone away. He wiped sweat off his forehead. "That *was* a rush." He smiled with relief and handed the vial up to Jerry.

"You want some?" Jerry said to Dewey.

"Yeah, right," said Dewey. "And then I'll put in a Bee Gees tape. And right after that maybe I'll have you put your tongue in my ass."

Dewey and Jerry laughed.

"Hey, Toothpick," said Dewey. "Where we meetin' this guy?"

"By that footbridge down near the basketball courts."

"He got good weed?"

"My brother says he does."

"What's his name, anyway?"

"I don't remember," said Jimmy. "Dimitri Carrots, some shit like that."

Dimitri Karras drove out of Northwest toward the District line. He turned the dial of his radio to 102.3, found his station, WHFS. The deejay played a road-themed set: Lowell George's "Willin', " Elvin Bishop's "Travelin' Shoes," and Danny O'Keefe's "Drive On, Driver" in succession. The station had broken artists like Little Feat and Springsteen early on in Washington, the latter sparking Karras to catch Bruce one night at the Childe Harold, a club date that truly lived up to its subsequent legend. HFS had turned Karras on to new music he otherwise would have missed; he always said that HomeGrown Radio was just another reason he would never leave D.C.

Karras stopped on Cameron Street in Silver Spring, went into Eddie Leonard's for one of their messy steak-and-cheese subs. He had heard their ancient jingle ("Eddie Leonard's Sandwich Shops/You should tryyyyy 'em") on the radio a few minutes earlier, and something primal had been awakened in his gut. He ate his sub, studying the robin's-egg blue wall on which cartoon drawings of all the sandwiches ran circularly around the store. There were two Latinos at the next table and a family of Latinos across the room.

The two Latinos argued loudly about the recent Forman-Frazier fight, one of the men jumping out of his chair, throwing a hook and a cross at the air. The other man, whose pants were stained crotch to knee with urine, yelled something in broken English about Frazier's manager prematurely forcing the TKO. Karras had seen the fight: Foreman had punished Frazier in the fifth, put him down with a hook and a right cross, put him down for the last time with a left-right combination that knocked him clean off his feet and left him hanging on the ropes. Frazier had taken a seven count and claimed he was fit to go on, but his eyes said something else. His manager had been right to throw in the towel.

The Latino family left hurriedly, the father's arms around the shoulders of both of his little girls. Karras left ten minutes later, the two men still arguing about the fight as he went through the door.

Karras drove out to Sligo Creek Park, cut the Karmann Ghia's engine in a lot off Dennis Avenue near some basketball and tennis courts. He watched a four-on-four pickup game for a little while, waiting for his customers to show. Out of the eight, only three of the kids had a game. One of them in particular, a boy of medium height and build, was active on both ends of the court and knew how to drive the lane.

A jacked-up green Firebird pulled into the lot. Karras made eye contact with the driver and walked over a nearby footbridge that spanned the creek. He stood on a path near the start of the woods, withdrew an ounce from his pants pocket, watched the three boys approach. The driver of the Firebird had a solid build and a cocky walk. The tall one breathing through his mouth looked stupid. The third one wore a long-sleeved shirt in the heat, which only flagged the fact that the boy was insecure about his scarecrow build. Karras flashed on an image of himself at seventeen, thinking, It's tough to be a kid.

"Hey," said the cocky one.

"Hey," said Karras. "Who's Noah Castle's brother?"

"Me," said the skinny kid. "Jimmy Castle."

Karras looked around quickly, extended his hand for what looked like a shake, passed the bag of weed from his palm to Jimmy's. The tall stupid-looking one handed Karras a tightly rolled tube of cash. Karras put the cash in his pocket without a glance.

The four of them stood there for a few moments, none of them saying a word. Jimmy Castle shuffled his feet.

"Fifty bucks an OZ," said the cocky one, stepping forward hesitantly. "It better be good."

"You got any complaints, you know where to find me," said Karras.

"My brother says he sells good herb," said Jimmy to the cocky one.

"Always," said Karras, forcing a smile. "You guys enjoy yourselves, hear?"

Karras left them standing on the path, walked over the bridge toward his car. He rubbed at an itch on his face. It wasn't like he was hanging around outside the local high school wearing a trench coat, pushing drugs. It wasn't anything like that at all. The way it was, Karras knew Noah Castle, an usher at the Janus who drank regularly at Mr. Eagan's in the neighborhood, pretty well. *Noah* had told him that his brother and his brother's friends were looking to score a bag of dope. *Noah* had said it would be all right. And anyway, there wasn't anything wrong with smoking a little pot now and then. This was something that Karras truly believed. Kids were gonna smoke it, and they had as much right to smoke it as anybody else. They were gonna get it somewhere, if not from him than from someone else. . . .

Karras drove quickly from the park. It made him uncomfortable to be out of the city, even for a short period of time. He'd go downtown, talk to this Stefanos character, see what the old bird had on his mind.

Crossing the District line, Karras exhaled evenly. He found Blue

Öyster Cult's eponymous debut in his carrying case, pushed the eight-track tape into the deck. "Then Came the Last Days of May" began, Buck Dharma's familiar fluid guitar lines filling the air. Though it was awfully sad, Karras deeply loved that tune: a song about friends and money and a drug deal gone wrong.

FOURTEEN

Clarence Tate parked his ride outside Meridian Heights, an apartment building gone condo on 15th Street, just east of Meridian Hill Park. He stayed in his black Monte Carlo after he had killed the engine, listening to the Stylistics going into the last verse of "Betcha by Golly, Wow," Russell Thompkins's falsetto and the harmony on the chorus giving him chills, like the Lord was doing the singing himself.

When the song ended, Tate got out of his car and crossed the street. Behind him, some tough-looking kids were entering the park; the brothers and sisters around town who were politically inclined had begun referring to Meridian as Malcolm X Park, and the name had started to stick, but what they really needed to concentrate on was cleaning the place up. Tate owned a condo in Meridian Heights and was concerned about the falling property values in the neighborhood.

He entered the building's small lobby. The old white guy who had been hired as security, Andy something, he was an okay dude but also a stone lush and therefore always either in search of a drink or down in the boiler room sleeping off the bottle he had found. Never at his post in the lobby, though, which pissed Tate off to the max. All these strangers were in town for the big July Fourth weekend, walking the streets, carrying on, gettin' all liquored up, and doing who knew what else, and there wouldn't be any security to speak of in the Heights to fend off any crime. Tate was fond of Andy and all that, but he knew Andy would be partying just as hard as everyone else come Sunday night. Harder, most likely.

The building had a staircase leading to the roof and an elevator that went, very slowly, to the top floor. Tate entered the stairwell rather than wait, as he was only going up to the fourth floor.

Tate had bought this place with his wife originally, and his little girl had spent her first few months here. But once his wife had gone off and gotten remarried to the street, Tate and his daughter had moved back in with his parents in the old neighborhood. Tate figured he'd rent the condo out, save some money like that, hope against hope that the Meridian Hill east area didn't go all the way to shit in the meantime and the condo would keep its value. He had a tenant in there now by the name of Enrique, who lived with a girl named Ruth. Enrique was cool, but he was struggling his own self, so Tate had to come around the first week of every month and personally collect. It was always about money, man, that was for damn sure.

Money. If he could only move those hot goods out of Marchetti's warehouse, take his cut, he could make a clean break from Eddie Spags. With Eddie striking girls now, dealing in reefer and blow, and especially with that bad nigger Cooper and his shotgun boys in town, the shit was just getting way too deep for Tate's taste. Tate wanted to live. And he didn't *even* want to think about making his little girl an orphan.

But everything took money, all the time.

A friend had told Tate about a group of brothers across town, dudes working out of a storefront who were paying top dollar for hot goods and buying in quantity as well. Tate would have to check into it, find out what that setup was all about. In the meantime, get up to the fourth floor, collect the rent check from Enrique and his squeeze. 'Cause that rent check, that was real money, too.

Wilton Cooper checked the address he had written down on the pad of paper, tossed the detail map on the backseat. He slowed the Challenger, pulled over to the curb on Davenport near 45th, parked beneath a big tree. He looked out the window at the house whose address matched up with the number he had on the pad.

"This it, Wilton?"

"This here's the number. Only Karras for this part of town in the D.C. book."

"Think he lives here?"

"Gonna find out right quick."

Cooper looked at the houses, modest and understated, on the block. Not too much serious money here, but enough to keep the real world behind that invisible fence. Driving in, he hadn't seen a brother or a brown man for the last few miles at least. Kind of place where everybody talks about the injustices of society, the need for education, rehabilitation over incarceration, all that. Guys wearing glasses without rims, reading the paper every morning with classical music playing soft in the background, talking over the fence to other guys who look like them about all the bad things happening out there, shaking their heads, talking, talking, talk, talk, talk. Neighborhood like this, where nothing bad ever happened, where nobody would know how to do a damn thing about it if something bad did, a couple of motivated niggers with guns could walk through a place like this and fuck some motherfuckers up at will. Course, they'd send in the cavalry soon enough to gun 'em down. Before they did, though, on the way to his doom, a man could have some fun. Cooper grinned.

"What's so funny, Wilton?"

"Nothin', little brother." Cooper glanced across the seat. "You ain't lookin' so good, you know?"

"I'm all right."

"You just sit tight, then. I'll be back in a little bit."

Cooper pulled his shirttail out to cover the butt of the .45 he had holstered behind his back. He got out of the car. He walked toward the house.

Eleni Karras had been watching from the window ever since the red car had pulled to a stop in front of her house. She watched the big *mavros* with the football-player chest get out of the driver's side and walk toward her place. Maybe he was selling something — though he didn't look like a salesman — or maybe he needed help. His *friend* needed help, that was it; the red-faced boy sitting in the passenger seat, he didn't look too well.

She opened the main door, looked through the glass of the storm door at the smiling *mavros*. It was a Friday afternoon, broad daylight. What could happen?

Eleni opened the storm door a quarter way. "Yes?"

"Yes, ma'am," said Cooper. "I was wonderin'. . . . Is this the Dimitri Karras residence?"

"Dimitri doesn't live here anymore. But, yeah, it used to be. I'm his mother."

Cooper laughed shortly in relief, shook his head. "Good. Was worried I had the wrong address."

"You —"

"I was supposed to meet Dimitri and Marcus here this afternoon. Least, I *thought* Marcus said here when I spoke to him on the phone this morning. All of us had plans to play a little basketball, see."

"You friends with Dimitri?"

"Not exactly. I was in the same outfit with Marcus overseas, few years back. Came into town for the Bicentennial celebration, thought I'd hook up with my old friend."

"You were in Vietnam with Marcus?"

"Proud to serve, too," said Cooper, extending his hand. "Name's Wilton Cooper, ma'am."

"Eleni Karras." She took his hand.

Cooper retrieved a handkerchief from his pocket, patted the sweat from his forehead. "Sure is a hot one."

"Oh, pardon me," said Eleni. "Please, c'mon in for a minute, cool off."

"Much obliged."

"Your friend want to come in, too?"

"I don't think so."

"How about we give him a little water?"

"Don't worry about him. He's all right."

Cooper walked through the open storm door, closed it and the main door behind him. It *was* cool in the house. Damn near cold, in fact.

"C'mon," said Eleni, with a flip of her hand.

Cooper followed her through a hall. She was a friendly woman, on the plump side but sturdy. A woman with a little weight on her, who asked the right questions at the door and, satisfied, was not afraid to let a black man into her house. Not a bright thing to do in his case, but Cooper liked her for that right away. Be a shame, really, if he had to go ahead and fuck her up.

"My husband was a veteran, too," she said, turning her head to the side and speaking over her shoulder as she walked. "Marine Corps."

"Semper Fi," said Cooper.

"Yes, Semper Fi."

They were in the kitchen. Eleni pointed Cooper to a chair at a Formica-topped table, in the middle of which sat a bunch of yellow flowers in a vase. She served him a tall, cool glass of water from the tap. He drank it down close to the bottom.

"Ah," he said. "I do thank you."

"You hungry?"

"Hungry?"

"Yeah, hungry. I made a little rice pudding this morning, still warm."

Cooper smiled. "I guess I could stand a taste."

She scooped some pudding into a glass dessert bowl, sprinkled cinnamon on top, placed the bowl in front of him with a spoon and folded paper napkin. She leaned her back against the counter at the sink, watched him take his first bite.

"Mmmm," said Cooper, pointing the spoon at Eleni. "This is *bad*."

"You don't like it?"

"Pardon, ma'am. What I mean to say is I like it just fine."

Eleni crossed her arms. "You just missed Dimitri, you know, little while back."

"Shame I did. Like I said, we had this game set up —"

"Dimitri talked about a game. But he said the game was for this evening."

"Marcus and me, we musta got our signals crossed." Cooper

scooped up another mouthful. "You know, the raisins, they really make this pudding."

"The raisins are key," said Eleni.

"Maybe I ought to give Marcus a call, see if we can't get this straightened out. You don't have his number, do you?"

Eleni's face screwed up on one side. "I thought you spoke to him on the phone this morning."

Cooper swallowed slowly, buying time. The Greek lady with the fat ankles was smarter than she looked. Hoped for her sake she didn't get too smart with him now. "I did, see. But that was this morning, when Marcus was at his crib. . . . His *apartment*, I mean. Marcus would be at work now, right, but it didn't come up in the conversation, where that is."

"He's got a record store," said Eleni, a quaver in her voice as she uttered the words, realizing just then that maybe the *mavros* was not a friend to Marcus and Dimitri at all. He had mentioned Marcus's apartment, but Marcus had a nice row house down on Brown Street. Wouldn't this Cooper fellow know that if he was a friend? Wouldn't he know that Marcus owned his own shop?

Eleni turned around, opened the cold spigot, began to rinse out a glass that was already clean.

"What was the name of that store again?" she heard Cooper say.

There's nothing to worry about, thought Eleni. If he's not really a friend, he's a bill collector, that's all. When you're in business for yourself, you have to dodge those guys all the time. She pretended not to hear Cooper's question and did not reply.

Cooper swallowed the last mouthful of the rice pudding, got up out of his chair. Okay, so now if the woman didn't want to talk, he'd just have to go and make her talk. And if he had to pull the .45, then of course he'd have to use it. Smash the barrel against her temple first, drag her ass down the stairs, put a bullet in her head down there. That old drill. He'd have to, much as he didn't care to, just to buy a couple of days more time. Shame for her, but the truth was it had been her son and Trouble Man who had started the ball rolling on the whole affair.

If they wanted to play, then everyone they *knew* was gonna play. That's just the way it was.

Eleni heard the *mavros* move toward her behind her back. She remembered how big and strong he had looked, coming up the walk. Okay, so he was a collection agent, looking for Marcus. "Leg breakers" — her husband, Pete, had called them that in the old days. Did they really hurt people that way?

"Ma'am?"

Cooper was right behind her. She could feel his warm breath on her neck.

"Real Right Records," she said, dropping the glass in the sink. She picked the glass up and set it on its base.

"What's that?"

Eleni Karras turned around. Cooper was standing there, holding up the glass dessert bowl near her face.

"I was just . . . you wanted to know where Marcus worked."

"Oh, that," said Cooper. "Thanks. But what I was really wonderin' —"

"Yes?"

"Could I get a little more of this puddin' to go?"

Eleni breathed out. "Sure . . . sure. I got a . . . I got a plastic container over here. You can give it back to Dimitri when you see him."

"Much obliged, ma'am. And could you fill it to the top?" Cooper smiled. "My friend out in the car, he's got a little problem with his teeth. Boy's on a soft food diet, if you know what I mean."

FIFTEEN

Dimitri Karras drove his Karmann Ghia down 14th Street, crossed Clifton, downshifted descending the big hill that was the drop-off of the Piedmont Plateau. He passed Florida Avenue, W, V, and then U. Fourteenth and U: one of the most legendary intersections in the city, the cross-street suburban whites always referred to when they were talking or joking about blacks. As in, "Hey, I thought I saw your mother last night down at Fourteenth and U," or "Where'd you get those shoes, man, Fourteenth and U?" Lame talk like that. It had been something once, a hub of black-owned business and music and nightlife for Washington's old Negro community. By the sixties it had become a hard four-corner home for pushers and junkies, criminals and whores. Then came the riots of '68. Now, 14th and U didn't look like much of anything alive at all.

Karras passed long-closed businesses, charred buildings, decaying projects, apartment houses now shells. Bars covered rock-shattered windows; slogans like "Say It Loud!" had been spray painted on plywood boards. Little had been rebuilt or reopened for the last eight years, since the fires and looters had ravaged the strip.

But Karras knew that 14th and 7th and all the other burned-down D.C. avenues had been sacrificed for something else. Things *had* changed, in the same way that a hard summer rain can clear the streets.

Eleni Karras had said that Stefanos's grill stood on the corner of S. It was there, marked by a rusted blue oblong sign encircled by mostly broken lightbulbs. The sign, in red lettering, read "Nick's." Karras parked his Ghia out front and walked into the restaurant.

Nick's was a run-down lunch and beer house with eight stools lined up against a counter. Behind the counter were a grill, sandwich board, soda fountain, two huge coffee urns, and a couple of coolers holding sodas, ice cream, and bottles of beer. Apparently there had once been some booths built in against the wall — you could still see the outlines where they had been removed — but they had been replaced by a narrow bracketed Formica counter where customers could stand while they put away their food and drink. Where the counter ended, an unplugged pinball machine was pushed against the wall. Beyond the pinball machine, just before an entrance to a back room, stood a jukebox. A black man holding a sixteen-ounce can of beer leaned against the jukebox, studying the selections. An Ohio Players number came from the juke.

Karras had a seat on a stool cushioned in a red color so faded it had gone to pink. A crisscross of duct tape kept the plastic on the stool from tearing any further.

"Nick," said a uniformed woman with a deeply creased walnut brown complexion. She was on the other side of the counter, leaning on it, smoking a cigarette and holding an unopened pack of Viceroys in her free hand. She did not approach Karras or even look in his eyes.

Two other black men with graying hair sat at the counter drinking from cans of Schlitz. Both of them had cigarettes going, too.

"Can't really bring myself to vote for a man from Georgia," said the man closest to Karras.

"What," said the other. "You gonna vote for that big block of nothin', Mr. Gerald Ford? Least that peanut farmer gonna bring somethin' new to the party."

"Ain't none of 'em gonna bring nothin' new," said the first man. "Anyway, I can't trust a man who smiles like that all the time."

The woman behind the counter stepped into her flat-heeled shoes and walked over to a set of swinging louvered doors that led to the kitchen. "Nick," she said over the top of the doors. "Got a customer out here."

"You too busy to serve him, baby?" said the first man, nudging his partner.

"On my break," said the woman. "If you had a job, you'd know what that was."

The men laughed. The woman returned to her spot, dragged deeply off her cigarette.

Karras pretended to study a grease-filmed Manne's Potato Chip sign — "Yeah, Manne!" — on the wall directly in front of him. That sign must have been hung there on the opening day.

A medium-sized man who had once been a big man pushed through the swinging doors. His chest sagged now and his shoulders slumped, and he walked with a slow, rolling gait. But his hands and wrists gave away his former size. There were a couple of Band-Aids on his fingers and smudges of dried blood on his yellowed apron. He saw Karras and smiled.

"*Thimitri* Karras, eh?"

"Yessir."

"*Yasou, re!* "

"Mr. Stefanos?"

"Nick. Tha's me."

Nick Stefanos shook Karras's hand. The hand was leather, and he still had a grip.

"Lemme look at you, boy." Stefanos stood back, smoothed back an errant gray strand of hair from an otherwise bald dome. His face was as loose and fleshy as an old dog's, flecked with age spots, with a faded pink scar on the right cheek.

"So how do I look?"

"Like your mother."

"That's what they tell me."

"You're a handsome boy, though, don' get me wrong. Just like your old man."

"Thanks."

Stefanos turned his head toward the kitchen. "Hey, *Costaki!* " he yelled. "*Ella tho, re!* "

A short, low-slung Greek with a wild head of gray hair and a thick, graying mustache burst through the doors. He was holding a carving knife tightly in his fist. His other hand was slick with grease and bits of meat.

"What the hell you want, Niko, I'm cuttin' up a little lamb!"

"C'mon over here, Costa. Say hello to *Thimitri* Karras, *o yos tou* Pete Karras."

Costa issued a lopsided grin, wiped his hand off on his apron, extended the hand to Karras. "*Miazi ti mitera tou,*" he said to Stefanos.

"That's what they tell me," said Karras.

Costa said, "So what can I get you, Karras? On the house!"

"Nothing, thanks. I just ate."

"Got a nice meatloaf —"

"I ate, thanks."

"Where you eat, huh?"

"Had a sub up at Eddie Leonard's."

"Eddie Leonard's," said Costa with disgust. "Might as well eat dog shit."

"He said he don't want nothin', Costa," said Stefanos.

"*I'll* have something, Costa," said the man closest to Karras. "Make me up a fish sandwich to go, will ya?"

"Anything on it?"

"Just hot sauce."

"I got some nice summer tomatoes, Nick jus' sliced 'em up this morning —"

"Just hot sauce, man. You gettin' deaf in your old age?"

"Hokay, *vre mavroskilo.* Comin' right up."

"*Sopa, re,*" said Stefanos.

The men at the counter looked at each other and grinned.

Karras watched the interplay between the two Greeks. Costa had just called the man a black dog, and Nick had told Costa to shut his mouth. They must have been doing the same dance down here for about a hundred years.

"Go make the man's sandwich," said Stefanos.

"I'm goin'," said Costa, who looked as if he had just sucked on a lemon.

"What," said Stefanos. "You got a problem?"

"Me?" said Costa. "I don't give a damn nothing." Costa went back toward the kitchen, turned back his head. "You take it easy, young fella."

"Yeah," said Karras. "You, too."

Karras tented his fingers on the counter. An electric fan in a high corner of the room blew dust and smoke around the place but did little to dispel the heat. The restaurant was kind of dark, too; a couple of high lights had gone out and had not been replaced. Well, that made sense. Which one of these old birds was gonna get up on a ladder to change a bulb?

"Thanks for comin' down."

"*Tipota*," said Karras with a shrug. He wanted to be outside, under a clear sky, breathing clean air.

"It *is* something," said Stefanos. "Young man like you, nice day like this, you wanna be doin' somethin' else, I know."

"You helped my family out plenty. So I'm here. Like I said, it's nothing."

Stefanos rested his forearm on the counter, leaned forward. "*O patera sou*, he was some kind of man. I don't just mean about him bein' a war hero. No sir, I don't just mean that. I mean about other things, too. He never even knew the kind of man he was."

"I don't remember him," said Karras.

"Tha's why I'm tellin' you, so you know."

"Okay."

"Hokay." There was an awkward silence as Stefanos moved his face around with a thick hand. "It's tough between a father and a son. Someday you gonna find out yourself."

"Mom said you wanted to talk," said Karras. "Something about your grandson."

"Yeah. That's what I'm gonna get to now." Stefanos looked away. "His name is Nick, jus' like me. I raised him myself. It don't matter the nuts and bolts of it, either, that's just the fact. I'm his father, and he's my kid."

"All right."

"But I'm an old man. The world's changed, and I don't understand it so good anymore. It's hard enough trying to talk to a son, but when you're that far apart . . ."

"Is he in trouble?"

Stefanos spread his hands. "What the hell I know, huh? He comes home every night, his eyes are all red, he's actin' funny. . . . I'm thinkin', maybe he's smoking that marijuana like all the kids are smoking it today. Maybe, what the hell I know, he's on all *kinds* of drugs."

It was Karras's turn to look away. He tried to think of something smart to say, decided to go ahead and say something, opened his mouth to speak.

"Nick —"

"*Mia stigmi*," said Stefanos, holding up one finger. "I'm not finished. Nick's got this job, see? He's a stock boy in some store uptown, unloads trucks, stacks televisions, carries air conditioners up and down stairs, like that. Works with a bunch of wise guys, I met 'em once, I figure they're all on some kind of drugs in that store, too, the way they act. But it's okay, it's good to have a job, it teaches you things about life. And it keeps the boy off the streets. Now he tells me he's leavin'. After July Fourth, gonna go down south and drive around with this friend of his he's been hangin' out with since high school. I ask him, 'When you gonna be back, huh?' and he's tellin' me, 'I don't know, *Papou*, gonna have an adventure and figure that out later on.' An adventure. Sounds like he's headed for trouble to me. Got a job, gonna start college in the fall, now he's gonna give it all up and get in a car and go on and have an adventure. Now, he's a good boy, and I'm not gonna tell you he's not. But I don't know, *Thimitri*, you gotta tell me the truth: am I *trelos*, worried about him like this?"

Karras looked at the confusion in the old man's eyes. "No, Nick, you're not crazy."

"I was wonderin', that's all. I don't know anybody I can trust to talk to who's close to the boy's age. I thought of you. You're a little bit older, you gotta have some more sense."

"It's okay, Nick. I'm glad you called."

"You'll go see the boy? Set him straight?"

Set him straight. Now a guy who deals weed to high school kids is gonna set another kid straight.

Karras said, "Sure."

Stefanos breathed out slowly. "*Bravo, re. Efcharisto.*"

"*Parakalo.*" Karras rubbed his hands together. "Where's Nick work, anyway?"

"Place called Nutty Nathan's, on Connecticut up there near Albemarle. Nutty Nathan's, funny name for a store, eh?"

"I know the place. Used to be the old Sun Radio."

"That's right."

"He on today?"

"Yessir."

"I'll go up there this afternoon," said Karras. "See if I can talk with him then."

Stefanos clapped Karras on the arm, then went to serve the two men at the counter another round of beers. The men were discussing a basketball player named Craig "Big Sky" Shelton, who had come out of Dunbar in '75. Except to light another cigarette and move it back and forth to her lips, the woman who worked for Stefanos had not moved an inch.

Stefanos walked back, his feet padding along a rubber mat. Karras watched him wince as he bent forward, leaning his arm back on the counter.

"This work must be gettin' kinda rough on you," said Karras.

"Not so rough," said Stefanos, smiling with his eyes. "Anyway, what the hell else I'm gonna do, eh?"

"I guess."

"You guess. Well, I *know*. This is *my* place here. I been serving these same people here for forty years." Stefanos lowered his voice. "Listen, you wanna hear somethin'? When they burned down this block, my place was the only one they left alone. Not even a rock through my window, *katalavenis*? People know me here, and I know them. All I'm tellin' you is, I *belong* here."

"Maybe so. Just be nice for you relax a little, that's all I was sayin'. "

"Ahhh," said Stefanos. "What the hell I'm gonna relax for, huh?"

"I just thought —"

"I *work*," said Stefanos. "That's what a man does."

Karras got off his stool. He shook Stefanos's hand.

"*Yasou, Thimitri.*"

"*Yasou*, Nick."

"You talk to my boy, hokay?"

"I will."

Dimitri Karras walked around the jukebox player, who leaned against the wall counter now and appeared to be sleeping on his feet. Karras turned his head back, saw Nick Stefanos moving slowly, one hip higher than the other, toward the louvered doors.

"What about that *psari*, Costa!?" yelled Stefanos.

"It's workiiin'!" yelled Costa, his voice echoing off the pressed tin ceiling of the store.

Karras passed beneath a Blatz Beer clock with a smudged glass face centered above the door. The time was off by several hours, and the clock's second hand had stopped. Karras opened the door and walked out to the street.

SIXTEEN

Nutty Nathan's stood on the west side of Connecticut just south of Albemarle Street, a few doors up from a Hot Shoppes that served as the centerpiece of a small commercial strip bordering the neighborhoods of Van Ness and Forest Heights. Across the street was the broadcast house of a local television station, WMAL, and a block north of that was a small piano bar named La Fortresse, revered by D.C.'s serious drinkers for its generous liquor-to-mixer-ratio.

Karras parked in a lot on the side of the building. Getting out of his car, he noticed a medium-sized man with muttonchop sideburns and a Fu Manchu mustache standing by the Dempsey Dumpster at the back of the lot, smoking a joint with one hand and holding a sixteen-ounce can of Colt 45 in the other. The man wore a loud gold sport coat and a matching gold patterned tie, and made no effort to conceal the malt liquor or the pot. He caught Karras's eye, wiggled his eyebrows, raised the can in a salute.

Karras walked around the building to the front of the store. He looked in the wide window where several air conditioners blew streamers against the glass. He went inside.

An Ichabod Crane look-alike sat on a console and watched a row of televisions, all tuned to the same station. He turned his head and glanced at Karras at the sound of the door's bell. The man was dead pale and had a frightening smile and wore a large wooden crucifix over his gold patterned tie and green shirt. His jacket was the same shade of gold as that of the man in the lot.

"Welcome to Nutty Nathan's," said the man. A tag clipped to his jacket read, "Hi, my name is Lloyd Danker."

"Hi."

"Something special for you today, sir?"

"Special? No, I don't think so. I'm looking for Nick Stefanos."

The man's smile went away. "Try the Sound Explosion. All the way in the back."

Karras walked past the bank of TVs, most of which appeared to be Sonys, that year's hot number. Yul Brynner's image — Brynner, with hair! — appeared on all the sets in a two-shot with a bored-looking Robert Mitchum. It was difficult to tell if Mitchum was asleep or awake. This was the one about Pancho Villa, though Karras couldn't remember its name, and Charlie Bronson was in it, too. It was Yul Brynner Week on Money Movie Seven, and MAL had been running Brynner pictures every day.

Karras went down a long aisle that split the store. Signage and accent striping gave him the impression that everything around him, including the merchandise, was either gold or red. He felt like he was peaking in a gold-and-red-tinted trip. To the right of the center aisle were major and small appliances, and to the left were televisions and stack-and-sell ACs. The ACs blew brightly colored tongues of streamers at him as he passed. He had gotten the message out on the sidewalk — it was mid-summer, and these guys had air conditioners to sell. Overkill seemed to be the intention at Nutty Nathan's

The aisle ended at a hastily arranged group of metal desks separated by cushioned dividers. An Arab-looking gentleman — his nose was large, his complexion rather dark — sat in a chair with his feet up on one of the desks. He appeared to be sleeping with a smile on his face. He opened his blood red eyes halfway, but only for a moment, and nodded at Karras slowly, very slowly, before closing them and issuing a deep and contented sigh.

Karras walked into a darkened area of the store housing cheap compacts and components, where a banner reading "Sound Explosion" hung. He heard "Any Major Dude Will Tell You" coming from a room separated from the rest of the stereo equipment by sliding glass doors. One of the doors was open, and Karras stepped inside.

A short wide-shouldered guy with his hair pulled back and banded in a ponytail stood in front of a receiver nodding his head to the music. The music sounded clear and bass-heavy; you could hear the pluck of the strings against the fret. In the darkness, the blue and orange display lights made the equipment look sexy and sleek. A row of floor speakers arranged in ascending height fanned out and seemed to embrace the ponytailed dude wearing a gold jacket.

The guy turned around, noticed Karras. "Hey."

"Hey."

"What's happenin', man?" Like the didn't-give-a-fuck cat out in the lot, this one obviously recognized Karras as a fellow stoner.

"Nothin' much."

Karras went forward, shook the guy's hand. His name tag said, "Hi, my name is Jeff Fisher." His jacket was soiled and smelled of cigarettes and weed. A coat-of-arms patch had been sewn on the breast pocket, an embroidery displaying a microwave oven, stereo system, and television set. His gold tie featured the same design; the tie looked as if it doubled on occasion as Fisher's napkin.

"My name's Dimitri Karras. I'm a friend of the Stefanos family. Is Nick working today?"

"He's downstairs in the stockroom on his break," said Fisher, whose mouth turned up in an ingratiating two-bong grin. This Fisher dude was higher than Neil Armstrong. A half-smoked cigarette was lodged firmly behind his right ear. "I'll get him if you'd like."

"That would be good."

"Wanna hear something first?"

Karras shrugged. "Okay."

Fisher lifted the dust cover of the working turntable, took the needle off of *Pretzel Logic*, slipped a cassette tape into a nearby deck. He went to a master switching box, pushed in a black button, then returned to a tall Marantz receiver and started punching buttons and twisting treble and bass dials mounted below the radio band. He moved quickly, excitedly, like every audiophilic pothead Karras had ever known.

"Gotta hear this through the 901s," said Fisher, jerking his head toward a relatively small Bose speaker that sat up on a pedestal base.

The music began. Karras recognized it as the intro to Curtis Mayfield's "If There's Hell Below," the one where Curtis is shouting, "Niggers . . . Whiteys . . . Jews . . ." against some acid guitar, bongos, and echo effects right before the jam really kicks in. But on this tape, the Curtis vocals had been mixed out, replaced by the voice of another black singer, this one in the Eddie Levert mold, the rhythm track just pumping along. It was the same song, basically, but with a different singer, and way different lyrics:

You Jewish bastards, you know your dicks are disasters.

You Nigger dudes, you know you fuck real rude.

You Chinese bitches, you know you like big switches. . . .

The song went along in that inventive vein, insulting every ethnic group with lewd, unrestrained glee while keeping straight on with the killer groove.

"What the fuck *is* this?" said Karras.

Fisher smiled. "Guy named Sam, used to work here, cut this track."

"It's bad."

"Damn right it's bad. Sam was bad, too. He was funnier than a motherfucker, man, and he could write some music and really sing."

"Was?"

Fisher turned down the volume. "Died about six months ago. His father shot him during a card game. Both of them were drunk." Fisher blinked his eyes, flicked some skin off his nose. "C'mon, I'll show you where Nick's at."

Karras followed Fisher out of the Sound Explosion. The guy from the parking lot was back in the store now and pitching a cheap Spectracon receiver, talking very fast to an older black man wearing a purple rayon shirt.

"Got to get the rebop on the bebop," said the salesman.

"Say what?" said the customer.

"Just sayin' this receiver can put it out."

The customer stroked the end of his Van Dyck. "How many watts this box got?"

"Box got lotsa watts," said the salesman. "I ain't kiddin' you, Jim."

Karras and Fisher moved out of the stereo department. Karras looked back at the jive-ass salesman with the muttonchop sideburns.

"Who was *that?*"

"McGinnes." Short and abrupt, like the name itself said it all.

They walked by the desk where the smiling Arab-looking gentleman sat sleeping. "And him?"

"Phil Omajian," said Fisher. "Our manager."

"He looks happy."

"Down freak. Stays out of our way, though. The best kind of manager you can have."

They entered a small room housing clock radios, irons, and a heavy metal desk holding paperwork and overflowing ashtrays.

"Hey," said Fisher, "I almost forgot. You need any sound equipment?"

"No, I'm all right."

"See me if you do. If I'm not here, we got this new young guy can help you out. Real nice guy. Name's Andre Malone."

"Okay."

Fisher pointed to a lit stairwell. "Nick's down there."

"Thanks."

Karras went down a shaky set of wooden stairs. The musty odor of damp cardboard hit him as he stepped onto a concrete floor littered with warranty cards and cigarette butts.

"Hello!"

"Back here," came a voice from deep in the stockroom.

Karras walked past rows of cartoned televisions and appliances, all up on pallets, toward the source of the voice. The basement ran the depth of the building and was lit dimly by widely spaced naked bulbs suspended on cords. Near the end of the center row, a teenage kid sat atop a Panasonic color TV carton, grease-stained restaurant wrap and a go-cup scattered around him, his legs dangling off the carton's side.

"Hey, man," said the kid.

"Hey."

The kid jumped down off the carton, landed cleanly on his feet. He shook his shoulder-length hair with a toss of his head.

"What's happenin'?"

"Nothin' much. My name's Dimitri Karras. Friend of your *papou's*."

"Nick Stefanos."

Stefanos put out his hand, gave Karras a soul shake. Karras had a look at the kid: on the thin side, wearing Levi's cigarette style, one turn up at the cuff — the same way Karras wore his — a pair of Sears work boots, and a Led Zeppelin T-shirt that replicated the cover of the band's debut. The kid smiled; like his grandfather, he had a friendly, wide-open face.

"Am I interrupting your lunch?"

"Nah, I just finished."

"Anything good?"

"I eat the same thing every day. Mighty Mo, Orange Freeze, and onion rings. Eat it the same way, sittin' on that very box."

"Creature of habit."

"I guess." Stefanos shuffled his feet. "Got a bonus, though, walkin' over to the Hot Shoppes today to pick up my food. Saw Isaac Hayes coming out of MAL. I guess he was doin' some kind of interview over there."

"How'd he look?"

"He was stylin', man! Isaac had those chains on his chest, with no shirt underneath, like he does on the albums."

"That's somethin'."

"Yeah."

Stefanos pulled a flat pack of Marlboros from his back pocket, shook out a bent smoke. He flipped open a book of matches, gave himself a light. Squinting through his exhale, he eyed Karras in a curious way.

Karras said, "I guess you're wondering —"

"You say you know *Papou*?"

"Well, not really. My father worked at Nick's grill in the forties."

"I don't remember him mentioning your dad to me."

"My father's been dead a long time."

"Sorry, man." Stefanos thumb-flicked ash off his smoke. "You look familiar, though. You go to Saint Sophia?"

"Not so much."

"Me either," said Stefanos. "Not so much anymore."

Karras said, "You ever play pickup ball?"

"At Candy Cane City sometimes. Me and my friend Billy get into some decent games every so often."

"Maybe that's it. Maybe you've seen me there."

"Could be it, yeah."

"So, anyway . . . I was talkin' to your grandfather. He asked me to stop by, introduce myself, say hello."

Stefanos blew smoke down at his work boots. "He's worried about me, right?"

"A little, I guess."

"That's what this is about. He's finally figured out that I like to get high."

"That's partly it, yeah. I'm not gonna lie to you."

"Well, what am I supposed to say? *Papou* and me, we got, like, fifty-some years between us. I love him, man, but how do I explain to a guy from his generation that *everybody* gets high? It's not like I'm sittin' around in somebody's basement all day, listening to *Dark Side of the Moon,* or somethin' like that. I work, I play ball, I chase after girls — gettin' high is just something I do when I'm doin' something else. I mean, *you* know, man! I can tell from lookin' at you that you get high yourself."

Yeah, and I deal it, too. And here I am, trying to give you advice.

"It's not just the reefer thing," said Karras.

"What, then?"

"He was talkin' about . . . You're goin' on some trip, right?"

"Oh, that."

"You leaving after the Fourth?"

Stefanos smiled with excitement. "The next morning. Billy's picking me up at *Papou*'s apartment on Irving Street. We're towing a ski boat down to Florida for this dude, and then we're just gonna drive around. See what we can see."

"Guess you'll be getting ready for it all weekend."

"Got a *lot* goin' on this weekend. Going down to the Town tonight to see that new one, *King Suckerman.*"

"One about the pimp?"

"Yeah. And then Sunday night's the party. I wouldn't miss the action down on the Mall for anything. In fact, we put off the trip till Monday just to stick around for the Fourth."

"How long you plan on being gone?"

"I don't know. That's part of the adventure! Why, you think there's something wrong with that, too?"

Karras tried to think of something responsible to say. The truth was, he didn't believe there *was* anything wrong with the kid's plan. He had gone out of town with no itinerary whatsoever more than a few times himself. A road trip, man, it could really do good things for your head. And Karras was tired of being a hypocrite. He had come out here, talked to the boy just as he had promised the old man. All right, he had done that. Now he just wanted to be finished with it and get away.

"No," said Karras. "There's nothing wrong with it, Nick. Have a good time, man. Enjoy yourself."

Stefanos crushed his cigarette under his boot. "Thanks."

Karras heard the sound of footsteps rapidly descending the wooden stairs. "Nick! Hey, Greek!"

It was the one named McGinnes, coming down the aisle in their direction, an electric charge in his goose-step walk. On the way, he retrieved a sixteen-ounce can of Colt from behind a carton, tore the ring off its top. He took a long pull from the can as he walked toward them.

"The bad dude's brew," said McGinnes, wiggling his eyebrows at Karras.

"Dimitri Karras," said Karras.

"Johnny McGinnes," said McGinnes. "What it *is?*"

They shook hands. McGinnes's eyes were electric, glazed and pink.

His Nutty Nathan's tie was thick as a clown's, knotted crookedly and match-burnt in several places.

"You need somethin', Johnny?"

"Just sold a Spectracon receiver to some *yom*. Gonna buy it on 'credik.' I can get that one myself. But you might want to bring up a KV-1910 when you get a chance. I sold the Sony to this Indian over the phone: he's gonna pick it up in a few."

"Want me to write his name on the box?"

"Okay. Write Singh on it. Or Patel. No, put Singh *and* Patel on there. That ought to shake him up. And bring up one of those Generally Defective ten-inchers while you're at it."

"The Portocolors?"

"Yeah. Void's up there right now, writing up another one of those pieces of plunder." McGinnes smiled. "But first, how about you and me get our heads up?"

McGinnes put the Colt can up on a carton. He took a film canister and a small brass pipe from his pocket and shook some pot into the bowl. He handed the pipe to Stefanos, put fire to the herb with a disposable lighter. Nick Stefanos coughed out the hit.

"Wanna get high?" said McGinnes to Karras.

"No, thanks," said Karras. "I'm good."

McGinnes gave the pipe another light, hit it hard, kept the smoke down in his lungs. He tapped the ashes out on his palm, slipped the pipe and the film canister back in his pocket.

"C'mere, Greek," said McGinnes, producing a Magic Marker from his jacket.

"What are you gonna do?"

"Just come here."

Karras watched McGinnes carefully draw a red dot in the center of the kid's forehead. For the Indian customer's benefit, thought Karras. That ought to shake him up.

"I gotta jet," said Karras.

"Good to meet you, man," said Stefanos. "Maybe I'll see you up at the courts sometime."

"Yeah," said Karras. "Maybe you will."

"Hold still, Jim," said McGinnes. "Gonna have us a red dot sale."

Karras backed away, walked the length of the stockroom, listening to the fade of McGinnes's giggle as he hit the stairs. The old man had been right: Young Nick worked with a bunch of wise guys. Well, at least the kid was having fun.

Out on the showroom floor, Karras could hear another Steely Dan cut coming from the Sound Explosion. He passed Phil Omajian, the smiling store manager, his eyes closed, his feet still up on his desk. McGinnes had apparently caught Omajian sleeping; a bright red dot had been drawn in the center of his forehead, too.

SEVENTEEN

"Yo. Mitri!"

"Hey, Marcus!"

Dimitri Karras sat behind the wheel of the Karmann Ghia, looking for a place to park. Marcus Clay had spotted him while walking down the sidewalk of McKinley Street on the way to the library.

"Hurry up and get your shit on, man, we're waitin' on you. I just went and called you from a pay phone to find out where you were at."

"I'll be right there," said Karras, hitting the gas and pushing the Ghia up to the top of the hill. He found a space, changed beside his car, and jogged down McKinley, cutting right at the rec center alley to the area behind the library.

The game was to be played on a fenced-in outdoor court. Since this was Chevy Chase, the asphalt was free of glass and debris, the hoops had been strung with chains, and the court was lit by powerful overhead lamps.

Karras passed a row of kids and more kids behind them, all jammed up against the fence. Someone had set up a portable eight-track player, and the Commodores' "Gimme My Mule" was playing loudly, with the emphasis on treble over bass. A teenager wearing painter's pants and a painter's cap was doing the robot next to the box while a couple of his friends looked on.

For an early evening summer contest in the Urban Coalition league, the place was packed. Though loosely organized at best, league rules required that starters be registered. From there on in, though, anyone could get in the game as long as he cleared it with the team captain. Karras saw more players than usual, with an obvious number of ringers, as he entered the gate.

"Come on, Dimitri!" yelled Clay from across the court. "Get it on!"

Karras went over to Marcus, greeted a couple other players he knew who were standing next to the bench. He patted Clay on the arm. "Good to see you, man."

Clay looked into Karras's eyes. "What's up with you, man?"

"I don't know. Just had a weird day, I guess. I'll tell you about it later."

"You ready to play some ball?"

"Sure. But why so many people?"

"Adrian Dantley's supposed to show tonight."

"Damn."

They heard some commotion from outside the fence. A Mark IV with peace-sign covers on the headlights came to a stop and double-parked right on the street. A very big man got out of the driver's side and walked toward the gate, the kids outside the fence slapping each other five even as they moved out of the man's way.

"Who's that?" said Karras.

"Looks like Zelmo Beaty to me," said the player next to Karras.

"Utah Stars?"

"Last time I checked."

The game began. Karras caught the tip and took the ball to the top of the key. He bounced one in to Clay, who took the turnaround J from eight feet out. The chains danced as the ball went through the hoop.

The other team brought the ball up. They had a Greek kid by the name of Ted "T. J." Tavlarides, a former baseball pitcher for Wilson who could get possessed and drop the pill from way outside. When he got into a zone his boys called him the Mad Stork. He was in one tonight; on the next two possessions, he swished two in a row from twenty-five.

"I don't need no doctor," said Tavlarides to his defender, as the second shot dropped.

"Cover his ass," said the team captain to the player who had just been used.

Clay took a pick, slanted into the lane, came up against a wall of defenders, and dished a no-look over to Karras in the corner. Karras took the jumper, bricked it off the back of the rim. Clay skyed, got the rebound, whipped it out to Karras in the same spot. Karras felt the velvety backspin on the ball as it left his hands. He knew it was good, and it barely kissed the chains.

"Way to get up," said Karras to Clay as they ran the length of the court to get back on D.

"I always get up," said Clay.

"By Larry Brown," said Karras.

The two of them smiled, touched hands.

Adrian Dantley rotated in for Tavlarides, and Zelmo Beaty came in for Marcus Clay. On the next ball out, Jo Jo Hunter, a Player of the Year from Mackin, checked in for Karras. By the second half, when the sky had darkened and the overhead lamps had been turned on, many of the town's recent inductees to local basketball royalty had found their way into the game: Gerald Gaskins, Al Chesley, and James "Turkey" Tillman, all from Eastern's '74 championship team; Hawkeye Whitney, out of Demtha; and Tiny "Too Small" Jones, who could shoot the eyes out of the bucket most any time. Clay was in and out, and he performed respectably, but Karras never saw another minute of play. He was perfectly happy to ride the bench, watching up close the exquisite battle on the court, a night of ball in D.C. that Karras and many others would not soon forget.

When it was done, Karras and Clay walked out of the gate to the street, stopped at Clay's Riviera.

Karras said, "That was bad."

"No question."

"We on for tonight?"

"Yeah. I got Rasheed closing up. Let me swing by my crib, have a shower. I'll be over with Elaine in about an hour, okay? Give you time for you and your little . . . *friend* to get ready, too."

"Cool."

"And Dimitri. Don't be talkin' about the game all night, hear? It just plain bores the fuck out of my woman, man."

"All right, Marcus. I won't say a thing. You see that move Dantley made against Zelmo, though?"

"Mitri, man —"

"All right. See you in an hour, hear?"

Clay got into his Riviera, turned the key. Karras walked over to McKinley and found his ride. He slipped *Coney Island Baby* into the deck, listened to his favorite Lou while cruising through Rock Creek Park under a star-filled dome of night.

"Man," said Wilton Cooper to Bobby Roy Clagget, "what the *fuck* is that?"

A canary yellow muscle car came to a stop in front of the Northeast row house, its Hemi bubbling beneath the hood. Ronald Thomas cut the engine, stepped out of the driver's side. Russell Thomas climbed out of the passenger seat, left the door open in the street. Both brothers were smiling with pride.

"You like it, Coop?" said Ronald. "I mean, it's bad, ain't it?"

Cooper got up off the stoop where he had been sitting, waiting for the Thomas brothers to return with his new ride. He went to the back of the car, where the word "Daytona" was written across a wide black stripe, and put his hand on the elevated spoiler that sat up higher than the roofline.

"Like it?" said Cooper.

"Yeah, man, you know."

"I done told you, Mandingo, what I wanted was a nice fast Dodge. You told *me* your cousin knew a boy could get rid of my Challenger, hook us up with somethin' plated and new."

"Cuz *did* hook us up, Cooper. Can't get much faster than a Charger Daytona. You talkin' fast, this motherfucker flies, man. Got a four-twenty-six and a Dana rear."

"Oh," said Cooper, "I can see that the vehicle is fast. What *you* don't see, Ronald, is we might have the law on our asses right quick. What I was thinkin', when I told you to pick us out a new ride, was you'd have the presence of mind to get us somethin' more *inconspicu-*

ous and shit. Instead, you bring us this Big Bird—lookin' thing right here with a six-foot-high spoiler, looks like a motherfuckin' rocket ship."

"Got a pistol-grip shifter on it, too, Cooper," said Russell.

"Shut up, Russell," said Ronald.

"And by the way," said Cooper. "You ever seen a brother drivin' one of these? Uh-uh, man, and if you claim you have then you a lyin' motherfucker. Seen a few Chinese motherfuckers drivin' these things, maybe, or a bunch of 'em standin' around with the hood up, pointin' at the engine, talkin' fast, shit like that. But never any brothers."

"Look," said Ronald. "If you like, I'll go on back, see that boy we picked this up from. He had this other ride available, a red seventy-four Sport with accent stripes. Just like the kind Starsky and Hutch used to drive."

"Uh-uh, man. All the sissies in the joint was way into *Starsky and Hutch*. I'll just go ahead and pass on the Sport." Cooper looked at Russell, pointed to the open passenger door. "Close that wing, man."

Russell went around and shut the door.

Cooper eyed the car for a while, then turned to Clagget. "What you think, B. R.?"

"I know it's gonna get us some attention." Clagget's mouth turned up in a pus-lined, toothless grin as he studied the lines of the Dodge. "But it is kind of bad, blood. You know?"

"If you like it, little brother," said Cooper, "then I guess it's all right."

"What we gonna do, Cooper?" said Ronald Thomas.

"Time we paid a visit to Trouble Man," said Cooper. "B. R., go up to the house and bring the hardware on down."

"We leavin' now?"

"Yeah," said Cooper. "Right now."

Cooper knew he should leave town, right away, with the money and the drugs. Drive as far away from his doom as he possibly could.

Looking at the car, though, he felt a pleasant kind of calm. What'd that prison psychiatrist call it that time, when he was talking about how it felt to bust out of all your chains? *Liberated.* Yeah, that was how he felt: free.

He could do anything, now.

EIGHTEEN

Karras stopped off on P Street at the Fairfax Market for chips, onion dip, smokes, and a couple of six-packs of beer. He hit a liquor store for a fifth of Mount Gay rum and piña colada mix, and took it all back to his apartment at the Trauma Arms.

As he came through the door, Vivian Lee stood with her back to him, wiping down the kitchen with a damp sponge. She wore the red-and-white striped tube top Karras had bought for her, jeans ripped at the knee, and cork-heeled sandals. Karras stood in the door frame, studying the shine of her long black hair falling over her bare white shoulders.

"Hey."

"Hey," said Vivian, turning around. Her eyes looked a little funny, but not in that recognizable, just-stoned way. Beyond stoned, like they were looking back in on themselves.

Karras took the party materials to the counter. He watched Vivian scrub at a clean spot on the Formica.

"Have a good day?" said Karras.

Vivian laughed.

"My day was a trip," said Karras.

"Mine, too." Vivian laughed again. "Literally."

"Oh, yeah?"

"Ran into a couple friends at the circle."

"What, you dropped some acid?"

"Uh-huh. This guy I know, Danny? He had this blotter, man."

"You okay?"

"I'm all right. We went to a movie, man. Went and saw *The Man*

Who Fell to Earth, at the Dupont? Whew. Bowie was weird, man. I guess I didn't get it. Bowie was weird. I didn't get it, I guess."

"All right."

"Bowie was so fucking weird."

"Vivian, you okay?"

"I'm all right."

Karras put the beer in the refrigerator. He took his T-shirt off, rolled it, and hung it around his neck.

Vivian checked him out. "*You* look healthy."

"Thanks."

"You look really good."

"Thanks a lot. Listen, Vivian. I'm gonna take a shower, get changed. Marcus and his lady, Elaine, they're comin' over. You up for that?"

"Sure."

Karras said, "Your cigarettes are in the bag."

He took a long cold shower. It had been more than a few years since he had dropped acid. He had tripped plenty of times as an undergraduate, but he was past that now. He thought of the nineteen-year-old girl out in his kitchen, scrubbing away at a clean spot, out of her mind on blotter. He thought of the old Greek in the dingy grill on Fourteenth Street, and the old man's grandson, to whom he could not bring himself to give advice. He pictured the kids in the park, passing him money, him passing them back a bag of dope.

"Fuck," said Karras.

He closed his eyes.

But Dimitri Karras forgot all about who he had become once he smoked his first joint of the night.

Marcus and Elaine came through the door as he was tucking his Hawaiian shirt into his jeans. He cracked a beer for Clay, mixed a batch of piña coladas in the blender, served a tall cool one with an orange slice hung on the rim of the glass to Elaine. He opened a beer for himself and one for Vivian. The four of them stood in a circle and touched drinks.

"To the Bicentennial," said Karras.

"To equality," said Elaine, glancing at Clay.

"Party down," said Vivian.

They smoked a jay. It brought Karras out of his funk and calmed Vivian down. She had been going from one subject to the next with Elaine, who had patiently listened without a break while Clay and Karras went through Karras's albums. They settled on *Call Me*, which got the party off to a good start. Karras turned up the volume. Elaine and Marcus put down their drinks and began to dance. Karras and Vivian came out to the center of the room, joined them. They all did the bump to the title tune, then slow-dragged to Green's Bee Gees cover. Afterward, Clay got Karras alone.

"Hey, Dimitri. Elaine was askin' me, did you pick that shirt out for Vivian yourself, man?"

"What the hell?"

Clay grinned. "You know, that tube top she's wearin'."

"Marcus —"

"You got to admit, it would be just like a pussy hound like you to pick out a tube top for your lovely young houseguest. For easy access and shit."

"I found it in a store down the street," said Karras. "Thought it would look good on her, that's all."

"Oh, she does look fine. But I was wonderin', did you happen to get her anything more practical?"

"Well, there was this halter top, see —"

"Yeah, Dimitri. I see."

Duncan Hazlewood, the resident manager, and his girlfriend, Libby Howland, came through the unlocked door. Hazlewood had a fifth of scotch in his hand.

"We got tired of waiting for an invitation, damnit," said Hazlewood.

"You don't need one," said Karras from across the room. "Duncan, Libby, c'mon in. Glasses are in the cabinet, ice is over by the sink."

Another joint was lit and it went around the party. Karras had a good hit, then waved Clay over by his side. Clay knew what Karras wanted.

"Naw, Dimitri. I'm too high."

" 'Too High.' Stevie Wonder."

"I'm tellin' you, man, I don't want no shotgun."

Karras put the lit end of the joint in his mouth. He blew on the joint, sent a concentrated jet of smoke into the room. Clay stepped up, took the smoke into his lungs for as long as both of them could stand it.

"Now you do me," said Karras.

Clay coughed out his hit. "Aw, fuck you, man."

Karras went to his record collection, withdrew an album from the stack.

"Got *Bloodshot* if you want it," said Karras. "J. Geils."

"Jay North," said Clay.

"You tellin' me you're not into a little Jerome?"

"Go ahead, man."

"Even got the red vinyl, too." Karras did an impromptu duckwalk over to the stereo.

Vivian filled a bong hit while Karras put on the record. He dropped the needle on the third cut, "Back to Get Ya." Karras danced by himself to the first couple of verses, turned up the volume at the harp break.

"Do the robot, Mitri!" yelled Clay.

Elaine leaned against the kitchen wall, smiled, rolled her eyes as Karras went into his stiff, jerky dance. Duncan and Libby stood behind the couch, laughing and moving a little themselves. Vivian Lee lit a cigarette.

They all had another round of drinks and smoked a little more weed, and then Duncan and Libby decided it was time to go. Elaine, who had an eye for art, promised to catch Hazlewood's next show. Duncan and Libby left, arm in arm.

"Whyn't you put on a slow drag, Dimitri?" said Clay. "I'm tired of watchin' you try to get on the goodfoot."

"Whaddaya wanna hear?"

"You got 'Brown-Eyed Girl'?"

"Yeah, I got Van."

"I ain't talkin' about no Van. I'm talkin' about *the* 'Brown-Eyed Girl.' The Isleys, man."

"Yeah," said Karras, "I think I got that one."

He found *Live It Up*, placed the needle on the second track on side one. Marcus and Elaine came together immediately, her head on his shoulder. Vivian came to Karras.

They danced to the beautiful song, Ronald Isley's wistful tenor filling the apartment. Karras saw Elaine put her head on Clay's shoulder and close her eyes. He wondered if anyone would ever love him that way. Vivian ran her hands up and down Karras's back. She crushed her breasts against his hard stomach. He felt the vibration of her slow moan and the hardening of his cock in his jeans. Vivian looked up at him with damp eyes.

"Dimitri?"

"Yeah?"

"I gotta go to the bathroom."

"Want me to go with you?"

"Okay."

Karras followed her there because he knew that was what she wanted. Because that was what he wanted, too. He had told himself before that it was wrong, but he was high now and told himself that it was right. He felt Elaine's eyes on him as he passed.

In the bathroom, Karras closed the door behind him. Vivian faced him, leaned back against the sink. She shook her black hair off her pale shoulders, pulled the tube top down to her waist. Free, her lovely breasts bounced one time. He put his thumb and forefinger to the pink nipple of her right breast, squeezed it until her lips parted.

"Nice lollipops," whispered Karras, noticing his stupid, open-mouthed reflection in the bathroom mirror.

She's a kid, you fucking . . .

She crushed her mouth against his; he kissed her back. He felt his breath shorten and pulled her against his groin.

Her heard Elaine's voice, calling his name: "Dimitri! Dimitri, come out here!"

"Hold that," said Karras.

Vivian said, "I will."

He walked out of the bathroom, through the hall to the living room. Elaine was by the stereo, wide eyed, clumsily turning the music all the way down. Marcus had opened the door and was standing there, his head slightly bent, his hands hanging limply at his sides. A uniformed cop stood in the open frame.

"Hey, pull over, Ronald," said Russell Thomas. "I'll ask that blue freak on the corner where that shop is at."

"That okay?" said Ronald to Cooper.

They had been searching for the record store for the last fifteen minutes. Cooper had looked up the address in the yellow pages, but with the traffic on Connecticut Avenue and all that, even at this time of night, it was difficult to slow down, get a good look at the numbers on the storefronts without attracting attention.

Cooper said, "Sure, man. Go ahead."

Cooper and Clagget sat in the backseat of the Dodge, Clagget pressing the sawed-off tightly to his leg. Ronald drove, with Russell at his side up front. Ronald cut the wheel, stopped the car in a bus zone at Connecticut and Q.

A dark-skinned woman wearing white bells and a short-sleeved print shirt stood on the corner. She glanced at her watch impatiently, as if to let the men in the car know that she was waiting for someone to come pick her up. Behind her, a kid had set up a portable eight-track and an overturned hat on the sidewalk. The kid was robotting wildly to James Brown's "The Payback."

Russell Thomas leaned out the window, raised his voice so the woman could hear him over the J. B. He put a smile behind the voice. "Hey, girlfriend, what's goin' on?"

The woman looked away. She coughed into her fist and blinked her eyes. The Daytona was putting out some serious exhaust.

Russell tried again. "Look here, dark and lovely. I would never harm a sister as fine as you. See, baby, I'm from out of town —"

"Who don't know that," said the woman, suddenly staring Russell dead in the eye.

"Anyway, I was wonderin'. . . . Where go Real Right Records, sugar? We're just lookin' to cop some sounds for the weekend, and we heard that Real Right was the place."

"Real Right?" The woman's features softened. "Well, you're only a block away. Real Right is up there above R, on the right."

"Thank you, precious. I do appreciate it."

The woman fanned carbon dioxide away from her face as Ronald Thomas pulled away from the curb.

"Freak was way into me, man," said Russell. "Matter of fact, maybe afterwards, I'll have you drive me back here. A girl like that could suck on my jolly stick for real." Russell rubbed his dick through his purple pants.

"Russell," said Ronald, "one of these days, someone's just gonna go ahead and kick your monkey ass."

"Then their momma'd be wakin' them up out of their good dream," said Russell, "tellin' 'em it's time to get off to school."

Clagget tapped Cooper's shoulder. "Wilton?"

"Uh-huh?"

"That girl looked somethin' like Carol Speed. You notice that?"

Cooper said, "I surely did."

Clagget touched the cranberry riot of acne splattered across his face. "You know, Wilton, that woman's gonna remember our car."

Cooper nodded, staring straight ahead.

They drove slowly by the store. Through the window, Cooper noticed a young dashiki-wearing man, no one else. He motioned Ronald, told him to take a long swing around the block. They came back out on Connecticut where the young lady had been standing moments earlier. The dancing kid was still there. They drove north.

Twentieth Street broke off of Connecticut just above R, giving the avenue stores backdoor loading capability and dual window frontage. Cooper pointed Ronald up 20th. Ronald steered the Daytona into a space.

"Cut it, Ronald," said Cooper.

Ronald Thomas killed the engine. For a while, all of them watched the flow of tourists and Washingtonians out on the street. Then Clagget pulled two double-aught shells from the loops of his hunting vest.

"Whole lotta folks out tonight," said Clagget. He thumbed the shells into the shotgun.

"That Bicentennial thing," said Cooper.

"You got some kind of plan, Coop?" said Ronald.

"I'm gonna get myself in through the front door on Connecticut," said Cooper. "Now, B. R. and Russell: When that back door cracks open, I want y'all to get your asses out the car and into the shop. Ronald, you just sit tight. Fire up that ignition again when you see us all comin' out the back. Everybody down with that?"

None of them replied. Cooper pulled his .45 from the waistband of his slacks, pulled back on the receiver, let a round drop into the chamber. He replaced the gun, left his shirttail out over his slacks.

"Keep that hog's leg down, little brother."

"I will, Wilton."

Cooper said, "Let's take it to the bridge."

Cooper got out of the Dodge, walked around the triangular point where 20th and Connecticut converged, went quickly to the front door of Real Right Records, keeping his chin tucked in to his chest. He tried the handle, then rapped on the glass two times. He smiled at the young man who stood behind the island counter in the center of the store, counting out bills. The young man made a cutting motion across his throat, mouthed the word "closed." Cooper smiled again, did a "come on over" thing with his hand. The young man shrugged, put the bills in the register, closed the register drawer. He went to the front of the shop, turned a latch lock, opened the door enough to put his head through the space.

"We're closed," said the young man.

"I can see that, blood." Cooper noticed the red, black, and green Africa cutout hung out over the brightly colored dashiki. "But I got a wad of cash money in my pocket and a stone freak sittin' in the shotgun seat of my ride. Freak loves her Harold Melvin and the Blue Notes, man. Teddy's voice makes that man in the boat of hers fall in and drown."

The young man laughed. "Like to help you, brother, but I can't. My boss says not to let anyone in after closing time."

"Your boss want you to throw away potential ducats, too? 'Cause I got a Ben Franklin in my wallet, and I'm fixin' to spend half of it in your shop right quick."

"I don't know. . . ."

"What's your name, man?"

"Rasheed."

"Rasheed, brother, come on . . . you *got* to help me out with my woman."

"All right. Make it quick."

Rasheed opened the door, let Cooper in, flipped back the latch to where it had been.

"You got *To Be True*?" said Cooper.

"Yeah, we got it."

"Take me to it, man, so I can get on out of here and leave you to your J-O-B."

Cooper glanced behind him at the foot traffic on the street as he followed Rasheed Adamson to the Soul section of the store. When he was satisfied that they were partially hidden by an aisle divider, Cooper pulled the .45 from behind his waistband. He moved forward quickly and jammed the muzzle of the automatic savagely into Rasheed's kidney.

"Uh!" said Rasheed. "What the —"

"Nigger," hissed Cooper, "don't *even* turn around. Don't say nothin' 'less I ask you a question, hear?"

Rasheed nodded his head.

"Good. Where the lights at in this joint?"

"G-got a set by the door and a set next to the stockroom."

"To the stockroom, then." Cooper pushed in on Rasheed's kidney. "Go."

They walked close together into the stockroom. Rasheed

extinguished the store lights without asking; he knew what Cooper wanted him to do.

"All right. Now open that back door an inch."

"Why?"

"I ain't ask you nothin', nigger. I *told* you to open that got-damn door."

Rasheed deactivated the back door alarm by punching a numeric code into a grid. It was not a silent alarm, and he didn't want the man with the gun to panic. He then used his keys to turn a series of locks. He opened the door and stepped back.

A half minute later two people came through the door. One of them, a white boy, held a sawed-off shotgun at his side and the other, a black man, carried a revolver.

Cooper closed the door tight, did not lock it.

"Everything all right out there, B. R.?"

"Everything's cool, blood."

Rasheed checked out the white one called B. R. Maroon snap-button-fly bells and a jungle-motif maroon and green rayon shirt with long collar points. Boy had some Flagg Brothers–lookin' kicks on his feet, too, and a pale, fucked-up, toothless face.

"Good," said Cooper. "You okay, Russell?"

"Everything's chilly," said Russell.

Rasheed searched Russell's blank face for a hint of compassion. He saw nothing there.

Cooper turned to Rasheed. "What you say your name was again, boy?"

"Rasheed."

"Wilton Cooper's mine."

Rasheed's eyes widened slightly. He had taken a call from the mother of Marcus's Greek friend, Dimitri Karras, earlier in the night. She had been trying to reach her son to tell him that a man named Cooper had been over to her place, asking a lot of funny questions about Marcus. Rasheed had left a note for Marcus detailing the message out on the counter.

"Somethin' wrong?" said Cooper, noticing the change in Rasheed's expression.

"No," said Rasheed.

"All right. Now look here, Ra-sheed. We come here tonight to get back somethin' your boss took. Somethin' that was mine. I got nothin' against you, man. Shame it had to be you standin' here and not your boy Marcus Clay. But we gonna deal with the situation that we got. I just want to be clear: You don't tell me what I want to know, I *will* fuck you up. Understand?"

"Yes."

"I'm just gonna leave it up to you. It makes no difference to me."

"I understand."

"Good. Now take us to the place where the boss keeps the money."

Rasheed hesitated. The white boy pointed the shotgun in his direction.

"All right," said Rasheed. "Come on."

Rasheed felt unsteady on his feet. He noticed a shake in his knees. He said a short prayer as he led them to the island counter, prayed to God to let him be a man in the face of all this. To be a man, that was important; also, to honor his word with Marcus Clay.

"Money's in the register," said Rasheed.

"Open it," said Cooper.

Rasheed turned a thin plastic key on the face of the register. A small bell announced the opening of the drawer.

"Ding," said Russell with a wide grin.

"What you got in there, Ra-sheed?"

Rasheed stared into the drawer. Some light spilled in from the street lamps of Connecticut, but the store was awfully dark, and it was difficult to see. " 'B-bout a hundred, hundred and twenty, maybe."

B. R. Clagget stepped through an opening and got inside the island, stood a few feet from Rasheed. He cocked his hip.

"Sounds like you're a little short," said Cooper.

"What's that?" said Rasheed.

"You talkin' about a hundred and twenty. I was thinkin' more like twenty *thousand*."

"Shit, man —"

"Don't be cursin' Mr. Cooper," said Clagget.

Rasheed moved back a step, stopping on the throw rug that covered the trap door. He felt the rug beneath his feet. Standing there, protecting the money, it sent a rush of courage and pride into his spine. Rasheed stood straight. He imagined how it would be the next morning, standing around with Marcus and Cheek, telling the story of how he fooled these country motherfuckers, Marcus looking at him, admiration in his eyes —

"About that twenty thousand," said Cooper.

"Look, I swear to you, man, I don't know nothin' about no twenty grand. What we got in the register is what we got to get us started for tomorrow's business. I mean, I just made the deposit myself a half hour ago."

Russell Thomas took an album from its sleeve, sailed it across the room. It shattered against the Chaka Khan poster taped to the painted cinder-block wall.

"Hey," said Rasheed. "You don't have to do that."

Russell said, "You tellin' me what I can do, boy? I'll come over there right quick and slap the taste out your mouth."

"Talk about it, Russell," said Clagget.

Russell pointed to a black-covered album that sat face out on display. He held the album up so Cooper could check it out. "Hey, Cooper, look. They got *Wild and Peaceful.*"

Russell dropped the record, kicked the display over. Albums slid across the floor, many of them breaking into pieces. Russell got his shoulders behind another rack, pushed the rack over on its side.

"We need peace," said Russell. "We need uni-tee."

Clagget laughed.

"Hey!" shouted Rasheed. "There ain't no need —"

"Talk about the money," said Cooper, sharply cutting him off.

"I don't know. . . . I'm tellin' you, I don't know what you're talkin' about, man."

Cooper stepped forward. Rasheed took a step back. Clagget looked down at Rasheed's feet. He smiled and racked the shotgun's pump.

"You know what that sound is?" said Clagget.

"Huh?" said Rasheed, wincing at the sudden rise in his voice. He stared openmouthed at the sawed-off, now pointed at his face.

"That there," said Clagget, "is the sound of your own death."

Rasheed looked at Cooper, smiled weakly.

"Hey, blood," said Rasheed.

Clagget squeezed the shotgun's trigger. Flame erupted from the sawed-off's muzzle. Papers flew off the countertop and floated in the air.

"Damn," said Russell.

Cooper looked out at the avenue. The sound had attracted a few faces at the window. The pedestrians saw black men in the shop and quickly got on their way. He figured one of those good citizens would be on a pay phone real quick.

"Little brother," said Cooper. "You didn't even give the boy a chance to speak."

"Didn't need to," said Clagget, pointing at the floor. "Look."

Cooper looked down to where Rasheed had been standing. The rug had been moved aside when Rasheed stepped back. There was the outline of a trapdoor cut into the hardwood floor.

Cooper got down on his haunches, lifted the piece of wood. He pulled out the cash box, opened it. He counted out ten thousand dollars joylessly, folded the money, put it in the pocket of his slacks.

"Cooper," said Russell. "We best be on our way."

All of them could hear the sound of a siren now in the distance.

"Get the money out the register, B. R."

"Right," said Clagget.

Cooper stood over Rasheed's body. The double-aught shell had cleaned off the side of the boy's face. It looked as if an animal had taken a bite from Rasheed, crown to jaw. Chunks of brain and clumps of damp hair dripped off the shelving beneath the counter. The blood looked black in the absence of light.

"Boy?" said Cooper softly, looking at the corpse. "Didn't your people ever tell you? White man gonna find a way to fuck you up every time."

"Got it," said Clagget, holding up a short stack of bills.

"All right," said Cooper. "Let's go."

The three of them ran out the back door, guns drawn. A couple of people on 20th had been hanging around since the shotgun sound had reached the street, and these people backed up quickly at the sight of the men. One of them, a student in his twenties, got on his belly and slid beneath a parked car.

Clagget dropped the sawed-off behind the front seat, got in first. Russell and Cooper were in soon after. Ronald had cooked the ignition and was pumping the gas against the clutch.

"Go on, Ronald," said Cooper. "Show us what Big Bird can do."

Ronald Thomas eased off the clutch pedal; the Daytona screamed away from the curb. The four of them were pinned against their seats as Ronald pulled back on the pistol-grip gearshift and caught long rubber in second. He double-clutched out of the Florida Avenue right turn. The Dodge fishtailed for fifty yards before straightening out on the way to 16th.

"Whewee," said Cooper.

"That was bad, Wilton!"

"Yes it was," said Cooper.

Bobby Roy Clagget yelled, "Man, we're blowin' this town all to *hell*!"

"Bo Hopkins," said Cooper. "Right?"

"*The Wild Bunch*," said Clagget, nodding his head.

Russell extended his hand, palm up, to the backseat. "You're one crazy white boy, man! You all right." Clagget slapped Russell's palm.

Cooper found his Salem longs on the seat at his side. He lit one for himself, lit one for Clagget.

"Hey," said Russell to Ronald. "Gimme one of them double-O's."

Ronald drew the deck of Kools from the visor, shook two out of the bottom of the pack.

The bright yellow Dodge with the big spoiler hit eighty miles an hour going east across the city. The men inside it were laughing loudly and giving each other skin. They could no longer hear the sirens of the police cars and ambulances converging on the record store at Connecticut and R.

NINETEEN

arcus Clay told Elaine to take the Riviera back to their row house in Mount Pleasant, that he'd meet her there. He and Karras left Vivian Lee at the Trauma Arms and jogged the two blocks to the store.

Clay and Karras were let through the police barricade and into the shop. Red light flashed intermittently on the cinderblock walls from the cherry-tops parked out on the street. A big man with a ruddy face stopped Clay as he came through the door. The man wore a plain khaki raincoat, though it was neither raining nor cool. The grip of his .38 curved out from beneath the coat's wide lapels.

"You Marcus Clay?"

"Yeah."

"Farrelly. Homicide."

"How'd y'all find me so quick?"

"You got an employee list posted in the back with numbers. We tried you at your home number first, couldn't get an answer. Tried a Mr. Cheek next, got him. He said you might be with Karras. Cheek gave us Karras's number." Farrelly moved his chin toward Karras. "That Karras?"

"Yeah."

"He work here?"

"No."

"Then he needs to stay out of everybody's way. Tell him not to leave, though. Might want to have a few words with him myself."

Karras heard Farrelly's instructions. He stepped back against the nearest wall. He didn't move.

Farrelly said to Clay, "You up for this now?"

Clay said, "Yeah."

"Over here."

Clay followed Farrelly toward the center island. He noticed but did not stop to touch the overturned displays and damaged inventory spread about the floor. Cheek was in a corner of the store, his shoulders jerking, tears running down his face. A uniformed cop stood next to him staring straight ahead.

They were through the opening and in the island now. Farrelly got down on one knee and pulled back the sheet. He looked up and into Clay's expressionless eyes.

"Rasheed Adamson," said Clay.

"Your employee?"

"Right."

"Matches his wallet ID," said Farrelly. He stood up and nodded shortly toward a small man in a gray suit wearing rimless bifocals. "Okay. Cover him up."

Farrelly said to Clay, "You want a coffee?"

"Don't drink it."

"I'm gonna get me one," said Farrelly. "I'll meet you in the backroom in five. Okay?"

"Sure. You through with Cheek over there?"

"Yeah, he's done."

"I'm gonna tell him to get on home."

"Fine. Five minutes, Clay."

"Right."

Clay went over to Cheek, put his arm around him, moved him away from the uniformed cop, talked to him, got him settled down. Cheek left the store without a word.

Clay saw a cop he had come up with in Shaw, a muscular guy named George Dozier, standing in street clothes by himself in the middle of the Jazz aisle. He went over to Dozier and the two of them shook hands.

"George."

"Marcus. You all right, man?"

"Yeah. What you doin' here, George?"

"Heard the call on my police-band at home, recognized the address. Came over, wanted to make sure . . . make sure it wasn't you."

"Thanks, man."

"Ain't no thing."

"You in homicide now?"

Dozier shook his head. "Doin' an undercover thing."

"You can find shit out, though, right?"

"I hear things, Marcus, yeah."

"Keep you ears open wide for me, man."

"You comin' to church on Sunday?"

"I'll be there."

"All right, then, Marcus. I'll see you in church."

Clay sat in his chair at the desk where he did his paperwork in the backroom. Detective Farrelly sat on the edge of the desk. Farrelly held a lit filterless Chesterfield in one hand and a Styrofoam cup of steaming coffee in the other.

"Rasheed Adamson," said Farrelly. "Good kid?"

"Yes."

"Better than good, I'd say. He's clean as hell. We checked him out."

"Rasheed was good all the way."

"No enemies, I guess."

"None."

"How about you?"

"How's that?"

"Enemies. You got any?"

"No."

"Wilton Cooper," said Farrelly.

Clay's heart kicked. He tried to keep his face from twitching. "Say what?"

Farrelly studied Clay's face. "We found a handwritten note out there on the floor, right in the middle of a bunch of papers that had been blown off the counter. The note said that a Wilton Cooper had gone by Dimitri Karras's mother's house today, lookin' for you. The same Karras who's out there right now, right?"

"That's right."

"Just checking." Farrelly cleared his throat. "The note was signed by Rasheed. I guess Karras's old lady called the store." Farrelly hotboxed his Chesterfield, stared down at Clay through his exhale. "So, Wilton Cooper. You know him?"

"No."

"You're sure."

"Yes. I don't recognize the name. And I know he ain't no friend of mine. Must be some salesman, or a bill collector, maybe, somethin' like that."

"You got trouble paying your bills?"

"Every small businessman I know's got trouble with his payables."

"I'll give you that." Farrelly drained his coffee. "Well, we'll check on this Cooper. See about priors, or if he's got any outstanding paper on him. If Cooper comes up goose eggs, then it looks like we're talking about a simple armed robbery gone wrong. The register and the cash box in the floor were emptied out. I assume you got insurance."

"Yeah."

"How much you normally keep in that box?"

"Whatever the day's take was."

"So what, a grand?"

"Less on most days. Three, four hundred."

Farrelly breathed out slowly. "Well, the perps left plenty of prints, that's for sure. Made a lot of noise, left a lot of prints, drove out of here like bats out of hell in a bright yellow car. We're talkin' to some witnesses right now. Funny, this crew didn't seem to give two shits about leaving clues behind."

"You think you'll get 'em, then."

"Hard to tell. The easy ones end up being hard, and the hard ones sometimes go the other way." Farrelly put his hand on Clay's shoulder. "You okay?"

"I'm fine."

"The forensics guy out there, Snipes, he was lookin' at you when you IDed Rasheed. Noticed how unemotional you were. Pointed it out to me when I was getting my coffee, like it meant something. Like maybe you were involved. An insurance scam, something like that. I didn't answer him because I knew he wouldn't understand. Snipes was never in the service."

"So?"

"You were."

"How'd you know that?"

"I was in the Big One myself. And my son did a tour of Nam. You get so's you can look at a man and tell if he's served or not. Fellow your age, that would place you in Vietnam. Am I right?"

"Yeah."

"What branch?"

"Look —"

"It's not important. It's okay." Farrelly got off the desk, straightened his raincoat. "After a while — after you've seen all that death, I mean — it gets to be like you're wearing a mask. But it's still just a mask. The fear and the turning in your gut, they're still there. So, anyway . . . I was just asking to make sure you were doing all right."

"Thanks, Detective."

"Make it Doc."

"Okay, Doc. Thanks."

"I'm going to talk to your friend for a few minutes, then you can go. We'll secure the premises for you. You go straight home, hear? Mix yourself a stiff one —"

"I will."

"And try to get some sleep."

Detective Doc Farrelly found Karras standing against the wall. While Farrelly was questioning him, Karras noticed Clay emerge from the backroom and walk with purpose to the Rock section of the store. He saw Clay lift several records out of the H bin and carry the records over to Soul. He watched Clay file them carefully in place.

"That's all," said Farrelly.

"What?" said Karras.

Farrelly said, "You can go."

Karras and Clay drove through Rock Creek Park, the top down at Marcus's request. They listened to the rush of the wind, the buzz of the small engine working from the back of the car, nothing else. Neither of them spoke. The air was thick with humidity, dampening the seats and filming the windshield. Karras gave the wipers a swipe to clear the glass as he turned off Beach Drive and headed toward Arkansas Avenue. Just before Arkansas he hooked a right, downshifted, took the winding hill up to Mount Pleasant.

Karras stopped in front of Clay's row house on Brown. A light shone in the second-story window that faced the street.

"Marcus?"

"What."

"That detective told me about the note. It was Cooper —"

"I know."

"Cooper was in my house. With my mother, man."

"I said I know."

"I didn't let on to that detective that I knew who Cooper was."

"Neither did I."

They listened to the crickets and the hiss of tires running north and south on 16th, one block east.

"Marcus?"

"What."

"I'm sorry, man."

"Shut up, Dimitri." Clay turned to Karras, spoke softly. His eyes were moist in the light. "Just shut your mouth, man. Don't want to hear about who's sorry, whose fault it was. Don't want to hear none of that. You can't undo death. The only thing that matters is what happens next."

"Marcus —"

"I don't want to talk about a damn thing tonight. Just want to close my eyes and hold on to my woman. I just want to do that, and think."

"Okay."

Clay shook Karras's hand. "You take it light, hear?"

"Yeah. You, too."

Karras watched Clay take the steps up to his house. He waited for Marcus to go inside, but Clay stopped on the porch and stood in the light of a yellow bulb and did not move. Karras waited a little while longer and drove away.

When the VW was out of sight, Marcus Clay had a seat on the top step of his porch. He cried until he couldn't any longer, then wiped his face clean with the tail of his shirt. After a while Clay stood up, straightened his shoulders, and walked into the house.

Dimitri Karras entered his apartment. Vivian had thrown away the empty beer cans and washed out the glasses, dumped the ashtrays and wiped the place clean. There was nothing to suggest that a party had been thrown here earlier in the night. Karras had crashed immediately at the sight of the cop standing in the door; now he was completely straight.

He extinguished the lights and went through the hall to his bedroom. Vivian Lee lay beneath a single cover, her bare shoulders visible, the curves of her nude body defined against the thin cotton fabric, her hair black as ink spilled out atop the white of the sheet.

Karras stripped naked and got under the sheet. He reached over and clicked off his bedside lamp. Vivian turned her body so that it touched his. He felt the weight of her breasts against his back.

Pearl slats of moonlight fell into the room. Karras listened to the tick of his wristwatch and studied the light inching across the floor. Time passed like this. He thought he might remain awake all night. But as the sky outside his window began to lighten, his eyes grew heavy, and Karras went to sleep.

TWENTY

Clarence Tate looked through the warehouse window down to the street. A nerve rippled along his right eye. He had read in the morning *Post* about the slayings on the Howard County farm, and he had read, deep in Metro, about the awful murder-robbery at Marcus Clay's Real Right Records. Now he would find out if all his fears were true.

"Eddie?"

"What?"

Marchetti's eyes were glued to *Soul of the City*, the local Saturday morning dance show on channel 20.

"Cooper just got here."

"So? He called, said he'd be stopping by, didn't he?"

Tate hadn't mentioned the killings to Marchetti. It wouldn't have done anybody any good to get Eddie all emotionally riled. Maybe Cooper wasn't involved. There was still an outside chance that this was all some freaky kind of coincidence. Maybe Cooper was just coming over one last time to say good-bye.

Tate said, "You ought to see the ride he pulled up in."

"Got rid of that red Mopar?"

"Traded it in for something a little flashier."

"Flashier than the Challenger? His prerogative, I guess."

Tate took in the car, spoke softly. "Boy just don't give a good fuck about nothin'."

"Say it again?"

"Nothin', Eddie. Looks like him and that skinny white kid are coming up alone."

Marchetti shrugged. "Buzz him in, then."

Tate watched the two Bamas lean against the yellow car. The better built of the two offered the stupid-looking one a cigarette while Cooper and the white boy walked across the street. Tate went to the office door and waited for them to ring the bell. When he had let them in, he went over to the television set and cut the power.

"Hey," said Marchetti.

"No distractions, Eddie," said Tate.

A moment later Cooper and Clagget entered the office.

"Mr. Tate," said Cooper, smiling. "Mr. Spags."

"Wilton," said Marchetti, getting out of his chair to reach across the desk and shake Cooper's hand.

Tate studied the boy in the high stacks who leaned his narrow frame against the wall, his face whiter than before, his eyes sunk deep. He seemed weak, almost too weak to stand on his own two feet.

Cooper had a seat, put his feet up on Eddie's desk. He pulled a pack of Salems from his breast pocket, lit one, tossed the match to the concrete floor. He dragged deeply, let some smoke pass through his nose, blew a ring and power-blew another through the first.

"Well," said Marchetti, "how are we doing?"

"Oh, we doin' fine. Look here." Cooper let the cigarette dangle from the side of his mouth, raised his hips, reached into the pocket of his jeans, withdrew a rubber-banded roll of bills. "Can't get a damn thing out these jeans once I'm sittin' down. Last pair of these disco blues I'm gonna buy, you can *believe* that."

"What's that?" said Marchetti, pointing his chin at the bills.

"Half your money, Spags." Cooper tossed the roll onto the desk. "After I took my fifty points, of course."

"You got the twenty G's back from Clay already?"

"Like I said, only half."

"He give you any trouble?"

"*He* didn't, no." Cooper lowered his eyes in theatrical remorse. "Had to kill one of his employees, though. Nice kid, too, one of those Marcus Garvey brothers. Guess you could say that boy was just unlucky to be where he was at."

"Kill?" said Marchetti.

"B. R. did it," said Cooper, jerking his head toward Clagget. "Blew the face off the young brother with his shotgun. Those double-aught shells sure did make an awful mess."

The color drained from Marchetti's face. Tate stayed where he was, standing behind the desk with his back against the wall, his arms folded across his chest, his fists balled tight.

"You okay, Spags?" said Cooper. "You lookin' as pale as my young friend B. R."

"I, I'm all right."

"Sure you are. I mean, you *did* want me to recover your money, didn't you?"

Marchetti spread his hands. "I'm just . . . Look, I'm just doing a little business in this town. Brokering a few deals, understand? I don't know anything about killing —"

"Now you do," said Cooper.

"But —"

"Here it is. You deal with men like me, you gotta deal all the way. I mean, you want to run with the big elephants, you gotta pee in the big bushes. Right?"

Marchetti shook his head. "This is over."

"Naw," said Cooper. "Not yet. Got to recover the rest of that ten thousand for you, Spags."

"I don't need any more money."

"Funny thing is," said Cooper, "neither do I. Got a whole suitcase full of it back where I'm stayin'. Know what else? Got a shitload of blow, too. Got everything I need and more. But, regardless, I'm gonna get the rest of that money from Trouble Man. 'Cause right now? I'm just plain having fun."

Marchetti glanced over his shoulder at Tate, then back at Cooper. He squirmed in his seat. "What do you mean you got the money *and* the blow? I thought —"

"You thought. Ain't you read the paper today, Spags?"

"We don't want to know about that, man," said Tate.

"Know about what?" said Marchetti.

"Your boy Clarence — excuse me, I mean Clar*enze* — *he* reads the newspaper, I bet. There's this story in this mornin's edition, you ought to check it out, 'bout how all these bikers got themselves doomed out on some Howard County farm."

"You —"

"Oh, yeah. Killed 'em like animals, Spags. Larry and his woman and all the rest."

Tate pushed off from the wall. He put a hand on Marchetti's shoulder. "Why you tellin' us, Cooper?"

" 'Cause we're partners, that's why. *I'd* call us partners, anyway. The law, they'd probably call the two of you 'accessories.' But I'd like to think of all of us as bein' on the same side."

"Ain't too careful of you," said Tate. "The more people you tell, the better chance that someone's gonna talk about it later on."

"You're smarter than that, Clarence. Way smarter than your boss, if you don't mind my sayin' so, Mr. Spags. You recognized the kind of person I was the first time you laid eyes on me, man. You know that if I ever even had a notion that you turned me in . . . well, you know what I'd do. Even if I were to be incarcerated, I'd find a way. Always someone on the outside owes an influential inside nigger like me a favor. And it wouldn't be just you I'd rain on. I'd find your kin, too."

"I ain't got no kin," said Tate.

"Oh, yes you do. You got 'Daddy' written all over your face." Cooper smiled. "What you got, man? Little boy? Cute little girl?"

Tate said nothing. But his face betrayed him.

Cooper said, "*Girl*, huh?"

Again, Tate did not respond. Cooper looked at him and laughed.

"Well," said Cooper, getting out of his chair. "We best be on our way. Just thought we'd stop by, give you one of them progress reports."

"What're you going to do now?" said Marchetti, a catch in his voice.

"Now? Gonna try and relax today, get ready for the big party to-morrow night. Think about how I can hook up with Trouble Man, get the rest of our jack. Mind, gonna be a little more difficult now, what with all the violence we done perpetrated yesterday." Cooper looked at Tate. "Clarenze, maybe you can put us up with T-Man. Y'all played ball together, right? Maybe he'll listen to you. You could hook us up someplace quiet, where I could go on and . . . *conclude* our business."

"Maybe I could," said Tate, with narrowed eyes.

"Go ahead and think on it. And Spags?"

"What."

"Gonna check on your Chinese girlfriend, too."

"That won't be necessary."

"What, you givin' up on her, man? Be a shame to let a fine piece of clevvies like her walk away. After all, it was her got the ball rolling on this whole conflict we got. I'll have to remember to ask that Greek boy what happened to her when I see him."

"Wilton?"

"What you want, little brother?"

"Let's go, blood. I don't feel so good."

"Yeah, you are lookin' a little peaked. C'mon." Cooper made a slight, mocking bow to Marchetti and Tate. "Later, fellas. Let's all keep in touch."

Cooper and Clagget walked from the office. A few minutes later Tate heard the rumble of the muscle car and then its fade.

"Clarenze?" said Marchetti.

"Not now, Eddie," said Tate. "I need to think."

The first thing Dimitri Karras did on Saturday morning, after he had put down half a cup of coffee, was phone his mother's first cousin, Homer Bacas, and ask him if it would be all right if Eleni spent the weekend out at his place in Burke, a Northern Virginia suburb of D.C. Homer had a nice house on Athens Road with a deep lot shaded by tall trees and a large vegetable garden featuring ripe, juicy tomatoes. Eleni always enjoyed her visits there. Homer said he'd invite her over for the Fourth and, without asking why, promised to honor Dimitri's request that he not mention to Eleni that her son had prompted the call.

The second thing Karras did was to gather Vivian Lee's few articles of clothing and toiletries, put them in one of his gym bags, and tell her that it was time to take a ride.

"Where we off to?" asked Vivian.

Karras said, "I'm taking you home."

Vivian looked vaguely betrayed, but there was something in Karras's tone that seemed to preclude further discussion. Karras finished his coffee and the two of them left the Trauma Arms.

They drove north on Wisconsin Avenue, out of the city. Vivian bent forward to light a cigarette in the wind, and when it had burned down to the filter she lit another off the first. She didn't try to argue or make conversation with Karras. Wisconsin Avenue became Rockville Pike.

"Go right up there," said Vivian, and Karras turned east onto Randolph Road.

They got over to Viers Mill and made another turn, entering a neighborhood of smallish houses originally offered to World War II veterans on the GI Bill. Vivian was in the place in which she had been raised. Her anger flared.

"This is about last night, is that it?"

"What?"

"The murder last night, at Marcus's record store. It was connected to those guys who were at Eddie's office, right?"

Karras shrugged. "I have no idea."

"Sure you do. You're worried about me. You don't think I can take care of myself."

Karras put on his shades. "I think you can take care of yourself fine. I just don't want you around anymore, that's all."

Vivian dragged on her cigarette. She tapped ash onto her jeans and rubbed the ash in roughly until it disappeared. She hit her cigarette, pitched it into the wind.

"You don't want me around."

"That's right."

"Why take me home, then? Why not just let me hit the streets?"

"I pulled you out of that place. You're my responsibility. I'm taking you home."

Vivian chuckled. "God, you're such a hypocrite. You wake up this morning and you decide that you want to be my daddy. But just last night you were ready to fuck me. So who are you, Dimitri? Or don't you know?"

"Where's your house?" said Karras.

Vivian said, "Just up ahead."

Karras parked across the street from a boxy one-story house with peeling white paint. A young man stood on the porch reading a racing form, a short pencil wedged behind his ear. A chain-link fence ran around the house, with herb and flower gardens taking up the entire front yard. A small pond sat in the middle of the herb garden, a miniature concrete temple by its side. Lily pads floated in the copper-colored water, and large goldfish flashed beneath the pads in the sun. An old Chinaman with a face like a walnut sat in a beach chair by the pond, staring into the water, and a Chinese woman who could have been fifty or eighty tended the flower garden nearby on her hands and knees. She looked over at the Karmann Ghia, stared at Vivian for a while without expression, then pulled some weeds from alongside a ground cover of purple phlox.

"My mother," said Vivian with contempt.

"Who's that in the chair? Your father?"

"My mother's father. He must be a hundred years old. My God, these people never die."

"They will," said Karras.

"Oh, there'll always be someone else to replace them. All my life we had ten, fifteen people living in that house. Relatives, friends, guys who worked in the kitchen at my father's restaurant. Sometimes I didn't know who they belonged to. You have no idea."

"So you had a lot of people around the house. And I bet a few of them even had the nerve to love you. Is that the worst you can say about it?"

"You don't understand."

The woman was looking at Vivian again from inside the fence. Vivian wiped her eyes dry with the palm of her hand.

"Go on," said Karras.

"I'll be out of here tomorrow. You know that, don't you? I'll be down on the Mall for the fireworks and I'll see someone I know and then I'll just be gone. I won't come back this time, either. I don't belong here."

"What you do after I split is your business," said Karras. "It makes no difference to me."

"Thanks. Thanks a lot."

"Listen, Vivian —"

"What? You're going to give me advice now? Jesus. Like I need advice from a guy like you."

"You're right. Go on, Vivian. Just go."

Vivian got out of the car, slammed the door shut. "You know what it is? You're old, that's all. Tired and old."

"I know," said Karras, but she was already halfway across the street.

He watched her walk inside the front gate. The mother said something to her sharply in Chinese, and Vivian ridiculed her loudly as she walked by. Karras could only guess what the mother had said; walking through the garden toward the house in her paisley halter top and tight jeans, her lips painted red, Vivian looked somewhat like a fifteen-dollar whore.

As she walked on, the young man on the porch made a comment, and Vivian knocked the racing form from out of his hands. He smiled, then stopped smiling as he looked across the street at Karras, straight into his eyes. Karras had no doubt that the young man would cut him, and take pleasure in it, if he ever saw him come around again in his sporty little car. Karras put the Ghia in first and pulled away from the curb.

On the way back into town, Karras stopped at a rec center on University Boulevard and watched a pickup game being played between five young men. Karras asked if they needed a sixth man and was invited into the game. None of his shots fell, and he was used on D. By the end of the game his teammates had stopped passing him the ball. He walked back to his car with a slight limp, listening to the laughter of the players still on the court. He had turned his ankle, and his left eye throbbed where he had caught a hard 'bow from an eighteen-year-old kid.

TWENTY-ONE

Jimmy Castle heard the honk of the Firebird. He buttoned the imitation pearl snaps on his favorite shirt and slipped his feet into his wedge-heeled shoes, leaving his room and taking the stairs up to the foyer of the house.

Standing in the foyer, he could see his mother in her bedroom, doing her traction, sitting up straight in the chair with her headgear on and facing the door.

"You leavin'?" she said, without moving her head.

"Yeah, Ma."

Dewey honked the horn again. Jimmy suddenly remembered where he had stashed his smokes the night before when his father had surprised him by coming downstairs. Jimmy had quickly tossed the cigs between the flour bin and the rice bin in the kitchen before his dad could see.

"You gonna be late?"

"No, Ma."

Jimmy went into the kitchen, opened the cabinet over the wall oven, stood on his toes, and felt around for his softpack. He pulled the cigarettes out quickly, sending a wooden bin out to the floor with a dull crash.

"What the heck was that, Jimmy?"

"Nothin'! It's all right!"

Some rice had spilled from the bin. Jimmy began to scoop it back in with his hand when he heard the horn again. Dewey had really landed on it this time. Jimmy left some grains of rice on the linoleum floor and slid the bin back in the cabinet. He slipped the pack of smokes behind his sock and headed toward the front door.

"Have fun, honey," yelled his mother.

"I will."

Jimmy looked back once more into the kitchen before opening the door. He saw the white rice on the rust-colored linoleum floor. He hesitated, thinking that he should go back and finish cleaning it up. His mom might come downstairs, slip on it, and reinjure her back. But he didn't want to piss Dewey off.

He left the house and jogged down the walkway to where the Green Ghost sat idling in the street.

They stopped at Country Boy on Georgia Avenue in Wheaton and picked up a couple cold six-packs of Schlitz. Jimmy used his older brother's draft card for ID, a formality for the old guy at the register, who had been selling beer to underage kids for years. Out in the Firebird, they tore the rings off three cans and got on their way. As soon as they hit the Beltway, Jerry fired up a joint. They smoked half of it down on the way to 95.

"You got the tickets, Jerry?" said Jimmy.

"Huh?" said Jerry. It was hard to hear Jimmy from the backseat; Dewey had *BTO 2* cranked up pretty loud.

"The tickets, man."

"The tickets?" Jerry faked a freak-out look, and Dewey laughed. Jimmy could tell that Jerry was just jacking him off. They had bought the tickets to the Rick Derringer concert at the Baltimore Civic Center a month back, and even though Jerry was kind of a burnout, he would never have left the tickets at home.

Jerry was lighting a match under the fat number again to give it another good seal. The windows were closed, making the smoke thick inside the car. It was hot, and sweat dripped down Jimmy's back beneath his long-sleeved shirt. Jimmy leaned forward, put his head between the buckets.

"Who's openin' for Derringer, man?" said Jimmy.

"The ticket says 'a Special Guest,'" said Jerry. "I bet it's fuckin' Edgar, man."

"That would be bad," said Jimmy, though he always got weird vibes now when he heard Edgar Winter. He had puked really bad one time listening to 'Frankenstein' after he and Jerry had smoked a bunch of green on top of a bottle of Strawberry Hill.

"You think Rick Derringer's a queer?" said Dewey.

"Huh?" said Jerry.

"Check out the cover of *All-American Boy*. The guy's wearin' makeup and shit."

Traffic on 95 was fairly heavy. Dewey accelerated, used the right lane to pass a green Pinto. He shot back across the middle lane and into the left, flooring the Firebird as he tilted his head back to drink the last of his beer.

"Dude," said Jerry, smiling, his head moving back and forth to the BTO.

"Hey, slow down, man," said Jimmy.

"Fuck you, Toothpick," said Dewey. He tossed the empty Schlitz can over his shoulder to the backseat, reached into the paper bag beside him for another.

Jerry Baluzy relit the joint. He hit it hard and passed it over to Dewey. Dewey took a hit, held on to the weed while a thought came into his head. He hunched down low and got comfortable in his seat.

"*King Suckerman* was bad," said Dewey. He had been thinking about the movie all morning and had put the depressing aspect of it out of his mind. "You know, it would be rough as shit to be a pimp."

"Yeah," agreed Jerry. "And if I was gonna be one, I'd be King Suckerman. 'Cause King Suckerman had *all* the bitches. The black bitches *and* the white bitches. Even had him a Chinese ho, too."

"Gimme some of that, Dewey," said Jimmy. He had noticed that the joint was getting pretty small.

Dewey turned his head, smiled at Jerry, held up the roach. His eyes were pink and dilated, and hair had fallen about his face.

"What, you want this, Toothpick? This thing's about the size of your dick."

Looking at Jerry, Dewey let his hand slip off the wheel. The Green

Ghost went off the road with the gas pedal pinned to the floor. The Firebird crossed the grassy center island and landed in the path of an oncoming tractor-trailer.

Dewey Schmidt screamed like a girl while Jerry Baluzy coughed a spray of blood against the windshield, his heart exploding in his chest. Just before the eighteen-wheeler hit, Jimmy Castle pictured his mother, and rice scattered on a kitchen floor.

TWENTY-TWO

asheed Adamson's viewing was held on Saturday night at the Jarvis Funeral Home on U Street. Dimitri Karras put a blue blazer on over a white shirt and yellow slacks. His only tie was a wide flower-patterned job in fluorescent colors. He skipped the tie and wore the long collar points of his shirt outside the blazer's lapels.

Upon entering, Karras stood in the back of the room, nodding to anyone who made eye contact with him but otherwise keeping to himself. Marcus Clay, Elaine Taylor, and Cheek walked in and went straight to a middle-aged woman wearing black who had been the center of attention since Karras had arrived. Marcus gave her a kiss, hugged her, and held her hand. Karras supposed that this was Rasheed's mother.

When Marcus and his party had moved away, Karras finally went forward and gave his sympathies to Rasheed's mother. She thanked him politely, though she seemed confused at his presence. He excused himself and stood by Rasheed's closed casket, taking in the scent of the surrounding bouquets of orchids and other flowers. Karras said a short prayer, did his *stavro*, and kissed the casket.

He walked over to Marcus, who stood to the side talking to Rasheed's brother, Al. Karras shook Marcus's hand, then Al Adamson's.

"Good of you to come, man," said Adamson.

"My sympathies," said Karras.

Adamson nodded. He wore a black suit with a black shirt and solid gray tie, a pearl-tipped tack holding the tie in place, and black alligator-skin shoes, shined to a high gloss. Adamson had a full beard and a shaved head. His shoulder muscles bunched to a thick neck. Karras could see the cut of Adamson's arms and chest beneath the tailored suit.

"You get your mom out the city?" said Clay.

Karras nodded. A look passed between Adamson and Clay.

"Dimitri?" said Clay.

"Yeah?"

"You don't mind, Al and me, we got a few things we need to discuss."

"Okay."

"Talk to you tomorrow, hear?"

Karras went to where Elaine stood, kissed her on the cheek. He left the funeral home and walked across U Street to his car.

"Saturday night," said Eddie Marchetti. "Nothing on."

"What's that?" said Clarence Tate.

Tate stared out the window into the darkness. He could hear the faint thump of bass from the disco down the street.

"I was just sayin' that Saturday is the worst night of the week for TV." Marchetti looked sadly at the Sony across the room. On the screen, a toothy white guy in a blue uniform was smiling at something another toothy white guy had said. "*Emergency.* Christ."

Tate walked across the room and turned off the set. He had a seat in front of Marchetti's desk.

"Eddie, we need to talk."

"About what?"

"About figuring out what to do about Wilton Cooper. About cutting our losses here. About getting rid of that inventory back there and closing up shop. I think it's time to discuss it, don't you?"

"Take care of it, Clarenze. That's what I'm overpaying you for, right?" Marchetti smiled weakly.

Clarence Tate shook his head. It wouldn't help to say anything else. Tate would have to figure everything out his own self. Eddie was just plain hopeless.

Marchetti stared at the Sony's gray tube. "I wish it were Sunday, Clarenze. *Kojak* night."

"Damn, Eddie —"

"What, you don't like Kojak?"

"I like him all right."

"Kojak knows how to dress."

"Man's got some bad vines," admitted Tate. "I'll give you that."

"You got a favorite *Kojak*, Clarenze?"

"Not really."

"*I* got a favorite." Marchetti leaned forward.

Tate sighed. "Go ahead, Eddie."

"Okay. There's this Mafia guy, and he has a son, a real loser. For one reason or another the son puts a hit out on Kojak, kills someone else along the way. Now this Mafia guy, he and Kojak, they go way back, but because of the kid the don's lost Kojak's respect. The Mafia don, he tries to talk Kojak out of going after the kid. He makes the mistake of calling Kojak Theo — trying to hit a nerve, for old time's sake and all that. The camera moves in on Savalas, who corrects the guy by saying, 'It's Lieutenant Kojak.' Like, you don't know me all that well anymore to be callin' me Theo. Really powerful shit. Anyway, in the end Kojak guns the kid down in the street. Some lady comes by and says, 'Who was that guy?' meaning the kid. And Kojak says, 'He was nobody, lady. Nobody at all.' I'm tellin' you, Clarenze, every time I see that one show, I get the chills."

Marchetti's eyes went somewhere else. He rubbed his jowls.

"You know, Clarenze, I never wanted no one to get hurt."

"I know it, Eddie."

"I only wanted to come down here and make a name for myself so I could go back up to Jersey with my head up. I was afraid that if I didn't do something to show my family, I'd end up a nobody myself, y'know what I mean?"

Tate nodded, waited for Marchetti to go on. But Marchetti didn't say anything else, and Tate stood out of his chair.

"Hey, where you goin'?"

"Home, to relieve my parents. Gonna put my little Denice to bed."

"Clarenze —"

"Huh-uh, Eddie. I need to be there for her before she goes to sleep."

Tate was halfway across town, driving east in his Monte Carlo, when a plan began to form in his head.

TWENTY-THREE

I n all of Marcus Clay's twenty-seven years, he had never seen so many Maryland and Virginia license plates on a Sunday morning in the District. As he drove his Riviera across town to church, it seemed that every suburban family and carload of college kids was headed into D.C. The Metrobuses were full, too, and people of all ages and colors were walking down the streets, carrying coolers and blankets folded under their arms. The big celebration had begun.

At the All Souls Baptist Church, the pews were all occupied, but as soon as the service ended the parishioners headed out quickly, eager to change into shorts and T-shirts and get their spots on the Mall or settle into the choicest picnic areas of Rock Creek.

Outside the church, Clay saw George Dozier head down the polished concrete steps to his ride, a brown Mercury Marquis, parked out front on the street.

"Hey, George!" called Clay.

Dozier stopped, turned around. "Marcus."

Clay went down to where Dozier stood, his keys in his hand. "George, man, I been looking for you."

"Here I am. But I'm kind of in a hurry. My mom put me in charge of the barbecue today."

"Shoot, George, *everyone*'s in a hurry today. I need to talk to you, man, about Rasheed's case. You told me —"

"Yeah, I know."

"Look, George, I tell you what. We're just a couple of blocks from U Street, right? How about I buy you lunch at Ben's?"

Dozier thought it over. "I can't spare more than fifteen, twenty minutes, Marcus. Don't want to get Moms upset."

"I won't keep you, man. Let's go."

Clay knew that Dozier couldn't resist a free lunch at Ben's Chili Bowl. What kind of real Washingtonian could?

"So — pass me that hot sauce, George — the other night, you said you were working some undercover thing."

"Yeah, that's right." George Dozier looked down the counter at Ben's, packed with folks in church clothes and others who were casually dressed. "Been working on something right here in Shaw the last six months or so."

Clay used a knife and fork to cut a portion out of his chili burger. Dozier had a couple of chili dogs on a plate in front of him. He picked one up and took a healthy bite.

"Mmm," said Dozier.

"What kind of thing you got goin' on?"

Dozier wiped his mouth. "Been runnin' this citywide scam down on these thieves. Got a storefront operation set up on Twelfth, between U and V. Call it G and G Trucking Service. A bunch of us cops in plainclothes sit behind a long counter, take the walk-in trade. You wouldn't believe it, man: Once the word got out on the street, *everyone* in this town who had stolen goods to sell started coming in to see us. They think we got a high-end fence operation going on. We tell 'em we work for some Jew, but the Jew, he's out of town. All kinds come in: office burglars, home burglars, pickpockets sellin' credit cards, stickup boys, junkies, you name it. Lot of 'em selling guns. Chief Cullinane says half of them's recidivists —"

"Recidivists?"

"Repeat offenders, back on the street."

"How you know that?"

"We got their names, numbers, addresses, all that. Been runnin' this operation for the last six months. Next week we're gonna shut it down, go to their homes or where they're stayin', arrest them then."

"Now wait a minute, George. How'd you get this cast of characters to give up their names and addresses to a bunch of plainclothes cops?"

Dozier was finishing up his first dog. He swallowed, then gave Clay a wide grin. Clay could picture the same exact smile on little George Dozier's face back when the two of them were alley-running kids.

"Here's the beauty of it, Marcus. We held a raffle."

"A raffle?"

"Yeah. You believe that shit? Raffled off an El Dorado, man, and don't you know that damn near every man walked in that joint filled out a card. Called it the GYA raffle."

"What's GYA stand for?"

"Got Ya Again. You remember back in February, when those white cops grew their hair kinda long, impersonated Mafia dons, ran a similar operation down? It was all over the papers and the TV, called it the Sting?"

"Sure, I remember."

"Well, this here's the same kind of thing. So we decided to use those initials: GYA, for Got Ya Again."

"Funny so many would fall for it the second time around."

"That's what a lot of the brass in the department said, that it wouldn't work. And there was that unspoken thing, since it was all brothers runnin' this operation, that we wouldn't have the brains or the wherewithal to pull it off. But we *are* pulling it off. Got over a million dollars in goods already recovered, Marcus."

"Congratulations, George."

"Yeah, I'm proud. Gonna be a boost for my career, and for a lot of other good brothers, too."

Clay ate his burger and waited for Dozier to finish his second chili dog. Dozier used the rest of the bun to mop the fallen beans and sauce off the plate.

"George?"

"Yeah."

"You hear anything on Rasheed?"

Dozier nodded shortly, looked down at his clean plate. "Heard plenty, Marcus."

"You got friends in Homicide?"

"Yeah, but they're careful about givin' out too much. No, I found out what you were lookin' for by talking to the FBI and ATF boys we got working with us on the GYA thing. Got close to a couple of them these last six months."

"The Feds are involved?"

"Uh-huh, and those Federal boys work fast. Turns out the group that robbed your store are wanted for a whole lot of shit, and not just in D.C."

"Like what?"

"There was this shotgun murder at a drive-in this past week, down in North Carolina. A car registered to a Wilton Cooper was seen driving the suspect, white boy named Bobby Ray something-or-other, away. Then on Friday was that slaughter up in Marriottsville, near Baltimore. You read about that, right?"

"I read it."

"Whoever did it burned the place down, but they got the tire markings, the shells, and some shot patterns, and they matched the double-aught loads. Same as the Carolina kill. Same prints, too." Dozier looked Clay square in the eyes. "Same everything as in your shop."

"Damn."

"Uh-huh. This Cooper is one bad nigger, on the for real side. Was some kind of king inside the walls of Angola. One of the suspects, got a yard-long record on him, was incarcerated with Cooper down there. This suspect's got a brother, and they think he's with them, too."

"What about the white boy?"

"No paper on him, but everyone makes him as the main triggerman. Way it appears, he just plain likes to kill. Question is, what connects them, motivewise, to you? Or was it something they had against Rasheed?"

"Rasheed was good. I don't know why they picked my store, George. I wish I did, but I don't."

"Well, they're gonna get 'em."

"Got a good lead, huh?"

"Shoot, man, they left a trail so bright, blind man could see it. Had this girl they asked directions to the night of the murder, she described the car they were drivin' down to wraparound stripes on the rear quarter panel. I saw the girl myself on Saturday, giving her statement in the station. Dark-skinned girl, looked like Carol Speed."

"Carol Speed. She the one played with Pam Grier in that prison movie set down in the Philippines?"

Dozier nodded. "*The Big Bird Cage.* Anyway, the way she described the ride, it was like they picked out the most noticeable set of wheels they could. Like they were lookin' to get caught."

"What were they drivin'?"

"Chrysler product with a big-ass spoiler on the back."

"Plymouth Superbird?"

"The sister version, by Dodge. Daytona Charger. Kind you usually see Chinese boys drivin'."

"So everyone thinks they're still in town?"

"Yeah. They found Cooper's original vehicle, a red Challenger, stashed in a wooded area in Bladensburg, someplace like that."

"Should be easy to spot 'em."

"All the local law enforcement's got the description of the men and the car now. Like I say, they'll get 'em. I just hope to God they do before those boys hurt someone else." Dozier looked at Clay, Clay's eyes fixed and staring ahead. "You all right, Marcus?"

"Yeah, George, I'm fine. Thanks for looking into it, man."

"I don't know what you can do with it."

"Can't do nothin'. Just tryin' to make some sense out of all this, for my own piece of mind." Clay took his wallet from his back pocket, signaled the aproned teenager who stood beside the grill.

"Hold on, Marcus." Dozier spoke to the grill man. "Young fella? How about another one of these chili dogs."

"Damn, George. I thought Moms was waitin' on you to get the barbecue going."

"She is. But I don't get in here as much as I used to. You come to Ben's, you might as well go ahead and fill it on up."

"Good dogs," said Clay.

"Like to make you cry."

Marcus Clay crossed Connecticut Avenue on foot, hit the sidewalk, walked north against the flow. He stepped around a tourist carrying a miniature American flag mounted on a stick, and bumped into her husband, who wore plaid shorts and athletic socks pulled up to the knee.

"Pardon me."

"Excuse me," said Clay to the tourist, and that's when Clay saw Clarence Tate standing in front of the locked door of Real Right Records.

Clay went to his storefront, stood eye to eye with Tate. "You lookin' for somethin', man?"

"What all good people are lookin' for," said Tate, spreading his hands palms out. "Peace."

"I don't need no abstracts. I'm askin' what you're doin' here for real."

Tate shrugged in a loose way. "Came to talk to you, Marcus, that's all. Figure we got a mutual interest in working this thing out."

Clay looked around him, past the loiterers and the pedestrians. Traffic inched along amidst a shimmering heat mirage in the street. "Cooler and quieter inside," he said, motioning his head toward the store entrance.

"You askin' me in?"

Clay unlocked the door and said, "Come on."

TWENTY-FOUR

Dimitri Karras looked out the front window of his apartment late Sunday morning. One block west, a mass of pedestrians moved slowly up Connecticut; Karras saw an opportunity to off the rest of his weed. He made a cup of coffee, scaled out the remainder of his dope, bagged it at the cable-spool table in his living room. He did a couple of bong hits and left the Trauma Arms.

Karras wore baggy, lightweight cotton trousers with deep pockets in which he kept his OZs. A Hawaiian shirt worn tails out covered the bulging pockets. He went down to the circle and sat on the edge of the fountain, talking to a couple of people he knew and looking out for narcs. He didn't usually ply his trade in the open here, but he knew the cops had better things to do on the Fourth, especially *this* Fourth, than to bother with a low-level dealer like him. After a while Karras saw an eager guy named Don Goines who was bone dry and offered to take the dope off his hands for retail. Karras made the deal sitting on a bench at the edge of the circular concrete walkway. He pocketed two hundred in twenties and went on his way.

He bought a Sunday *Post* and another cup of coffee and returned to the circle, where he had a seat on an unoccupied bench. Karras read the A section, then Book World, and then Metro, his routine. Halfway into Metro he came upon a story detailing a Saturday accident on 95 in which a car carrying three boys had collided with a tractor-trailer head-on. All three boys and the driver of the truck had been killed. Open alcohol containers, marijuana, and paraphernalia were found in the car's wreckage. The boys were Silver Spring residents, and one of them was named Jimmy Castle.

"Hey, Dimitri, what's goin' on?"

"What?"

Karras looked at the face in front of him: a law-firm messenger he knew named Mike, or Mick, something like that. Karras hadn't noticed his approach.

"Dimitri, you okay?"

"Yeah, I'm fine."

"You don't look so good, dude. You're whiter than a fuckin' sheet."

Karras looked down. He had dropped the Metro section, and it lay in the grass at his feet.

"I'm all right."

"Hey, Dimitri." The messenger lowered his voice. "I'm lookin' to cop."

"Cop?"

"Yeah, I'm lookin' for some smoke, man."

"I'm done with that," said Karras. "I'm cooked."

"You look cooked, dude," the messenger said, but Karras was up and walking away.

Karras had a beer at Benbow's and a second one right behind it. He knew he could get drunk very quickly on an empty stomach, if that was his intent, but Karras was not a drinker, and he was still rational enough to realize that getting drunk would neither bring Jimmy Castle back to life nor change what he, Karras, had done. He drank a third beer anyway and stepped out into the heat.

Karras badly wanted to see Marcus, but he couldn't face him yet. He thought of going to a movie, but he had seen the feature at the Janus, and there was the possibility that Noah Castle was there, ushering the show. Of course Noah wouldn't be working, not one day after his little brother's death. But Karras didn't care to take the chance.

Karras stood in the middle of the Connecticut Avenue sidewalk. People went around him, all of them moving south. He began to feel nauseous out in the sun. He walked back to the Trauma Arms and took the steps up to his apartment, stopping once on the stairs to get his breath. Inside, he went straight to the bathroom, where he vomited his beers and morning coffee into the toilet. The beer bile stung shooting through his nose. He pulled himself up and washed his face with cool water from the sink. He staggered out into his bedroom, dropped onto his mattress, closed his eyes, and fell asleep.

"So," said Marcus Clay. "*Talk* about it."

"It's about Wilton Cooper," said Clarence Tate.

Clay said, "I figured it was."

"Want you to know somethin', man, straight off."

"Go ahead."

"I had nothin' to do with what happened in your shop."

"Never thought you did. Was your boss, though, that brought those boys north."

"He didn't know nothin' about the consequences. Eddie's just simple like that."

"He's responsible, just the same."

"In the same way that you're responsible. You and your Greek friend."

"Tell me somethin' I *don't* know, Tate."

They stood on the sales floor, Tate with his back against the Soul rack, Clay straight up with his arms folded across his chest.

"Okay," said Tate. "It was Cooper's bitch killed your employee. The ugly white boy with the Zayre's-lookin' vines pulled the trigger."

"I know it."

"Wasn't just your employee they dusted. They killed a bunch of bikers out in Howard County as well."

"I know that, too."

"Cooper's crew is just a killin' machine."

"Uh-huh."

"You know all that."

"That's right."

"But you haven't told the cops what you know."

"Right again," said Clay. "And neither have you. Otherwise, you'd be talkin' to them right now and not to me."

"Yeah. I'm talkin' to you."

"You know where Cooper's at?"

Tate nodded. "I got the number where they're staying, over in Northeast. Take about a couple of seconds for the police to be over there and bust that door down."

"But you're not gonna call the police."

"No."

"Why not?"

" 'Cause Cooper threatened the life of my baby girl."

Clay unfolded his arms and leaned back against a rack. Now he stood eye level with Tate.

"You got a daughter?"

"Yeah." Tate smiled. "Girl named Denice. Prettiest little thing you ever did see."

"Why not have her mother take her out of town until it's over?"

"She ain't got no mother. The woman who bore her lives on the streets. She started spikin', fell in love with that shit. Forgot all about the love she had for her daughter. *I'm* raising my girl now. Anyway, it ain't never gonna be over."

"Cops raid that joint, they're gonna put Cooper and the rest away for life. You won't have to worry about no threats he made."

"That's bullshit, Marcus, and you know it is. Wilton Cooper's one of those niggers got so he loves the inside. On the street he's hunted. But inside those walls he's something else. A hero, man. Incarceration doesn't punish a man like Cooper. The longer the bit, the greater his reward. He can have anything done, have *anyone* smoked from in there."

"I hear you, man."

"Question I have for you is why haven't *you* been talkin' to the cops?"

"Who's askin'? Your boss pullin' your strings, or you come here your *own* self?"

"Just me," said Tate.

"Okay," said Clay. "I thought there might be a better alternative than the kind of justice the courts gonna deal out to Wilton Cooper. Thought I might have the opportunity to meet with the man, face-to-face, before the law gives him his gift, puts him where he wants to be."

"Then we're thinkin' the same way."

Clay said, "What'd you have in mind?"

Tate pulled a folded piece of paper from his pocket. He motioned Clay, and the two of them went to the island in the center of the store. Tate placed the paper on the counter, used his fingers to smooth out the folds.

"I ain't much of an artist," said Tate. "But this here's a place where I thought I could arrange it so the two of you could meet. It would have to be tonight."

"During the fireworks."

"Right. On account of all that noise."

"You think you can get him to come?"

"I think he's waitin' on my call. Truth is, that's why he's hangin' around D.C. He don't give a *fuck* about the money you took. It's all about you."

Clay stared at the crude pencil diagram. "All right, Tate. Like I said: *Talk* about it."

They planned for the better part of an hour. Clay went in the backroom and phoned Elaine, told her he'd be home a little later in the day. When he came out, he saw Tate flipping through the C bin in Soul.

"What you lookin' for, man?"

"*Give More Power to the People.*"

"The Chi-Lites. You mean you don't own that?"

"I wore the grooves down on my original."

"Well, it's on order," said Clay.

"Can't let that inventory build up, right? Got to turn it quick."

"You know it. I'll put it aside for you when it comes in."

"Thanks."

Clay watched Tate withdraw an LP, read the liner notes on the back. "You're into that neoclassic sound, huh?"

"That what they call it? Shoot, man, I just love good music."

Clay looked Tate in the eye. "Let me ask you something. Why's a smart guy like you workin' for a dumb-ass like Eddie?"

"Just happened, I guess."

"That doesn't explain why you stay."

"I don't intend to be with him much longer. Tryin' to make this one last score, you want to know the truth. Lookin' for a fence to take this big load we got. Eddie and me, we got this deal. Gonna split the take on that one and go our separate ways. And there's another thing. I know it sounds like bullshit, man, but I just don't believe in walking out on a man after I've made a commitment to him."

"It don't sound nothin' like bullshit to me," said Clay. "Matter of fact, I could use a man like you right here."

"Say what?"

"I'm offering you a job. You can start on Tuesday morning, when I get this place clean and opened back up. Got a lot of plans, Clarence. Soon as we get rollin' here, I'll be lookin' for another location. Gonna need a good man to manage it for me, and the one after that, too."

Tate smiled. "Thanks, man. But like I say, I been counting on that money from the fence."

Clay rubbed his jaw. "Okay. How about this? I'll find a fence for Eddie. Let me take care of that. Eddie'll make whatever he can make. In the meantime, I'm gonna give you a grand, out of that ten thousand I got left, to come to work for me right away. Call it a bonus, Clarence. Call it anything you want."

"Thousand dollars?"

"That's right."

"Need to think on it, man."

"Think on it hard."

"I will."

Clay wrote his phone number on a slip of paper and handed it to Tate.

"You call me later, hear?"

"Soon as I talk to Cooper."

"Right."

They walked to the door. "Where you off to now, Clarence?"

"Got something to take care of for you over at Meridian Heights."

"Then?"

Tate shrugged. "Go home, I guess. See my little girl."

"No celebration tonight?"

"Ain't *my* independence day," said Tate.

"I heard that."

"Anyway, tonight's Sunday, right? Round ten o'clock tonight, I usually be watchin' *Petey Greene's Washington*."

"Petey Greene's somethin'. "

"You *know* he is.

"Marcus —"

"Don't say it. Don't be wishin' me no good luck. It's *all* luck, man. If there's one thing I learned overseas, that's all it is."

"All right, man."

"All right."

They shook hands. Clay unlocked the door. He let Tate out and watched him walk down the street.

Clarence Tate double-parked his Monte Carlo across from the Meridian Heights condo on 15th. On his left, people milled about and partied in Meridian Hill Park, staking out their spots for the evening's festivities. The park sloped from the edge of the plateau to the beginnings of downtown, and its high ground afforded a clear view of the city, the monuments, and the Mall. Meridian Hill was a prime viewing point for the city; the park was going to be happening tonight.

Tate went up the steps, entered the condo building. Andy, the security guard, was not behind his desk. A bulletin board where notices and local ads were hung was mounted near the elevator. On the board, a handmade flyer advised residents that the doors leading to the roof would be padlocked on July 4, as insurance restrictions prohibited parties and other group activities on this, the most desirable of outdoor party nights. Tate went back out to the street.

A boy dribbled a basketball on the sidewalk out front, putting it through his legs and around his back, occasionally punctuating a particularly good head-fake with a simulated, get-up J. Then he went back into his dribble. The kid, Tate thought, had pretty good moves.

Tate approached the boy. "Hey."

"Hey, wha's up."

The boy gave Tate a quick appraisal but did not stop dribbling the ball.

"Want to make some money?"

"Ain't dealin' no drugs."

"I ain't ask you to run no drugs, boy. I'm talkin' about straight-up money for five minutes' worth of honest work."

The boy stopped dribbling. "What I gotta do?"

Tate made a head motion. "Step on over to my short."

They went to the black Monte Carlo. Tate reached inside, withdrew a brown paper bag wrapped around a bottle. He pulled a twenty-dollar bill from his slacks and showed it to the kid.

"Okay," said Tate. "Here's what I want you to do. 'Bout seven-thirty, eight o'clock tonight, when the sky starts to darken up, I want you to take this bottle of scotch into that building over there."

"Meridian Heights?"

"Yeah. There's a security guard works the desk inside."

"Old white dude. I seen him."

"That's right. I want you to give the bottle to the white dude. Tell him you found it out here on the street, that you got no use for it, something like that. Be friendly, man, like you mean it. Wish him a happy Fourth of July."

"Okay."

"He might be down in the boiler room by then. You know where that is?"

"You mean where the rats are at."

"But you know where it is."

"Uh-huh."

"Now, for all I know, he might already be deep into a drunk. Even if he is, I want you to give this bottle to him anyway."

"What you got in that bottle, some kind of poison and shit?"

"Watch your mouth, boy. And no, it ain't nothin' like that. I mean the man no harm. Just a plain old bottle of King George scotch is all it is, still got the seal on it. Like I said, it's a present, that's all."

The kid wiped his runny nose. "If there ain't nothin' to it, why you not takin' it to him your *own* self, then?"

"You want the money or not, boy?"

"I want it."

"Then do as I say." Tate handed the kid the bottle and the twenty-dollar bill. "One more thing, now. Anybody asks about me later on, you never seen me or talked to me, hear?"

"Sure."

"I come around here once a month, might want you to watch my M. C. from time to time while I got it parked on the street."

The kid stuffed the twenty into his pocket. "Cool."

Tate placed his hand on the kid's shoulder. "What's your name, boy?"

"Michael Hill."

"Look here, Michael. You handle that basketball pretty good."

Michael smiled. "Gonna play in the NBA."

"I believe you will. But don't forget about readin' those books, hear? Tough as it is out here, a man needs some kind of edge. Schoolin' will give it to you. And stay away from those knuckleheads be tellin' you it's uncool to learn."

"What my mom says."

"Your moms is right."

"Take it easy, man," said Michael, before he turned.

"Yeah, young brother," said Clarence Tate, watching the boy cross the street. "You take it easy, too."

Dimitri Karras woke to the sound of the phone ringing by his bedside, his shirt soaked in sweat, his hair wet on his forehead. He checked his wristwatch, saw that he had been asleep for hours. He closed his eyes, tried to remember if he had dreamed. The phone continued to ring. He reached over and snatched it out of its cradle.

"Yeah."

"Mitri."

"Marcus. What's up?"

"You all right, man?"

"I'm fine. What's up?"

"I gotta see you, man."

Karras didn't ask for an explanation. There was something in Marcus's tone that he had never heard before.

"Now?"

"Soon as possible. We need to talk."

"Okay," said Karras. "Where you want to hook up?"

"I'll meet you on the beach. Say, a half hour?"

"Right, Marcus. I'll see you then."

The line clicked off to a dial tone. Karras racked the receiver and sat up on the edge of the bed.

TWENTY-FIVE

Sherril Drive dropped away from upper 16th and wound down through the park, the serpentine road sloping steeply, leveling out at a bridge that crossed Rock Creek. Karras navigated the turns, parked the Karmann Ghia next to Marcus Clay's Riviera in a small lot.

Karras walked back over the bridge and took a bridle trail into the woods that rose and dipped alongside the creek. He hiked for a quarter mile, encountering no one, then jumped off a small embankment to a narrow strip of white sand at the water's edge. Marcus sat in the sand, his legs outstretched.

"Marcus."

"Dimitri. Thanks for comin', man."

They had been meeting at this place since childhood, a quiet, neutral spot in a park that had become an unofficial north-south dividing line separating the city by income and race. In the summer the oaks were full across the creek and blocked the view and muted the car sounds of Beach Drive. The water moved slowly here, and the air felt cool in the shade of the trees.

Clay said, "Have a seat."

"I'll stand. I been sleeping all day."

"Was gonna say, you look like you just crawled out of bed. You don't look so good."

"I know it." Karras dug his hands into his pockets. "Why'd you call me out, Marcus?"

Clay stood up, brushed sand off his tailored jeans. He found a flat stone and skipped it across the creek.

"I'm gonna ask you again, Marcus. Why'd you call me out?"

"All right." Clay turned to Karras. "You want it short and to the point, here it is. I'm squarin' off against Wilton Cooper and his boys tonight. Thought you might want to know."

"Squaring off."

"Gonna meet him face-to-face, the way he wants. The only way he understands."

"You know where he's at?"

"Clarence Tate knows. Tate's settin' it up."

"And you trust Tate."

"Yes, I do."

"Shit, Marcus, you know where Cooper and the rest of them are, why not just turn 'em in?"

"For what? So they can rehabilitate Cooper? Maybe they gonna rehabilitate that white boy got death in his eyes, too. You think?"

"Aw, hell, Marcus, *I* don't know."

"I know. I *know* what's got to be done. You can *believe* that."

"What the hell are you talkin' about, man? Revenge?"

"Revenge is a little boy's game. I'm talkin' about somethin' else."

"Justice," said Karras. "You've got some warped idea about justice. That's what this is about. Right?"

"That's right."

"Christ."

"Listen. Cooper came into my store, wrecked it, and took one of mine. And it wasn't just Rasheed they killed. They did those bikers out in Howard County, the ones were on the TV news. Blew up their shit on their own turf. Greased a man down in Carolina as well, and those are just the ones I know about. Those boys are on a killing spree. Someone's got to put a stop to it, and I'm not talkin' about puttin' them in handcuffs and leadin' them away to a warm bed and a hot meal. I mean stop it for real. Rasheed Adamson, he stood up for me when the time came. Now I gotta go on and do the same for him."

"Just you," Karras said bitterly. "You're gonna face these guys yourself."

"Not by myself. Rasheed's brother will be there. Thought you might want to come along, too."

"No," said Karras quickly. "Not me."

Clay said, "Suit yourself."

Karras walked to the edge of the creek, watched the run of brown water. "You think I like letting you down, Marcus? Is that what you think?"

Clay spoke softly. "You ain't never let me down, Dimitri. You always been a friend. But you just ain't the type to step up. To step up and *do* something, I mean. In the end, I guess I didn't expect you to join me. I just thought you might want me to give you the chance."

"The chance to kill a man. The chance to get killed. That's what this is. You can forget it, man, because it's not for me."

"Like I said, suit yourself."

"Right."

"You might want to get the girl out the way, though. At least do that. This doesn't work out, they're gonna come lookin' for Vivian, just for sport."

"I did it already," said Karras. "I took her home."

"Yeah, makes sense. You were done with her, I guess."

"I never fucked her, Marcus, if that's what you mean."

"Congratulations, man. You held back on gettin' a nut with a nineteen-year-old girl. Takes a real sensitive stud to make a sacrifice like that."

"Look, Marcus —"

"Next thing you know, you'll be tellin' me you're givin' up dealin'."

"I am," said Karras. He turned from the water to face Clay. "I'm through."

Clay looked into Karras's hollow eyes. "What *happened* to you, man? You ready to talk to me about it now?"

"What happened? I finally fucked up." Karras's voice shook. "I sold a bag of dope a couple days ago to Noah Castle's kid brother. The kid was in a car accident on Saturday with his friends. All of them got killed."

"What's that got to do with you?"

"The paper said they found dope and paraphernalia in the car. The kid was in high school, Marcus. I might as well have put a gun to his head myself and pulled the trigger."

"Bullshit, man. That's bullshit. You don't know what happened in that car. And that boy would have found a way to cop his herb whether you sold it to him or not. Anyway, where they grow it, people be dyin' over that shit every day. You ever stop to grieve about that? I mean, what'd you *think* all this time, Dimitri? All these fine times we been havin' these last few years, gettin' high, easy pussy anytime you want it, all that? You go up a mountain, man, sooner or later you gotta walk back down. Sooner or later you got to pay. Didn't you think there'd be a downside to all of this?"

"No. I guess I didn't think there would be."

"Yeah. You never have stopped to think. Long as I've been knowin' you it's been that way." Clay gave Karras a sad smile. "I remember the first time my mother brought me over to your neighborhood. Up till then, I had rarely been west of the park. You took me over to your playground, where we got into a game. All your other friends, they were trying to talk black around me, act street, put on a show for the nigger from Shaw. Not you. You didn't do it then and you've never done it since. At first I thought you were avoiding who we were. Then I started to wonder if you even noticed the differences between us."

"I noticed. But what? You tellin' me because you're black and I'm not we can't be friends?"

"We *are* friends. I love you like a brother, man, *you* know that. But the fact is, you've been sleepwalkin' through your whole life."

"Marcus, man —"

"I'm sorry, Dimitri. I thought that this time you'd be ready to step up. I shouldn't have expected so much."

"I'm sorry, too."

"Yeah, well." Clay checked his watch. "Gotta get out of here, man. You with me?"

"No."

"All right, then," said Clay.

Karras turned his head, listened to the crack of twigs beneath Clay's feet. The sound began to fade. Karras stared at his reflection, broken in the ripples of the creek. He looked behind him at the path on which they had arrived.

Marcus Clay was gone.

Wilton Cooper took a swig of Near Beer, looked at B. R. Clagget, naked and facedown on the bed. Dried blood was streaked on the boy's buttocks from where Cooper had withdrawn. The copy of *Pimp* was still in Clagget's limp hand; he had been reading it for a few minutes after Cooper had had his way with him, before he fell to sleep.

Cooper hadn't meant to be so rough. He surely hadn't meant to draw blood. But the boy was a weakbody to begin with, and now he was down with the fever, full-blown. Still, Cooper thought it his right to take a little ass from the boy. After all, could be the last nut he got for a long while. From this boy, anyway.

The phone rang on the nightstand. Someone answered the extension downstairs, then yelled for Cooper to pick it up. Cooper lifted the receiver, waited for the click-off sound of the extension.

"Yeah."

"Cooper?"

"It is me."

"Clarence Tate."

"Clar*enze*. What's up?"

"Got ahold of Marcus Clay."

"Okay."

"Clay wants to meet."

"Got his attention, huh?"

"Yeah. He wants to hand over the rest of the money. Tried to just give it to me, but I told him it wouldn't work. Told him that you wanted to see him face-to-face."

"You did good."

"I did what you asked. There's an apartment house on Fifteenth Street, just east of Meridian Hill Park, called Meridian Heights. Got a roof entrance and no security guard. I took care of that. Told Clay you'd meet him on the roof. You can take the elevator up to the top floor, then walk another flight of stairs to the roof."

"Why Meridian Heights?"

"I own a condo there. Know the layout, and it's safe. Public but not too public, if you know what I mean. Gonna be a bunch of noise around there tonight. Case *you* make some noise, no one'll notice."

"You always did strike me as smart."

"Can't be all that smart, talkin' to a man like you."

Cooper laughed. He stopped laughing and said, "Clarenze?"

"What."

"Just don't want any misunderstanding here. If this is some kind of setup —"

"It ain't no setup."

"If it *is*. I'm gonna pay a visit to your little girl — or someone I know will — and believe me, we gonna party down."

"Nine-thirty tonight," said Tate. "The fireworks'll be gettin' off by then."

"Nine-thirty," said Cooper. "Tell Trouble Man I'll be there."

Cooper racked the receiver. He went over to the bed and shook Clagget's bony shoulder.

"B. R. B. R., wake up."

Clagget rolled over on his back, exhaled slowly, opened his eyes. His breath was sour and held the promise of death.

"What, Wilton?"

"Rise and shine, little brother. We goin' out."

"Marcus."

"Yeah."

"It's Clarence Tate."

Clay put his hand over the phone, looked toward the bathroom where Elaine was showering. The bathroom door was ajar, and Clay lowered his voice.

"Talk about it."

"I set it up," said Tate. "They'll be on the roof of Meridian at nine-thirty. If they're smart, they'll be there sooner, and if you're smart you'll be there sooner than that."

"I hear you. Anything I need to know?"

"Like I told you before, the white boy is sick with something. Weak. That's Cooper's Mary, so I figure Cooper will stick with him. Most likely the two of them will use the elevator, then take the stairs the rest of the way. The elevator's slow —"

"You told me."

"All right. Take some chain cutters. They got the door to the roof padlocked."

"Okay. Anything else?"

"He talked about my daughter again on the phone."

"Relax."

"Kill him," said Tate.

"That's the idea."

"And after you kill him, kill him again."

"Better get ahold of your shit, Clarence."

"I can't help it, man. I want that devil out of my world."

Clay said, "I'm gonna do the best I can."

The shower stopped running. Clay hung up the phone. Elaine came from the bathroom wrapped in a towel. Clay stared at her as she went and stood before her mirror, rubbing lotion on her arms. She saw him in the reflection, his eyes still on her, and she turned to face him.

"What's wrong with you, Marcus?"

"Nothing, baby," said Clay, trying to smile. "You're just so goddamn beautiful, that's all."

Dimitri Karras felt strange, sitting in his favorite chair. Over the years, the seat cushion had conformed to his body, but this evening it was hard for him to find comfort there. The room was hot, and there was too much noise coming up from the street.

He moved to the couch, cleaned some pot in the overturned top of a shoe box, filled the bowl of the bong. He lit a match but did not put fire to the weed. He watched the flame burn down until it reached his fingers, blew the match out. He studied the smoke rising off the match.

Karras leaned back and closed his eyes.

On those occasions when he was looking for answers, Karras thought that it would be especially nice to have a father. If he had a father, he could take a walk with his father now, ask him about choices, direction, the steps you had to take to become a man. But Karras had no father. And Marcus, *he* had never had a father. It was another thing the two of them shared. Another reason, he supposed, that the two of them had gotten to be friends, and stayed friends. Why they had always stuck together, looked out for each other, too.

Behind his closed eyes, Karras pictured Marcus, standing alone.

The picture changed. Now he saw his mother, leaning against the sink, her arms folded, the bird building its nest behind her outside the kitchen window. Wilton Cooper was in the kitchen, too. He was smiling, and he was walking toward her. His shadow crawled up her chest and blackened her housedress as he approached.

Karras felt his heart thump in his chest. He tried to make the images of Marcus and his mother go away, but they would not.

When he opened his eyes the living room had darkened, and the sky outside the window had gone to slate.

Dimitri Karras went to take a shower, because that was what a man did before he dressed to leave the house.

"Where you going with that tool, Marcus?"

"Out."

Clay walked toward the front door with a set of chain cutters in his hand. Elaine was on his heels, crossing the room swiftly. He had tried to avoid her for the last half hour, but now her anger had boiled up to where he just had to go ahead and walk. He decided not to answer her rather than lie.

"Why are you being so evasive? You got something going on with Dimitri, is that it?"

Clay stopped at the door. "Look. I told you, I'm going out. That's all I got to say."

Elaine stood a few feet away, her arms folded across her chest. "Listen to me, Marcus. You and me made a promise to be together on everything from here on in, and for a long, long time. I want a future with you. I want to have your babies —"

"That's what I want, too."

"And now you're walkin' out of here all mysterious, with some kind of purpose in your step, you can't even tell me where it is you're off to. I'm no fool, Marcus; don't go treating me like one. This has something to do with Rasheed's death, doesn't it? You're on some kind of revenge trip, isn't that right?"

"Not revenge." Clay put his hand on Elaine's arm. "Look, baby . . ."

Elaine pulled her arm out of Clay's grasp. "Don't 'baby' me. Don't you soft talk me. You're gonna stand there and disrespect me like that, not even give me a chance to plead my case? Look at me, Marcus!"

"I am."

"You're never going to get as fine a woman as the one standing before you right now. I swear to you Marcus, you go out this door like this, I am *not* gonna be here when you come back."

"I love you, Elaine," said Clay. "You *know* I do. And I want all the things you want, for the both of us. That's what I've been workin' so hard for, and that's what I'm gonna keep workin' for, hear? Now, whatever you decide to do, that's up to you. But I've got to go now."

"Marcus —"

"Don't say nothin', baby. I've got to go."

He left the house, closed the door behind him. At the bottom of the steps he turned and looked at the light in the second-story window. He went to the Riviera, opened the door, and dropped the chain cutters behind the front seat.

Clay turned the ignition key, pulled out of his space. He drove down to Newton, hung a right. Coming out of the turn, he saw a white man with shoulder-length black hair and a black handlebar mustache, leaning against a small car. Clay slowed the Riviera to stop, put his head out the window.

"Hey," said Clay.

"Hey."

"Come to say good-bye?"

"Comin' *with* you."

"Decided to step up, huh?"

"That's right. Cooper made a play on my mother. And there's no way, Marcus . . ."

"What?"

"There's no way I'm lettin' you go up against him alone."

Clay eyes softened. There was pride there, and admiration, too. It had been a long time since Karras had seen Clay look at him like that.

"Well," said Clay, "get in."

"We takin' your ride?"

Clay nodded. "We're gonna take a real car tonight. Besides, tall as you're lookin' right now, you'd have trouble squeezing into that toy of yours."

Karras walked around to the passenger door, dropped into the shotgun bucket. He looked across the seat at Clay.

"What now?" said Karras.

"Gonna even up the odds."

"We got a few more comin' with us?"

"Don't need a few more," said Clay. "Just Al."

Marcus Clay pulled back on the shift, put the Riviera in gear.

TWENTY-SIX

ilton Cooper carried the suitcase holding the money and the drugs. Bobby Roy Clagget followed him down the stairs, a duffel bag in one hand, the other hand holding the banister for support. Clagget wore the coffee-stained pleated white baggies with a clear blue plastic belt cinched tightly at the waist, his blood-smudged baby blue rayon shirt patterned in navy blue seashells, and multicolored stacks with four-inch heels. Cooper, who felt that a man on his way to a gun party needed to be styling, had gone dark and classic: a maroon polo shirt tucked into reverse-pleated black slacks with canvas jazz oxfords on his feet.

They reached the bottom of the stairs and stood in the foyer of the house. Open doors gave to a cheaply furnished living room, where the Thomas brothers sat with their cousin Doretha and her two kids. Cooper and Clagget entered the room. Doretha brought the children into her arms at the sight of them, sat straight in her chair, managed to force a trembling smile.

"Ronald?" said Cooper.

"Yeah, Coop?"

"You and your brother get your shit together. We checkin' out."

Ronald and Russell rose from their seats simultaneously. Russell stabbed his Kool out in an ashtray and picked up a gym bag with an Adidas logo printed on its side.

Cooper withdrew a roll of green from the pocket of his slacks, counted out three hundred-dollar bills in an elaborate manner. "Here you go, baby." He dropped the bills on a particle-board lamp stand next to her seat.

"Thank you kindly," said Doretha, a thin, spidery woman with glaucomic eyes.

" 'Preciate your hospitality. Hope we didn't put you out."

"Oh, no," said Doretha. "No trouble at all."

"We'll be leavin' town tonight," said Cooper. "Don't expect we'll be seein' you again. But just so we don't misunderstand each other —"

"I don't know you no way," said Doretha, nodding her head, not looking into Cooper's eyes. "I never laid eyes on you in my life."

Cooper smiled, gave Doretha a little bow. "Was a pleasure makin' your acquaintance."

Ronald said, "See you around, Dodo. Say hello to Uncle Lee for us, hear?"

Russell nodded to Doretha and the children. All the men left the room and exited the back door of the house.

Doretha held her younger daughter, who had begun to cry, tightly against her chest.

"Let it out," said Doretha, patting the girl's back.

At the end of the alley, two boys watched while another boy lit an M-80 and rolled it under an overturned trash can. The boys ran away, the trash can lifting from the force of the explosion. In a nearby yard a family of four held Roman candles and marched in a wide circle. A string of firecrackers went off two blocks away; over the sound, Cooper and his men heard a drunken man screaming at a woman and the woman's pathetic, sobbing reply.

"Ain't nothin' but a house party tonight," said Russell.

"There it is," said Ronald.

Cooper jerked his head toward the car. "Get it uncovered," he said.

Ronald rolled the canvas tarp back off the Daytona. He and Russell folded the tarp and dropped it over the fence into Doretha's yard.

Cooper placed the suitcase in the Charger's trunk, retrieved Clagget's hunting vest, shut the lid. He tossed the vest to Clagget and the keys to Ronald.

"Want me for the wheel man?" said Ronald.

Cooper nodded. "Y'all sit up front. Me and B. R. gonna chill in the back."

They got into the car. Clagget set the duffel bag between him and Cooper. He unzipped the bag, reached in, passed Ronald his short-barreled .357 and Russell his revolver. Ronald checked the load, wrist-snapped the cylinder back in place. Russell opened the Adidas gym bag, pulled out the Baggie of cocaine. He dipped his pinky nail into the blow, did two jolts, fed Ronald the same way.

"Bad freeze," said Russell.

"Who you tellin'?" said Ronald, and the two of them touched skin. Cooper strapped both holsters under his arms, checked his .45s, fitted them, drew them quickly, fitted them again. Clagget thumbed shells into the sawed-off, slipped four more through the loops of his vest.

"Kick it over, Mandingo," said Cooper.

Ronald brought the car alive.

They drove down the alley, the sputter of the dual exhaust cutting the air. Russell reached into the sun visor, pulled free a fresh pack of cigarettes. He packed the smokes against his palm, then tore a hole in the bottom of the deck.

"Gimme one of them double-O's," said Ronald.

Russell Thomas withdrew two Kools. He lit Ronald's, lit one for himself.

Marcus Clay took Irving Street and then Michigan Avenue across town. The traffic thinned considerably as they headed east, though in all the neighborhoods through which they passed people had gathered on porches and others stood in groups, drinking beer, smoking cigarettes, leaning against cars in the street. Around Brookland, Clay slapped in a cassette that kicked off with "Little Child, Running Wild," his favorite Mayfield jam. By the time the song ended, they had parked in front of an open garage in a small commercial strip at the edge of the residential district near the north-south railroad line. Clay and Karras got out of the Riviera and walked across the street.

Al Adamson was under the hood of a canary yellow, suicide-door Continental, one droplight illuminating his cluttered double-bay garage. He stood up straight, cleaning his hands on a rag, and walked toward them.

Adamson wore a black fishnet T-shirt tucked into black plain-front flares. The flares ended an inch shy of his oilskin work shoes, revealing black thick-and-thin socks. Adamson's arm muscles rippled as he wiped his hands clean; his deep brown smoothly shaved dome shone in the light.

Adamson glanced at Karras's Hawaiian shirt, his eyes momentarily lighting with amusement. When he looked over at Clay his eyes had hardened and his mouth was set tight.

"Marcus."

"Al."

"You found the ones killed my brother?"

"On our way to meet 'em right now."

Adamson said, "I'll just go ahead and get my shit."

He went into a room at the back of the garage. Clay and Karras stood by the Lincoln, not speaking, listening to the tick of an STP clock mounted on the cinder-block wall. Karras didn't have to ask what Al Adamson had gone to retrieve; he already knew. The knowledge frightened him and excited him at the same time.

Adamson returned with an olive green pack. He set it on the tool bench against the far wall. Karras and Clay went over to the bench.

"Got two forty-fives and a thirty-eight Special," said Adamson.

"You and me on the automatics," said Clay. "Give the revolver to Karras."

"Here you go, man." Adamson handed Karras the .38. "It's ready to go."

"That's it, huh?"

Adamson nodded. "Point and shoot."

Karras held the gun loosely. He stared at it, turning it in his hand. Clay took a .45 from the pack, released the magazine, dry-fired toward the wall. He palmed the mag back in the butt and holstered the Colt behind his back.

Adamson holstered his the same way. He lifted a sheathed Ka-bar knife from the pack, got down on one knee, used the knife to rip his pant leg open six inches up the seam. He resheathed the knife, put his foot up on the bench, grabbed a roll of duct tape, tore off a strip. He taped the sheath tightly to the side of his calf, put his foot back down, shook his pant leg over the knife.

"That'll do it," said Adamson.

"You bring gloves?"

"Three sets, in the pack."

Clay said, "We best be on our way."

Adamson reached up, steadied the droplight, counterclockwised the bulb a half turn. Karras was still staring at the gun in his hand, like he was wondering how it had gotten there, when the garage went to black.

By nightfall over a million people had converged on the Mall. Traffic below Pennsylvania Avenue, from 12th to 23rd, had come to a stop hours before, and the gridlock had begun to spread north. Motorists parked their cars and abandoned them on the 14th Street bridge, blocking a major route to and from Virginia; many Metrobuses stopped running, stranding riders well into the night; children's faces, and the faces of their parents, were smashed up against the windows of the packed, newly opened Metro trains. A thousand boats floated in the Potomac River, their occupant's eyes fixed on the darkening sky.

On 16th Street, the horns and raised voices of exasperated drivers could not make the traffic move.

"Better get over to Fourteenth," said Karras. "Go south, then come on up Fifteenth to the Heights."

Clay said, "Right."

It took fifteen minutes to get around the block. Then they were on 15th and going up the hill, going slowly so as not to hit the pedestrians standing in the street. They heard a crack like summer thunder and saw a color mix reflected in the windshield's glass.

"Fireworks have started," said Karras.

"Yes they have," said Clay.

"That's the fireworks," said Karras. "Isn't it, Marcus?"

Clay said, "Relax."

Clay stopped in front of Meridian Heights, let the motor run. People moved in and out of the shadows in the park to their left, laughing and shouting; sparklers sailed through the air, died before they hit the ground. On their right, the entrance to the condo building was lit and empty.

"That it over there?" said Adamson from the backseat as he tightened a pair of black driving gloves over his hands.

"That's the place," said Clay.

"Where you gonna park the Buick?"

"Be up a ways, on the street."

"Anything else you need to tell me 'bout the setup?"

"I think I covered it."

"I'll be goin' in first."

"Figured you would."

"Get that door opened for you."

"Chain cutters are on the floor, Al."

"Got 'em. Where you gonna be?"

"Me and Karras will be at the top of the stairwell, waitin' on Cooper."

"And I'll be on the roof, backin' you up."

"Al?"

"No need to say nothin', Marcus."

"Go ahead, then, man."

"Gonna get some," said Adamson, clapping Karras on the shoulder before exiting the car.

They watched him move across the street, quick and low as a cat, the chain cutters in his hand, the asphalt beneath his feet flaring yellow from the fire of a rocket overhead. And then Adamson had vanished into the building just as quickly as he had sprung from the car.

"He can really move," said Karras, the sound of his own voice calming his nerves. "I guess it came in handy for him over there."

Clay stared at the entrance to Meridian Heights. "Yeah, he can move. Was always the first one in the jungle, too. *Volunteered* for the point every time. Never wanted to depend on no one else, I guess. You can't fault him for it, though. I mean, after all, he managed to do something a lot of others *didn't* do."

"What's that?"

"He came back alive."

Karras looked at Clay. "You know something, Marcus? That's the first time you ever talked to me about Vietnam."

Clay shrugged. "First time you asked."

He gave the Riviera gas and headed up 15th.

Marcus Clay parked the Riviera in front of a hydrant two blocks north. He killed the engine, slipped his hands into the black driving gloves, touched the handle of the door.

"You gonna leave it in a fire zone?" said Karras, gloving his own hands.

"Fuck it," said Clay. "Ain't no cop gonna bother with a parking violation tonight. Come on."

They jogged down the block, took the steps up through the entrance to Meridian Heights. The lobby was quiet and buzzed with fluorescence. Clay noticed the security guard's empty desk and chair; Tate had delivered on his promise.

"The elevator, Dimitri. Let's go."

They went through the open doors. The light was yellow in there, or it appeared that way, reflecting off the yellow walls, and the car bounced slightly as they stepped inside. Karras pushed the button for the top floor. The doors closed.

"It's slow," said Karras as the car ascended to the second floor.

"Counting on that," said Clay, looking at his watch.

Karras drew the gun from behind his back. He hefted it in his hand. "Marcus?"

"What?"

"I don't even know what to do with this."

"Like Al said, point it and shoot. And don't be pullin' that trigger or yanking back on it. *Squeeze* that trigger, hear?"

"When?"

"I'll tell you when."

The elevator came to a stop. Walking out into a gray-carpeted hallway, they came to a door with a flat black sign on it that read, "Roof." Clay pushed on the door, and Karras followed.

They stood on a landing in a darkened stairwell. The stairwell ran floor to floor, descending to the ground level and beyond to the basement. Up above, on another landing at the end of a short flight of stairs, the door had been opened to the roof. Through the door they saw sparkling fingers of green and red reach out and then fade into the night.

"Up there," said Clay.

They took the stairs up to the last landing. Clay found a light switch behind the door, flipped it. A forty-watt bulb washed anemic light onto the landing.

The padlock and broken chain lay coiled on the concrete. Clay kicked the chain against the wall.

"Where's Al?" said Karras.

Clay said, "On the roof."

A heavy sound echoed in the stairwell from far below, and then the indecipherable voices of two men.

"Get behind the door," said Clay.

"Marcus," said Karras. "I'm —"

"I know it, man," said Clay. Before he extinguished the light he added, "I am, too."

Ronald Thomas eased up on the accelerator as he neared Meridian Heights on 15th.

"Park this bitch on the street," said Cooper.

"Right here?"

"Park it."

Ronald double-parked beside a tricked-out Chevelle, hit the blinkers. Russell dumped a mound of blow onto the crook of his thumb, hit it all at once. He laid out a mound for his brother, and Ronald took it in. Russell wiped blood off his upper lip and stuffed the Baggie in the glove box.

"Y'all ready?" said Cooper.

"Readier than a motherfucker, man," said Russell. His eyes were jittery and bright.

Cooper said, "Let's take it to the bridge."

They climbed out of the Dodge and crossed the street. B. R. Clagget ran alongside Cooper, the sawed-off pressed tightly against his leg. He caught his heel on a step leading into the building, and Cooper grabbed him under the arm to prevent his fall. Clagget felt light as paper in Cooper's grasp.

"Come along," said Cooper.

"I ain't feelin' so good, Wilton."

In the fluorescence of the lobby, Clagget looked waxy and gray, the vomit of acne purple on his sunken cheeks.

"Never you mind. Soon as we get out of this town we gonna get you strong again."

"Tonight?"

"Yeah, little brother. Tonight."

Ronald and Russell stepped forward as they came to the open elevator.

"Uh-uh," said Cooper. "You and your brother take the stairs."

"All right, Coop," said Ronald. "See you up there, man."

Cooper said, "Right."

"Marcus," whispered Karras.

Clay said, "Hush."

They stood shoulder to shoulder behind the door. From outside the time between explosions grew shorter; the silence was filled by the conversation of the men coming up the stairs. The men were taking the stairs more rapidly now, and the concrete beneath Clay and Karras's feet began to vibrate as the men advanced.

Underneath the driving gloves, Karras's hands were hot, slick with sweat. He had one hand behind him, wrapped around the grip of the .38. Sweat pooled in the collar of his shirt and snaked down his back. He could hear a thin wheeze in Clay's breathing. Then the wheezing stopped. Clay had stopped breathing, that's what it was; Karras stopped breathing, too. The men had rounded the corner of the top-floor landing and were coming up the last set of stairs toward the door that gave to the roof.

Marcus looked through the crack between the door and its jamb.

In his rectangular tunnel of vision, he saw Ronald Thomas pass. Russell passed next, his face flashing blue. They stepped outside and turned a corner, and then they were gone.

Clay pushed against Karras's shoulder. Karras stepped out from behind the door and pressed his back against the wall. He exhaled slowly and took in a lungful of thick, damp air.

"Move it," whispered Clay.

"Where?" whispered Karras.

Clay pointed his chin at the top of the stairs.

TWENTY-SEVEN

The Thomas brothers stood on the roof, facing south. The roof was nearly clear: There were a couple of overturned beach chairs, three empty beer cans, and an air-conditioning system, duct work and compressors and such, that cluttered the northernmost end. Ladders leading down to fire escapes hung on the building's east and west walls.

Below, in the park, people moved about, holding sparklers, lighting off cones, firecrackers, and cherry bombs. A bottle rocket shot up above the trees. Beyond the park and downtown, the fireworks rose above the Mall, flowering and exploding now relentlessly, coloring the monuments, coloring the Thomas brothers and the roof.

"Whew," said Russell, stumbling back a step.

"What?" said Ronald.

"I am *tripping,* Ronald. All this blow is just fuckin' up my head!"

"There it is."

"Look here. I gotta run some water through my pipe."

"Don't let me stop you."

"Need a little privacy, though."

"What, you shamed about somethin'?"

"Shamed? Shoot, man, I'm right proud!"

"Go ahead, man."

" 'Cause you *know* I got some weight."

"Just go ahead."

Russell drifted, lighting a Kool along the way. Ronald drew his .357. He watched his brother walking slowly, putting that dip into it the way he always had. Ronald smiled.

Russell went behind the air-conditioning ducts, stood at the building's edge. He let the cigarette dangle from the corner of his mouth while he unzipped his fly. Russell pulled his cock out and let a hard stream of piss fly over the ledge.

"Ahhh," said Russell. "God*damn*."

Being higher than a motherfucker and taking a good-ass pee: It occurred to Russell just then that he'd never felt happier in his life.

The elevator crept toward the top floor. Wilton Cooper racked the receiver on one .45, then the other, reholstered them both. He looked over at B. R. Clagget, narrow of shoulder, wasted, hunched in the corner of the car. He nodded at Clagget's weapon.

"You best ready that hog's leg, little brother."

"My movie. Gonna take it all the way to the last reel, blood."

The car came to a stop. The doors opened to the hall.

"How you want to play it, Wilton?"

"The Greek'll be with him. Kill the Greek, soon as you get a chance. Marcus Clay is mine."

"After we get the money?"

"This ain't got nothin' to do with money. Kill 'em all, straight away."

They walked out into the hall, found the door to the stairwell. Cooper gave it a push.

The stairwell was dark as they entered, darker as the door closed behind them. From where they stood they could see the open door past the landing above and the rockets spreading fire in the square of night.

A light came on abruptly, and Clagget shielded his eyes. Cooper looked to the top of the stairs and smiled. Clay and Karras stood there, guns at their sides.

"Trouble Man," said Cooper.

"Cooper."

"Takin' the high ground, like a good soldier."

"Cooper?"

"What."

"You ain't got much time. I wouldn't be wastin' what you got left talkin' all that bullshit."

"What *would* you have me do, then, Clay?"

"I was you, I'd be prayin' there's a God who forgives."

Al Adamson rushed forward from behind the air-conditioning ducts, the Ka-bar knife in his hand, and slashed Russell Thomas's throat clean through his windpipe.

A wave of blood arced over the building's edge. Russell crumpled like a marionette whose strings had been released, his head flopping back against his shoulders as if hinged.

Adamson wiped the Ka-bar off on his black slacks, put his foot up on a square of ductwork, and sheathed the knife. He walked out from behind a large compressor.

Thirty feet away, Ronald Thomas stood with his back turned, gun in hand, watching the fireworks. Adamson pulled his .45, jacked a round into the chamber.

"Turn around slow!" yelled Adamson.

Ronald did it.

"Now drop it or use it," said Adamson.

Ronald raised the .357.

They faced each other, guns pointed, expressionless. A barrage of rockets ripped across the sky.

Ronald Thomas fired his gun; Al Adamson fired his. Twin muzzle flashes flared in the night.

Cooper said, "You hear that, Clay?"

Clay nodded.

Cooper grinned. "Even with all those rockets and shit, the sound of a gun stands out. I guess you brought along some help. My money'd be on the Thomas brothers, you want to know the truth."

Marcus Clay did not respond. Clagget slipped his finger inside the shotgun's trigger guard, wrapped his hand around the pump. Karras snicked the hammer back on the .38 and aimed the gun at Clagget's chest.

Cooper laughed shortly. "You lookin' a little shaky, Greek boy. By the way, was pleased to make your momma's acquaintance. Like a woman with a little back to her. Maybe I'll look her up again, soon as we're done."

Clay said, "You gonna talk all night, Cooper?"

"All right," said Cooper, "I guess we ought to just go ahead and get this done. Seein' as how y'all got all your shit drawn and ready, and we standin' here, basically at a disadvantage, maybe you're thinkin' now that things are gonna go your way. But here's how *I* see it —"

"No," said Clay. "Here's how it *is.* Your sissy ain't racked that pump yet, number one. Would be like him to wait for the drama rather than to come prepared."

Cooper's smile died.

Clay said, "And that leaves you and me." He leveled his gun at Cooper.

Karras shifted his weight, sweat dripping from his hair to his eyes. He tried to blink away the sting.

"Shoot him, Dimitri," said Clay.

"Marcus," said Karras.

"You know your boy ain't gonna use that gun," said Cooper.

"Shoot him *now,* Dimitri!"

Karras did not move. The pipes cried in the stairwell below.

Clagget racked the shotgun's pump.

"Aw, shit," said Cooper. "Here we go, T-Man."

Cooper crossed his arms as Clagget brought the shotgun around.

Karras closed his eyes, pulled back on the trigger of the .38.

There was a deafening explosion. Clagget fell back, the shotgun flipping from his grasp and clattering down the stairs.

The automatic in Marcus Clay's hand kicked three times as Cooper's fingers grasped at the grips of his .45s.

A high-pitched tone sounded in Karras's ears. Through the gun smoke, he saw Clagget writhing on the floor. A black hole showed in the thigh of the kid's white slacks, and blood was shooting from the hole with the force of water flowing from a hose. The blood was washing over the walls and splashing back on Clagget. He was in a heap and holding his fingers over the hole, but the blood was finding its way through, and Clagget's face was blue and stretched back.

"Marcus."

"Shut up."

Clay went down to the landing. Cooper was sitting up, his back against the wall, his maroon polo shirt flapping at the sucking wound in the center of his chest. One elbow was white and shredded where the second round had hit, and two fingers were gone from the right hand where the third bullet had taken them off. Cooper stared into Clay's eyes, his own eyes glassy, his mouth open as he tried to take in breath.

Clay looked down at Clagget. He had seen a femoral artery wound before, in the war. The blood was everywhere now, overflowing the lip of the landing. Clagget had stopped trying to stanch the flow. He let his head fall back in the crimson pool.

"Come on, Dimitri."

Karras didn't move.

"Come on," said Clay. "They're done."

Karras stepped around the dying men and followed Clay. Their shoes made blood prints on the stairs.

Clay got behind the wheel of the Riviera. Karras dropped into the shotgun bucket, lacing his fingers tightly and resting his hands in his lap. Clay looked in the rearview mirror and smiled.

"Marcus."

"Al."

Adamson sat low in the backseat. He shook a cigarette out of a pack and put fire to its end.

Adamson blew smoke out the open window. "You make out all right?"

"Yeah. You?"

"Uh-huh. One of 'em had a little life in him after it went down. Followed me halfway down the fire escape, took a blind shot at me in the dark. He ain't gonna last but another minute or so. I gut-shot his ass, blew some shit out his back, too. He's gone."

Clay and Adamson's eyes locked in the rearview.

Adamson nodded to the back of Karras's head.

"He all right?"

Clay thought of the first time he had killed a man.

"He's all right," said Clay. "He'll be fine."

"Get all your shit, then," said Adamson, "and put it in this bag."

Adamson passed the olive green pack through the opening in the buckets while Clay removed his shoes. Clay looked inside the open flap at the chain cutters and Adamson's gear. He dropped his own shoes, gun, and gloves in the pack.

"Now you, Dimitri," said Clay. "Take them Clydes off, too."

Karras did it, and Clay passed the pack back to Adamson.

"Better get goin'," said Adamson. "Don't know if you noticed it or not, but you're parked in a fire zone."

"Where we off to, man?" said Clay.

"Anyplace where there's water," said Adamson, "provided you can get to it. Need to get this shit to the bottom of a river right quick."

Clay drove to the next intersection, turned right, and headed east.

Ronald Thomas came out of the alley clutching both hands to his stomach. He felt as if his insides were falling out on him, right there. His hands were slick with blood, and his trousers were soaked with it down past the crotch. It hurt like a motherfucker, too. God*damn* did it hurt. He had never taken a bullet before, and he had no idea it could put a hurting on you this bad.

Ronald had lost his gun just before dropping down from the fire escape. No matter. All he had to do was get to the Dodge. He had the keys in his pocket; at least he had been smart enough to keep them on him. Maybe Russell was waiting for him there — Ronald hadn't seen Russell on the roof since he had gone off to take a piss.

He hoped Russell had been smart enough to slip away when he got a look at the bald-headed dude. It would be like Russell to do just that.

A cop was standing by the yellow Dodge.

Ronald knew he shouldn't have double-parked that Mopar out on the street. He turned his head and walked south on the sidewalk, standing as straight as he could manage without screaming out from the pain, and did a slant-step across 15th, straight into the park.

There were people everywhere in the park, laughing, clapping, talking loud, like this was the party they had been waiting for all their lives. The rockets above exploded without a break now, brightening the park with sunlight intensity. The faces of the people were unfamiliar, distorted in the colored light.

Ronald thought if he could get someplace quiet, a country kind of place, it would be all right.

He stumbled onto a concrete stairway, passing a group of people sitting on a statue.

"That nigger's drunk as a white boy," said a man, but when Ronald turned to look at him the man was just a dark face in a crowd of many dark faces, none of them friendly or warm.

Ronald lost his balance, cried out, tripped down the steps and rolled, landing on his back at the edge of a fountain. Everyone in the park stood then, cheering and applauding as the finale was loosed above the Mall. Ronald looked up: red, white, and blue diamonds burned across the sky.

Not here, Lord. Please, not here in front of all these strangers. I'm too far from home.

A young man nearly stepped right on him. He got down on one knee and saw the massive wound in Ronald's gut. Ronald put his hand on the young man's shirtsleeve, gripped it tight.

"Goddamn, man, you all right?"

"Where go my brother?" said Ronald.

"You just hold on, blood. I'm gonna get you some help. We'll find your brother, too, don't you worry about that. Just hold on."

The young man found an older man, who appeared to be sober and responsible, standing alone at the edge of the promenade.

"There's a man needs help. He's hurt real bad."

"Show me," said the older man, who read genuine fear in the young man's face.

The two men went to the fountain. Rubies and emeralds sparkled in Ronald Thomas's open eyes.

"Do something," said the young man.

"Ain't nothin' *to* do," said the older man. "This man is dead."

The explosions ended just as the red, white, and blue light stopped flickering on the cinder-block wall. Then there was a great cheering sound and scattered applause. Wilton Cooper guessed that the big celebration was done.

His eyes traveled down to his shirt. A small fountain of blood pumped out rhythmically from the scorched, ragged opening in the fabric. He let his head fall to the side. That was all he had the strength to do.

Bobby Roy Clagget, light as he was, had been lifted by the bath of his own blood and carried a foot to rest against the wall. Cooper could see the slow rise and fall of Clagget's birdcage chest. Clagget's thin lips were pulled up high over his gums, and his complexion was stark and marbleized, beyond blue. He looked as dead as any man Cooper had ever seen.

Cooper knew that he, Wilton Cooper, was dead, too.

What was Bobby Roy thinking? Cooper guessed that B. R. Clagget was just plain surprised. That he had been shot, and yes, that it was all about to end. If he thought himself to be the hero of his own private movie, then it didn't make sense — it *couldn't* make sense — that the hero would die. Hadn't the hero always walked away in the last reel?

Cooper coughed up a great black glob of blood that flopped over his mouth and came to rest on his chin.

"Wilton?"

"Yes, little brother."

"I'm dyin', blood."

Cooper issued a gurgling laugh. The blood was in his lungs now, and he was drowning in it. He stared at the cinder-block wall, the mortar lines erasing in the forty-watt light.

"Wilton?"

"Yeah?"

"It hurts," said Clagget in a small and childish way.

"What," said Wilton Cooper. "Didn't you think it would?"

TWENTY-EIGHT

arcus Clay drove across the city, taking the Sousa Bridge over the river and into Anacostia Park. Clay, Karras, and Adamson walked down to the picnic area, where revelers still gathered, drinking, laughing, listening to music, and getting high.

Adamson had the pack slung over his shoulder. He nodded toward the end of the manicured grass where the tree line gave to a thin forest that ran upriver.

"Think I'll take a walk in the woods, Marcus."

"All right, Al. You take care."

"Right."

Adamson looked at Karras for a moment, then turned and jogged toward the woods. He entered the black space between the trees.

Clay said, "Come on."

They walked down to the waterline, where they copped a joint from a Ward 8 resident their own age. Clay and Karras had a seat on the grass looking out across the Anacostia, the sky still bright in the west and thick with smoke.

Clay fired up the number. The two of them smoked it down without conversation, listening to Hendrix's *Are You Experienced?* coming loud from a Gremlin parked behind them in the lot. Clay smiled. Probably some blood, back in the world. The brothers over there, they did love their Jimi. Listening to the music, it made Clay think of Rasheed; the image of Rasheed kept the smile on his face.

"Marcus?"

"What?"

"How can you be grinning like that tonight?"

"Just thinking of young Rasheed. Picturing him, is all. All the energy he had, how opinionated he was. How he was always so certain that he was right."

"And now it's okay to talk about him in a good way, is that what you're saying? Because we took out the ones who took him?"

"Say it again?"

"You think we did the right thing."

"I know we did."

"*I* don't know," said Karras.

Across the river, boats had begun to return to their marinas, where brightly colored lights were strung along the docks. A houseboat threw a small wake that lapped at the bulkhead of the eastern shore.

"Dimitri?" said Clay. "You remember that time, I don't know, I was just out of high school, nineteen sixty-six or somethin' like that, I took that trip up to New York?"

"I remember."

"Yeah. Took the train up there to get in a city game with Earl Manigault. Was eager to try, you know. And I found that game, too, right on One Hundred and Thirty-fifth Street. I knew I'd find it, 'cause I wanted it too bad, had practiced all summer long just for the chance."

Karras almost smiled. "And he took your ass to school."

"You don't have to tell me. He damn sure did. That's when I knew — I *knew* — I didn't have it in me to be the best at ball. And that's when I decided to go ahead and go for something else. Course, the draft board had a different idea, sidetracked me a little bit. But I held on to that goal. To open my own business, build something for myself. And you know? I was right. I mean, look what happened to Earl. The streets claimed him, man, and here was a brother who could not be stopped on the court. But I think, what it was, he just didn't have the vision to move on and get where he needed to be with his life. Like he was in hang time *all* the time, and he didn't know how to get back down."

"What's your point?"

"You're still up there, too, Dimitri."

"Marcus —"

"Listen. Here's what I been playin' with in my mind: I want you to come work for me. I think you should."

"Aw, come on, man."

"I'm serious."

"What, you and me and Cheek and Tate? That's a bigger staff than you had before."

"Need someone with some rock knowledge in that place. Dupont Circle ain't exactly a hotbed of funk, man. Someone comes in lookin' for a Mo the Rooster LP —"

"Mott the Hoople."

"Whatever. And as far as overloading the staff goes, it ain't gonna cost me, 'cause I'm not promising you much to start. I'm talking minimum wage."

Karras looked over at Clay. "I don't know, Marcus. I'm not much for holding a job where you gotta be somewhere every day at some special time. I wouldn't want to let you down."

"I got faith in you, man. More than you got in yourself. It doesn't work out between us, you go your own way, that's fine, too. I'm talkin' about giving you a little stability right now, 'cause you need it."

"Thanks, Marcus. But I gotta think about it, okay?"

"Think on it, then. I'd like you in there Tuesday morning, nine sharp, when we open back up."

Karras lay back in the grass. He stared at the sky until his eyes grew heavy. When he heard Clay's voice again, it was difficult to tell if Karras had slept or just been deep into his high. The sky had lightened, though, and there were stars in it instead of smoke.

"Mitri, man."

Karras got up, resting on his elbows. The dewy grass felt cool against his bare feet. "What are we doin'?"

"Traffic should be easin' up by now. I gotta get my ass home."

"Al back yet?"

"Al ain't comin' back. Let's go."

It took an hour to get to Mount Pleasant. Clay let Karras out at the Karmann Ghia. Karras walked around to the Riviera's open window.

"What about tomorrow?" said Karras.

"Goin' to see Eddie Spags, early in the mornin'. Clarence Tate did me a big solid today. Gonna do one back for him. How about you?"

"I don't know."

"I'll see you Tuesday mornin', then, Dimitri. Nine A.M. sharp."

"I'll let you know."

"Got to do it, man. It's a new day."

Clay and Karras locked hands. They looked deep into each other's eyes.

"Take it light, Marcus."

"Yeah," said Clay. "You, too."

Clay drove on, turned the corner, headed west on Brown. He parked in front of his house, locked the car, took the steps leading to his porch. Glancing up, Clay saw the light burning in the window of the bedroom he shared with Elaine Taylor.

Looking at the light, Marcus Clay smiled.

TWENTY-NINE

Dimitri Karras waited for Marcus Clay's Riviera to take the turn onto Brown. He found his wristwatch underneath the driver's seat of the Karmann Ghia and checked the time: 5:10 A.M. Too late to get a good night's sleep. And there was nothing to do at his apartment, and no one waiting for him there. He got into his car and headed uptown.

People stood at bus stops on 16th, some still stranded from the night before. A few stray partyers wandered on side streets, staggering, talking to strangers, holding on to lampposts. Others sat on their lawns or were stretched out sleeping atop cars.

Karras drove over the District line into downtown Silver Spring. He went into Tastee Diner, found a booth in the station of his favorite waitress, a kind elderly woman named Hannah.

Hannah placed a cup of black coffee in front of Karras. "Rough night, Dimitri?"

"Didn't everyone have a rough night?"

"Everyone but me, I guess. Worked a double shift. Shoulda seen the folks we had in here."

"I can imagine." Karras put the menu down unopened. "Two over easy with scrapple, Hannah, side of white toast."

"Be right up."

Hannah sat in the booth across from Dimitri while he ate his breakfast. In the booth behind him, a man played a Merle Haggard tune on the table's miniature juke.

"Your feet are dirty, Dimitri."

Karras looked under the table at the bottoms of his bare feet. The soles were close to black.

"Thanks, Hannah."

Hannah smiled. "And you could run a straight razor over that face."

"Thanks."

Karras paid up, leaving five on three-twenty, and walked out of the diner. The sun had come up, and the sidewalk felt warm beneath his feet. He crossed Georgia Avenue to the all-night Drug Fair and bought a pair of Japanese sandals for ninety-nine cents and also a pack of Marlboro reds.

Karras walked down Georgia a few blocks, going through the B & O tunnel that ran beneath the tracks, and went along the Canada Dry plant to a green area known as Acorn Park. He sat on a bench in the shade of an oak and lit a cigarette. He was not a smoker, and he grew dizzy after the second drag. He stubbed the cigarette out against the wooden bench.

He folded his arms, leaned back, and went to sleep.

When he woke, the day was hot, and the sun had crawled across East-West Highway and reached his feet.

He pulled his hair back off his face and buried his face in his hands.

"Mind if I get a smoke from you?" said a man in a torn T-shirt who stood before him.

"Keep 'em," said Karras, opening his eyes.

Karras stood up and walked the half mile back to his car.

At ten in the morning on Monday, Marcus Clay parked his Riviera behind a black Monte Carlo on Half Street in Southeast and walked across a hot, dusty asphalt lot. He pushed a faded yellow button beside a windowless door, heard a buzzing sound, turned the knob on the door, opened the door, and entered a narrow stairwell. He took the stairs up to another door, pushed on it, stepped into a large room.

Eddie Marchetti sat behind his desk, watching *Celebrity Sweepstakes* on the Sony. Clarence Tate sat on the edge of the desk, one leg brushing the concrete floor.

"Mr. Clay," said Marchetti in a businesslike way. He touched the remote, and the television clicked off.

"Eddie," said Clay, nodding one time. "Tate."

"Glad you could make it," said Marchetti.

"I said I would."

Marchetti pretended to arrange some papers on his desk. "So let's get down to business. You bring the rest of my money with you?"

Clay said, "No."

"How's that?"

"Couldn't bring something I don't have."

"Explain."

"Your assistant, Clarence here, he set up a meeting with me and Wilton Cooper, like he said he would. I met Cooper, gave him the ten grand. Then, later in the night, Mr. Cooper and his boys met with an unfortunate series of accidents."

"I know about the accidents. Any idea what happened to 'em?"

"One of those freakish things, I guess. Said something to the wrong guy, or fell into an armed stickup. Or maybe they got hunted by the friends of the bikers they smoked up in Howard County. You know about that?"

"I read the paper." Marchetti tapped his finger on the *Post* lying flat on his desk. "Got the final edition right here."

"You read it all?"

"Yeah, I —"

"Had you read it all, you'd know something else. They found Cooper's car outside the place he got murdered. Trunk was full of money and drugs. Some of that money was your ten grand, I'd expect. Or maybe the triggerman took your ten off Cooper after he got himself greased. Either way, I don't have it; that's plain as day."

Marchetti sighed. Tate shifted his hands in his lap.

Clay said, "You run with some bad people, Mr. Spags."

"Got to pay if you want to play," said Marchetti, giving it the hard-guy squint, the tough routine coming easy to him now that Cooper and the rest were dead.

"So," said Clay, "like I been sayin', I just don't have it."

"Well," said Marchetti, "you didn't come here just to let me down, did you? I mean, you owe me, after all the trouble you caused. Is it the girl? Is that it? You got Vivian waitin' to come in, out in the hall, right? Like a surprise."

"Sorry, Eddie. The girl is gone. Ran away from my Greek friend into the arms of a young buck she met on the street. Would've happened to *you* eventually, if you want my opinion. Anyway, Spags, a stud like you is way too much for a little girl like Vivian Lee. You ought to be lookin' out for a woman can match you as a man."

Marchetti's face brightened at the compliment. He sat up straighter in his chair. Then he looked at Clay oddly, studied his face.

"Wait a second," said Marchetti. "You came here for *something*, though, didn't you?"

"Matter of fact," said Clay, "I did. Figure I did owe you something for all the trouble I caused."

Marchetti lifted his double chin. "Go ahead."

"I know you been lookin' to off all that merchandise out of your warehouse, and I know how hard it is to get rid of the load you got. So I heard about this fence, dig, that's doin' some serious acquisition work in town. Under the roof of a place called G and G Trucking, on Twelfth Street in Northwest, between U and V."

"G and G."

"That's right. Went by there my own self, talked to the man behind the desk. Asked him some questions without using my own name. Implied I had some weight to move, if you know what I mean. He implied back that they could handle all I could truck on in."

"You think it's on the up and up?"

"Like I say, I don't know these cats. But he gave me no reason to doubt him." Clay reached into the back pocket of his pressed jeans, pulled out a sheet of paper. He walked to the desk and slid the paper in front of Marchetti. "Here you go, Spags. Wrote the address down for you and everything."

"Thanks. I'll look into it next week."

"Better get over there the next day or so. They're gettin' ready to close down the operation."

Tate reached over and took the paper off the desk. "I'll handle it, Eddie. Get a truck loaded up tomorrow morning and roll right over there."

"That's not a good idea," said Clay, looking hard into Tate's eyes.

"Why not?" said Marchetti.

"See," said Clay, "it's a bunch of brothers runnin' the operation. Word is, they been payin' top dollar to the white men been comin' in. Figure they can take the bloods for a lower price, I guess. Now, they see a man of your stature walkin' through the door, a Caucasian gentleman they figure knows how to negotiate professionally, they're gonna *have* to be a whole lot more generous."

"He's right, Clarenze," said Marchetti. "I better handle this one personally. No offense, of course."

Tate said, "None taken."

"Thank you, Mr. Clay," said Marchetti.

"Well." Clay reached across the desk, shook Marchetti's hand. "I best be on my way."

"Pleasure doin' business with you," said Marchetti.

Clay smiled, nodded meaningfully at Tate, turned and walked across the room. Tate watched Clay move with that head-held-high way of his, and Marchetti gave Clay a final once-over as he disappeared out the door. They listened to his footsteps on the stairs.

"You know, Clarenze?" said Marchetti. "Even with everything that went down, I like that guy."

"I kind of like him, too."

"Now all I got to do is turn over that merchandise and I'll be on my way."

"You leavin' D.C., Eddie?"

"I am. Gonna take my winnings and head back up to Jersey."

"Smart move. You want to know the truth, this ain't your town, Eddie. You don't belong here."

"I guess you're right."

Marchetti and Tate heard the Riviera's engine turn over outside the warehouse.

"You know something, Clarenze?"

"What?"

"I was lookin' at Clay just now, walkin' out of here? That's one big man, you know it? I never realized how big he was!"

"Up till now," said Clarence Tate, "neither did I."

THIRTY

At the top of Irving Street, on the corner of Mt. Pleasant, Dimitri Karras stood in the sun, leaning against the side of his Karmann Ghia. He checked the time on his wristwatch and saw that it was a little past eleven.

A hot wind blew trash across the street. An old man, nearly blind, stood at the bus stop and tapped his cane on the quartz-reflecting sidewalk. In the front yard of a nearby row house, a young Puerto Rican doubled over and vomited in the grass.

Karras turned his head.

A black '69 Camaro, jacked up in the rear, approached, coming fast up Irving. Karras stepped out in the street and flagged the car down.

The driver of the Camaro pulled over to the side of the road. The driver and his passenger had a short discussion, and then the passenger door opened. Young Nick Stefanos stepped out of the car.

Stefanos walked toward Karras. Karras watched a kid with longish blond hair get out of the driver's side and light a smoke. He tilted his chin up at Karras and smiled; Karras didn't like the smile or the kid's face.

"Hey," said Stefanos.

"Hey."

They shook hands.

"Dimitri Karras, right?"

"That's right, yeah."

"What's happenin', man?"

"Leavin' for your trip?"

"Just said good-bye to my *papou*. Me and Billy are on our way to pick up the boat and head south."

"Thought I'd catch you before you left."

"How'd you know —"

"Irving's one way headed east. You told me you'd be shoving off about eleven."

"Okay," said Stefanos, digging his hands in the pockets of his jeans. He waited for the older guy with the haunted face to speak.

Karras said, "I just wanted to talk to you, that's all."

Stefanos looked at Karras's wrinkled Hawaiian shirt, unbuttoned to the navel, the man's unclean face, his dirty feet. There seemed to be blood or something streaked on the man's jeans.

"You been up all night?" said Stefanos in a friendly way.

"Up?" Karras looked down at his shirt in surprise, as if he was seeing it for the first time. "Yeah, I guess."

Stefanos glanced over his shoulder at his smirking friend. "Listen, Billy's in a hurry —"

"I know."

Karras had planned to ask if Nick Stefanos knew the Castle boy. He had planned to tell him about the accident, tell him to take care. But he remembered then that the two boys had gone to different high schools. And in truth, he knew the conversation would be pointless. Stefanos was nineteen years old; he would not understand, or care to understand, the gravity of death.

"Nick," said Karras.

"Yeah?"

"I only wanted to tell you —"

"I know. 'Have fun.' You told me the other day."

Karras shifted his feet. "Look . . . what I really mean to say is, don't waste your time. You think you're just having fun and then ten years pass and you figure out that you haven't done a goddamn thing. All you've been is high, and you can't even remember what was so good about that."

"Right." Stefanos cocked his head and nodded slowly. "I hear you, man."

No you don't. Goddamnit, you don't.

Karras bit down on his lip. He reached into his pocket, pulled free a slip of paper with a shaky hand. "Anyway. I put my address on here for you. In case you want to write. I know you won't write your grandfather, but you can write me. A postcard'll do it, so I can just tell the old man I heard from you and you're okay. You can do that, can't you?"

"Sure." Stefanos took the slip of paper, looked at it. "Real Right Records. I bought a couple of LPs there once."

"I work there," said Karras. "That is, I'm going to be."

"Cool." Stefanos looked back at his friend once again. "Look, Dimitri, if that's it —"

"You gotta go."

"Yeah. I better go."

"All right," said Karras. "Go."

Stefanos went to the car, dropped into the shotgun bucket. Billy Goodrich had gotten back behind the wheel.

"Who was *that* guy?" said Goodrich.

"A friend of my grandfather's."

"Your pa*pa* send him to talk to you?"

"*Papou.*"

"Whatever. He send that guy to tell you to be careful and shit?"

"He's just a friend."

Goodrich smiled. "What'd he want, then, Greek?"

"I don't know," Stefanos said truthfully. "Come on, Billy, let's ride."

Goodrich cooked the 327 and pulled away from the curb. Nick Stefanos looked in the sideview mirror at Karras, still standing in the street, watching them drive away. The Camaro went over a rise and crossed 16th.

Stefanos glanced back in the mirror. Dimitri Karras was gone.

Nick Stefanos and Billy Goodrich picked up the Larson in Alexandria and put the boat on the hitch. Their next stop was a market, where they bought a cold six-pack of beer. Though it was barely noon, they grabbed two Buds out of the bag, pulled the rings, and tapped cans.

"To our trip, Greek."

Stefanos had a swig of beer as Goodrich turned the ignition.

"We got everything?" said Stefanos.

An ounce of Mexican sat in the glove box, along with a vial filled to the top with Black Beauties and a half dozen hits of Purple Haze; a plastic grenade hung from the rearview, and a Bad Company logo was taped, facing out, to the windshield of the car. Several Marlboro hardpacks were scattered on the dash. Plastered to the rear of the Camaro was a bumper sticker that read, "Mott the Hoople: Tell Chuck Berry the news."

"Everything that matters," said Goodrich.

Billy Goodrich laughed and caught rubber pulling out of the lot. Stefanos slapped *Sally Can't Dance* into the Pioneer eight-track deck. The druggy guitar of "Kill Your Sons" crashed from the Superthruster speakers.

They took a ramp leading to 95 South. Goodrich pinned the gas pedal, pushing the Camaro up to eighty-five. He began to talk to Stefanos about the movie they had seen together on Saturday night. But Stefanos wasn't really listening to his friend. He couldn't get the image of that Karras guy out of his head.

Nick Stefanos couldn't figure out why Karras bothered him. *He* would never get off the track like Karras. It wasn't like he was looking into his own future when he looked into that Karras dude's wasted, hollowed-out eyes. What had happened to Dimitri Karras, *whatever* had happened, could never happen to him. He was way too smart for that. And he had so much time.

"Hey, Greek!"

"What?"

"I'm talkin' to you, man! I was just sayin', the movie was badder than a motherfucker, wasn't it?"

There was little traffic on the interstate. They were on a long straightaway, the white lines bleeding into the horizon. Stefanos smiled, looking at the road ahead.

"Yeah," said Nick Stefanos. "*King Suckerman* was bad."

Also by George P. Pelecanos and along with
King Suckerman and *The Sweet Forever,*
part of his DC Quartet

The Big Blowdown

"Pelecanos has joined James Lee Burke and Lawrence Block at the high table of contemporary crime greats" *The Times*

Washington DC, 1946. For two local young men, Pete Karras and Joey Recevo, the easiest way to find work after the war is by turning to crime — providing a little muscle for a local boss, Mr Burke, who runs a protection racket with the Mafia. The trouble with Pete Karras is that he is just too soft on his fellow immigrants, and the last thing the boss wants is for his mob to get soft. The boys have to teach Karras a painful lesson that he won't forget and he pays the full price for compromising the boss's fearsome reputation.

Three years later Pete and Joey meet up once more and a final confrontation puts the meaning of friendship and honour to the ultimate test.

The first novel in the Washington Quartet which comprises *King Suckerman* (shortlisted for the 1998 CWA Golden Dagger Award), *The Sweet Forever* and *Shame the Devil*, *The Big Blowdown* features Pelecanos' inimitable trademark blend of music, drink, and sense of place; tautly plotted and infused with street talk. A sharply written crime epic that evokes the mean DC streets of the 1950s and delivers.

The Sweet Forever

"*The Sweet Forever* is the real deal; a dirty, human slice of raw American life" *The Times*

"The whole thing is so fast paced it locks you in a half-nelson and insists you read the whole lot from beginning to end. Without blinking" *Later*

"Welcome to the tough and violent world of America's hottest young crime writer . . . he just keeps getting better" *Uncut*

"The undisputed king of slick, hip-swaying inner city literature. And *The Sweet Forever* — which mixes Elmore Leonard's hip dialogue with Richard (Clockers) Price's grimy ghetto heart — is just the coolest, smartest, most vital novel we've read this year" *Maxim*

"Living history compellingly spelled out via street life, pop sounds, shoot-outs and an awesome appetite for dope" *Literary Review*

"Downbeat and street, he's well worth checking" *Straight No Chaser*